ON ANOTHER NOTE

The second book in the *NOTED!* series

Kathy J. Jacobson

LITTLE CREEK PRESS®
AND BOOK DESIGN

Mineral Point, Wisconsin USA

Copyright © 2016 Kathy J. Jacobson

Little Creek Press®
A Division of Kristin Mitchell Design, Inc.
5341 Sunny Ridge Road
Mineral Point, Wisconsin 53565

Book Design and Project Coordination:
Little Creek Press

Third Edition
April 2017

All rights reserved

No part of this book may be used or reproduced
in any manner whatsoever without written
permission from the author.

Printed in Wisconsin, United States of America

For more information or to order books:
kjjacobsonauthor@gmail.com
or visit www.littlecreekpress.com

Library of Congress Control Number: 2016939781

ISBN-10: 1-942586-14-0
ISBN-13: 978-1-942586-14-2

Dedication

For Kirsten—"my Marty"
and
in memory of
Godwin Pallangyo—"lala salama"

Chapter One

John and Jillian walked hand in hand toward the front door of John's huge Storybook-style home in Los Angeles.

Just minutes earlier, Jillian had stood at the top of the large circle drive, her eyes clouded with tears, waiting for a taxi to take her away from her home of the past year—and from John. She had thought it best to run away from this place and her feelings. But earlier that afternoon, she had come to the conclusion that she was about to make the biggest mistake of her life—and that it was too late to do anything about it.

Jillian had resigned herself to the idea that soon she would be gone from this place, never to return. She had been staring down the driveway watching for her ride, when Lucy, John's orange-haired cat, suddenly bolted out of the house toward her, followed by her master. They showed up just in the nick of time, as the cab arrived only minutes later.

John had written Jillian two notes—the first of which had simply said, "Please stay." When she had responded with a note asking "why," his note back to her had said:

I think I'm the right person.

Jillian had to think for a moment about those words, then recalled a conversation they had had a few weeks prior. John, knowing that Jillian had a daughter, had asked about her husband. Jillian had mentioned that she had never been married, and John had bluntly asked her "why not?" She told him that she guessed she had never fallen in love with the right person. They had both fallen silent after that, as neither of them had had much success in matters of the heart—in loving the *right person*.

As Jillian deciphered the meaning of John's note, her heart went from a dead stop to ready to break the sound barrier in a matter of seconds. She responded to John with one final note, one they had both written to each other over the past year. It simply said:

NOTED!

As they stepped up to the door of John's house, John released Jillian's hand for a moment and held the door open for her to enter. She crossed the threshold and stood in the marbled foyer, looking around as if she had never seen it before, rather than standing in a room she'd been in almost every day for the past year.

They each gently dropped Jillian's suitcases to the floor and faced one another. Now John took both of Jillian's hands in his and just looked at her with those warm, dark brown eyes. They had a gleam in them that she had not seen before, and there was something else about them—they seemed happy—and hopeful.

Jillian was the first to speak. "I didn't think I'd ever see this place—or you—again," she said quietly.

John and Lucy had been gone from the house the entire day. At first Jillian had been relieved that he wasn't there. But later, when she realized that her leaving was a mistake, she had wished and prayed that he would return, but it didn't happen. She hadn't known that John and the cat had come home during the brief time she had retrieved her suitcases from the guest cottage—her residence of the past thirteen months—and dragged them wearily to the circle drive to wait for the taxi.

John's eyes locked onto Jillian's. "I thought I'd never see you again, either. I tried to stay away—to let you go like you wanted—but I couldn't let you go without at least asking you to stay, so I came back," he said.

"I'm glad you came back—and I'm so glad you asked," she said softly. She could feel her eyes beginning to moisten again. Jillian, who was not one to easily cry, had shed more tears in the past few days than in the last ten years combined. "I'm so sorry, John."

"For what?" he asked, looking even more deeply into her eyes and tightening his hands around hers.

"For doing all the things I tell everyone else not to do," referring to the advice she gave in her blog for the broken-hearted. She had realized earlier that day that she was great at giving out advice but terrible at following it.

"I was afraid," Jillian admitted quietly, lowering her eyes for a moment.

"I understand," John said sincerely, and in her heart, she knew that he really did.

"Thanks for not giving up on me, and for giving me another chance," Jillian said, looking up once again.

John began to gently rub his thumbs over her hands as he held them. "Thank you for giving me about a hundred 'another chances' over the past year. You never gave up on me, Jillian, no matter what ridiculous thing I did—or said—or didn't say."

John was being truthful about that. He had not been a happy man when she arrived to work at his home as a live-in house helper, but she had known from her past experience in nursing, that "hurt people, hurt people," and she had been kind and forgiving many times over.

"Let's call it even, then," Jillian said. She had an overwhelming desire to kiss him, but controlled the impulse.

"I will, if you will," said John.

"Deal," Jillian replied.

"Deal," John repeated, and they squeezed each other's hands and shook them slightly, as if to shake on it, their eyes never leaving the other's.

Then John pulled her into an embrace. Jillian's heart was pounding wildly against her chest. She was sure that John could feel it as she pressed against his body, and wondered if he could hear it, as it was banging in her ears. She felt small and lost in his strong arms. She didn't want it to end, but she thought she would forget herself if this went on much longer, so she pulled back gently.

Jillian glanced at the suitcases on the floor, and John's eyes followed hers.

"Where would you like me to put those?" John asked.

There was a fleeting temptation to say you can take them right up those stairs, but Jillian had been down that road before. This time she wanted to do everything the right way.

"How about the cottage? At least until the new helper gets here," Jillian suggested.

"There isn't going to be a new helper, at least not a live-in one." He paused. "I just couldn't bear the thought of someone else..." His voice trailed off. Then he said tenderly, "I'm just so glad you're here."

"Me, too," she said.

John looked into Jillian's eyes, and she felt like he was looking straight into her soul. Then he lifted her hands to his lips and kissed them lightly.

Jillian wondered at that moment how she could have been so foolish. She had almost left this man, and this place. She must have been out of her mind, and then thought to herself that if John kept on kissing her hands, she would definitely be out of her mind.

"John, do you think we should tell our families about this change of plans?" she asked. She thought contacting their loved ones would be a good excuse for a little separation. Besides, she was dying to tell her daughter, Marty, a medical intern in Senegal, that she was staying after all. Marty had sensed that Jillian was afraid, and that that was why she was leaving. Jillian thought that her daughter, her most precious gift from God, would be glad to hear that she had changed her mind.

John smiled that brilliant smile of his. "I think I have a nephew in Chicago who will be one happy man—just like his uncle," he added, squeezing her hands tightly.

John's nephew, Tommy, and Jillian had become quite close over the past few months. She often gave him updates about his uncle, and he in turn had been her source for learning about John's likes and dislikes. They had met in person just weeks before, when John had collapsed from a brain tumor no one knew that he had. Tommy had flown out to Los Angeles, and their relationship had been taken to an entirely new level. He had credited Jillian with bringing his uncle "back from the dead," and had been crushed when he heard the news that Jillian was leaving.

John offered to carry Jillian's bags back to the guest cottage, but she suggested he call his nephew instead. She also didn't think he should lift such a heavy bag yet. Even though his surgery had been accomplished using a wonderfully non-invasive procedure through the nasal passage, he still had to take it easy for a while, including watching how much weight he lifted.

John headed for the phone in the library, but not before giving Jillian one last hug. She started back to the cottage. She had carried the suitcases out of the cottage to the front circle drive by herself, and she could carry them back. As she began pulling the largest one, carrying the laptop case over her shoulder and the smaller bag in her hand, she was amazed how different they felt now. When she had taken them to the driveway earlier to leave, they felt like they were filled with cement. Now they felt as light as feathers.

Jillian grabbed the key to the guest cottage on her way through the kitchen. Less than an hour before, she had sadly placed the very same key on the counter next to the notepad. The notepad. She thought about how for the first two-thirds of the year she had worked for John, notes were the primary form of communication between them. It was difficult to remember now how it had been back then. They had both changed so much over the past year, each prying open the other's heart without even realizing that it was happening.

Before Jillian tried a video call to her daughter, she called her friend Karen, whose home she had been on her way to when the taxi arrived. Jillian had planned to stay at Karen and her husband's house until she found an apartment. Karen was ecstatic for Jillian when she heard she was staying, sensing that her friend hadn't really wanted to leave her job and home—or her employer.

Jillian had met Karen at a book club, introduced to her by Drew, an accountant she had dated over the past year who was now decidedly just a friend. Karen had known from the start that Drew was not the one for Jillian and had surmised that Jillian's heart belonged to another, even if Jillian was not prepared to admit it. Karen had become Jillian's best friend in California—at least her best female friend.

Karen likewise adored Jillian, crediting her with her desire to go back to college and finish a degree, as well as with being the one who encouraged her to renew a spark with her husband, Robert. Jillian still felt she had little to do with it, but Karen was adamant that all of this was inspired by Jillian, so she gave up fighting against it.

Next, Jillian tried to call Marty to video chat. When she didn't answer, Jillian sent her a text message telling her to go online for

Kathy J. Jacobson

a video call right away if she was able. Often, unless Marty was in the middle of an emergency or a meeting, that strategy worked, and this time was no exception.

Marty answered, her expectant face filling the computer screen.

"Hi, Mom. I was just thinking about you. This was the day, wasn't it?" referring to the day that Jillian had planned to leave.

"Well, it was *going* to be the day," Jillian said, a huge smile spreading across her face.

"I haven't seen you smile like that in months," Marty exclaimed. "Spill it, Mama."

Jillian went on to tell her daughter the story—most of it anyway—leaving out some of the more personal details. Jillian told her daughter that she had been right. She had been afraid—scared to death, actually. When Jillian thought John might not survive on the night he had collapsed, she could hardly breathe. She didn't think she could stand the hurt of losing someone she loved—again. But she had finally decided, almost too late, that she was ready to give love another chance.

Marty was just about to begin an overnight shift at the hospital, so she had to cut the call short. Usually, that would be cause for disappointment, but not on this occasion. Jillian couldn't wait to get back to the house—and to John. She checked herself in the mirror. She pulled a brush out of her bag and ran it through her hair, then found her toothbrush. Jillian felt an odd mix of pure exhaustion—she hadn't really slept in days—and sheer happiness—she couldn't seem to stop smiling.

It was an incredible feeling to realize that she might be able to share her heart with someone—someone very special. She closed the door to the cottage behind her and headed back through the yard toward the house and—Jillian felt down deep inside—toward her future. She looked up at the setting sun and the heavens, and just prayed two words—*thank you*.

Chapter Two

Jillian walked into the kitchen through the back door, as she had hundreds of times over the past thirteen months, but this time, it felt different. She sat down on one of the stools at the counter and waited for John to finish his call. Lucy came prancing into the room, and Jillian picked up the soft, orange feline and told her that she was staying. As if on cue, Lucy began to purr.

Moments later John came in, smiling after his conversation with Tommy. Jillian still had trouble believing that until just recently, John would not talk on the phone to anyone—not his friends, not his agent, and not even his beloved nephew. He had been a sad, hurt, and scared man who had cut himself off from anyone who had ever cared about him.

Jillian slid off the stool and stood. "How did it go?" she asked, even though she was pretty sure of the answer, as John was grinning from ear to ear. That grin of his! It was one of his best features, she thought, and she had loved it ever since she was a nineteen-year-old watching him on television in the popular medical drama, *O.R.* While the other girls were attracted to the young interns on the show, she liked the more mature, more serious character John had played. Her friends teased her, saying her was "too old" and "too boring."

It was funny they should call him boring. One article she had read about him shortly after her arrival suggested that that was the main reason his relationship with his on- and off-screen love, Dr. Pamela Prine, played by actress/former Olympic swimmer, Monica Morgan, had failed. Jillian thought her old friends, and Monica Morgan, were crazy. To her, there was not a thing that was boring about John D. Romano.

"Well, the first thing I'm supposed to do is give you a big hug from Tommy, if that's okay?" John said, his grin widening as he moved closer to her.

Jillian's heart started its gymnastics again. "I suppose," she said teasingly, trying to sound nonchalant, which was the exact opposite of reality.

John hugged her again, firmly but gently, for a long moment. It would have been okay with Jillian had they just stood in that spot holding one another for the rest of the evening, but he backed away and searched her face.

"May I take you to dinner?" John asked.

It was six o'clock, but it felt like it was midnight to Jillian. She nodded, but asked, "Is there somewhere we could go just as we are? I don't think I have the energy to get all dressed up. I haven't slept very well lately."

"Neither have I," John said honestly. "We could do something simple and unhealthy for once—burgers, pizza..."

"Pizza!" Jillian exclaimed. "How about the place the pizza came from—the kind we had when we watched the bowl game?" John had ordered from what he had deemed his favorite restaurant in Los Angeles, and possibly the entire country. It had been New Year's Day when they had watched his alma mater, and team he had been a quarterback for in college, Northwestern, win a bowl game. It was the best pizza Jillian had ever tasted.

"Well, it is just a little 'hole in the wall,'" John said, sounding apologetic.

"I like little 'hole in the wall' restaurants," she said, and meant it.

John's face lit up. "I believe you. Let's feed Lucy and then go," he said, smiling again. Jillian suddenly realized that she had seen John smile more in the last hour than she had in the last year.

They fed Lucy her special food and brushed her coat. They closed up the rooms they didn't want her in while they were gone, then headed for the garage. Jillian wondered what the cat would think about this new "situation." Lucy was used to John's undivided attention, pretty much "twenty-four, seven." So far, the cat seemed to adore Jillian, but that might change if she had to share her beloved master with her.

They hopped into John's Land Rover and drove toward the city. They were both quiet, both processing the events of this tumultuous day. Both had gone from feelings of utter despair to incredible highs of hopefulness in a matter of hours.

They arrived at the small, but busy restaurant in an Italian neighborhood. A young man, who was the host, welcomed them. He was "new," according to John. The man wrote their names down on a long list. It appeared that they were going to have to wait quite a while, until John came to the attention of the owner, who had just emerged from the kitchen. The gentleman obviously knew John very well, as the huge, smiling bear of a man lumbered across the room and threw his arms around him.

"Where have you been, Giovanni?" the man asked in a loud voice. "I've missed you, friend!"

"It's a long story, Leo, but I'm back now." John explained, grinning widely.

Kathy J. Jacobson

"I see that," the man said as he held John by the arms, examining him closely, "and you look wonderful—*happy!*" The way the man said it, he sounded like he was surprised.

Then the man turned his attention to Jillian. "And who is this lovely woman with you who is making you so happy?" Jillian felt the blood rushing to her face *again*.

"Leo, this is Jillian," John said.

The burly gentleman hugged Jillian just as he had John, and she hugged him back.

"Nice to meet you, Leo," she said, smiling.

"The pleasure is mine," he replied. "I have a special table for you two. I'll take you to it myself." Leo led them to a quiet little table in a corner near the back of the restaurant. Jillian wondered whose spot they were taking, but she was so hungry by this point that she had to admit she didn't really care.

Leo brought them a bottle of wine on the house, and some crusty Italian bread and olive oil. There was a candle in a wine bottle burning on the dark, heavy wooden table. It was a relaxed atmosphere, and there was something uniquely intimate and comforting about it as well. Jillian loved everything about this place, and said so.

"This is a very special place. Thank you for bringing me here. And Leo—what a sweetheart!" Jillian said.

John looked surprised and pleased at the same time. "I'm glad you like it. It's not everyone's cup of tea," he said quietly, looking thoughtful as he spoke. John was remembering the first and only time he had come to Leo's restaurant with Monica Morgan.

Monica had absolutely *hated* everything about it. Leo had tried to hug her, and she basically pushed him away. As they had eaten, Monica had complained—constantly and loudly. She didn't like the food. There was too much of it, and she was going to gain weight just looking at it. There were no tablecloths. There was no this, no that... The complaints had gone on the entire evening, causing John great embarrassment. They had never returned to the restaurant again. John had come by himself many times since then, but in the past two years he had not left his house. He had basically been a hermit, with the exception of his Monday morning runs to the pet store with his cat.

John and Jillian ordered pizza, some pasta, and salad. As Jillian said when they ordered so much, they could always take home any leftovers.

The meal did not disappoint, nor did the company. Jillian ate more food than she was accustomed to downing at one sitting. She chalked it up to having eaten very little over the past week. She had lost her appetite bit by bit, the closer her slated day of departure had come, and she was quite sure she was a few pounds lighter than her normal weight.

Another thing that made her want to eat was a touch of anxiety. She had to admit it, she was a little bit unnerved by sitting across from the man she had been thinking about almost non-stop for a year. She had always tried to pretend that it was someone else she was looking for, but her thoughts always seemed to return to John. When they did, she tried to tell herself it was anything other than attraction, and definitely not love, but the way she was feeling on this night, she realized she had only been kidding herself.

Jillian cleaned her plate and commented again on how wonderful everything tasted.

John smiled at her. "Are you sure you don't have some Italian blood in you?"

"I'm not sure of anything when it comes to my heritage," she answered, and she proceeded to tell John about being adopted and about the wonderful parents in whose love and care she had fortunately landed.

For the next hour, they exchanged stories about their families.

Jillian talked about what it was like to grow up on the farm, to be an only child, and how supportive and special her parents had been. She told him what a shock it had been when her father, Martin, for whom Marty was named, had gotten sick and died from cancer when Marty was four.

John talked about growing up in a Midwestern town that revolved around the auto industry, with his parents and older brother, Anthony. From the description of his family life John gave, it appeared that he was very close to his mother, who died two years after he graduated from college. She was a kind woman, and a woman of faith, but had had a number of chronic health issues for as long as John could remember.

His father and brother, as it sounded to Jillian, were closer to one another than John had been to either of them. John mentioned that after his football career ended, it seemed like his father and brother drifted out of his life. His father had never approved of his study of literature, calling it "useless." When John was unable to play due to a knee injury, there just didn't seem to be anything that bound them together anymore. John said even his high school sweetheart had ended their relationship when he was no longer a football hero.

John's father died about the same time that Jillian's mother had, and she already knew that John's brother, Anthony, had died ten years before of Alzheimer's disease. John had indeed experienced a good share of heartache himself over the years, Jillian thought to herself as she listened to his life stories.

They finished their meal and ordered tiramisu for dessert, along with espresso. Jillian wasn't too worried about whether or not she could sleep that night. She was more concerned about trying to stay awake in the car on the way home.

John and Jillian could have stayed sitting at that table forever, but they decided they should let someone else have a chance to eat, as the line for a table was still outside the door. As John paid the waiter, Leo came over to say good night to them. They stood up from the table, and again, Leo hugged them both, Jillian first, then John. As he released John, he whispered something to him that Jillian could not quite catch. John answered in a low tone, "I hope so."

John and Jillian were quiet again on the way home, but it was a comfortable quiet. Jillian didn't fall asleep as she had feared. Instead, she felt herself getting a "second wind." *Must be the espresso—or the company.*

When they arrived at the house, they pulled into the garage. John turned off the ignition, and they stepped out of the vehicle. As they did, the strangest feeling came over Jillian—like she was coming home—for good.

Before they went inside, John asked Jillian if she would like to go for a walk, if she wasn't too tired.

"That would be a very wise choice after what we just ate," she said, smiling and puffing out her cheeks.

John laughed, and Jillian smiled again, loving the sound of his happiness. John hit a button to close the garage door behind them before they headed down the circular driveway to the street. It was a beautiful, calm, and mild evening. Jillian had been here just over a year and was still amazed how nice it could be in winter. Back in Wisconsin, where she came from, it was fifteen degrees. Here, it was about sixty.

They walked close to a two-mile route, which was probably pushing it a bit. John was still not one hundred percent after his surgery in early January, but he was getting stronger every day. He was a man accustomed to hours of exercise a day, and Jillian knew that it had been frustrating and annoying for him to take things so

Kathy J. Jacobson

slow and steady. Just this past week he had been given the "green light" to use his incredible workout room once again, albeit on a very limited basis to start, and no weightlifting yet. It would be months before he could work out the way he had before his medical event.

They returned to the house and entered the kitchen.

"I need to get a new bike," John said, putting his keys down on the counter. John had had a bike accident the previous spring, caused by balance issues from the tumor. He had returned from his ride that day bloodied, angry, and very frightened. He had thrown his ruined bike, along with his helmet, into a heap on the curb for the trash collectors and had never replaced it.

"What are you doing tomorrow?" Jillian asked.

"Bike shopping?" John asked, reading her mind.

"Good idea," she said, like it had been his, "and maybe we could stop by my friend's house and get mine, too."

"Deal," John said. It was one of Marty's favorite expressions, and Jillian had introduced it to John. Ever since, it had become a favorite word in Jillian and John's conversations with one another.

As wonderful as the evening had been, Jillian's second wind was beginning to wear off, and she was fading fast. John must have sensed it. He moved closer to her and said, "It's been an interesting day."

"That's a diplomatic way of putting it," Jillian said.

"Oh, you know me. I'm all about diplomacy," he replied, with proper sarcasm in his voice.

Jillian chuckled and rolled her eyes. John, at times, was one of the most blunt people she had ever encountered, or perhaps *honest* was a kinder way of putting it. She didn't mind it when he was trying to be helpful, but she hadn't appreciated some of their earlier exchanges, which were more on the hurtful side.

She smiled at him warmly. "Well, the day certainly *ended* well. Thank you for dinner, and the talk, and the walk... and for everything, John," she added quietly. "But, I think I'd better call it a day. Even the espresso isn't working anymore."

"May I walk you to your door?" John asked, surprising her.

"I'd like that," she said.

John opened the back door from the kitchen to the patio, and they began walking toward the guest cottage. They passed the swimming pool, which was shimmering in the moonlight. As he had earlier in the day, John gently slipped his hand into hers. Jillian loved the feel of his touch and was wishing that it was a longer distance to her residence, as they arrived all too soon. Her heart was doing its workout again as they stopped at her door.

"Jillian, may I kiss you?" John asked, turning her toward him gently.

Jillian was pretty sure that no one had ever asked her that before. She thought about the last time she had been kissed by a man. It had been New Year's Eve. As a favor, she had accompanied Drew to a huge and loud New Year's Eve party thrown by some of his major clients. That night, he had grabbed and kissed her twice, once at the stroke of midnight and the other when he had dropped her off. Neither time had she appreciated it.

Jillian couldn't seem to speak, so she just nodded.

In contrast to the kiss from Drew, she didn't want this one to end. Afterward, John just held her. Jillian felt like they were breathing in unison, and she didn't feel like she could get close enough to him, even though their bodies were against one another's. *So this is what love feels like.*

John pulled back and looked at her. "Good night," he said.

"Yes, it was a good night," she said.

He smiled, kissed her forehead, and reluctantly began his walk back to the house.

Jillian went into her cottage and sat on the edge of the bed. As she did every night, she said her prayers, a habit since childhood.

Kathy J. Jacobson

She prayed for her daughter, her friends in Wisconsin and California, her friends back in Tanzania, and all those who were in need. And lastly, she prayed, as she had so many times over the past year, for God to give John whatever he needed—silently adding that she sincerely hoped the answer had something to do with her.

Chapter Three

The next morning, Jillian woke up and laid in her bed for a short while, just thinking. She wondered if yesterday had been just a dream, but as she glanced around the barren room, she decided it had indeed been real.

She had packed up everything and cleaned the cottage from top to bottom before her planned departure. Her bike was at Karen's, and her guitar was locked up in the music room at church. She suddenly wondered what she would do for employment or where she would live in the future. Maybe she shouldn't be too hasty about bringing back her bike. Perhaps she really should move into Karen's house after all. She and John had a lot of things to talk over, she thought to herself.

As she considered the options in her mind, Jillian was startled by a light knock on her door. She got up, quickly found her satin robe in her opened suitcase, and went to the door. She looked through the peep hole, saw that it was John, and opened the door.

"Sorry if I woke you," he said. "Would you like to join me for breakfast in the kitchen, in say, half an hour?"

Jillian smiled, "That would be nice. The cupboard is bare," she said, glancing behind her.

"That's what I thought. I'll see you soon, then," he said with a warm smile on his face.

Jillian, again, was impressed by his thoughtfulness. It had been evident even on the very first day she had moved into the cottage, when he had food items stocked for her because it was a holiday. His thoughtfulness, together with the way he listened to the things she said and remembered them, were some of the things she liked best about John.

Jillian jumped through the shower, dragging back into the bathroom many of the items she had packed up just the day before. Yesterday seemed like a lifetime ago rather than just hours.

Once more, she seriously wondered what she had been thinking when she decided to leave in the first place. Chances for real, honest love "didn't exactly grow on trees," as her mom would have said. Jillian thought about her mother and missed her so much. Her mom had told her that someday true love would find her when she least expected it. *You were right, Mom.* She felt both warm at the memory of her mother, but sad that she wasn't there to talk to, or for her to see what was happening in Jillian's life. *You would have liked John, Mom.*

Jillian dressed quickly, and rushed toward the house. She slowed down as she approached the door and stepped into the kitchen. John was at the counter near the sink, putting the finishing touches on a fruit and cheese tray. Very European—her first impression. He had some incredible-looking breads and croissants on a plate, along with some great-looking jams. He said he had gone down to the Farmer's Market earlier to buy them, which shocked Jillian. She had never known him to go to the market the entire time she had lived there.

"I hope a continental breakfast is okay," he said, carrying the food to the breakfast nook table. There were two place settings ready and waiting, along with a single yellow rose in a small vase on the table.

"It's more than okay," Jillian said, as she slid into the bench seat at the table. "I'm impressed," she continued.

"Don't be. I didn't make anything. I just… *gathered*."

Jillian was still impressed, and realized that she had never had any man, other than her dad, make—or *gather*—breakfast for her before.

"Really, John, this is perfect."

They continued their conversation from the evening before about their families. John was telling Jillian about the amazing bread his mother used to make. The kind he sent out for on a regular basis, and Leo's bread, were the closest to hers he had ever found, but no other could really capture it.

"I've never been able to find the exact same bread, anywhere," John said, a far-off look in his eyes again as he spoke of his mother.

"And you never will, John. There are some things that only moms can make. We might be able to follow a recipe and come close, but it will never be the same. Our mothers had their own special touch, and then there's the added ingredient, the most important of all—love."

John looked at her in a way that made her start to blush, so she changed the subject and went on to tell him about the fruit pies that were her mother's specialties. They were the best.

He countered by telling her about the homemade noodles and gnocchi that his mom used to make. Jillian made a mental note to see if Tommy had any of these recipes of his grandmother's that she could try, but realized she was getting ahead of herself.

"And of course—her cannoli," he said, "but you already know about that. You came as close as anyone ever could to making it like she did. That was really a special surprise, Jillian."

Jillian had made John's mother's cannoli recipe for him at

Christmas. *That's because it had the secret ingredient, John.* But she didn't have the nerve to say that out loud to him—not yet, anyway.

"You made breakfast—I should clean up," Jillian said.

"Not this time. You've done enough of that for me over the past year," he replied. His words reminded Jillian that they needed to have a practical conversation sometime during the day, about how long she could stay on the premises now that she was no longer employed by John as his household helper.

"But I was getting paid for that, John," she reminded him. But he would hear none of it, and shooed her away.

She told him that she was just going to go to the cottage to unpack a few things since he was occupied. Jillian watched him for a moment as he ran water into the sink and poured dish soap into it. She had never seen him like she had seen him this morning—preparing breakfast items, clearing the table, washing dishes—so real—so regular—so normal.

She started for the door. "Don't forget your rose, Jillian," he called after her, his eyes glancing at the flower in the vase on the breakfast nook table.

"Thank you," she said quietly as she took the simple vase and flower from the table. Jillian walked back to the cottage, smelling the rose along the way, still wondering if she was in some kind of really good dream.

Jillian hung up some of her clothes and put others in a pile to iron—one of her least favorite activities. She was just thinking about what to do about the future when her cell phone rang. It was the number for a nursing home she had recently contacted about possibly picking up some nursing shifts.

They told her that they were not in need of any nurses right now, but maybe she would be interested in doing a part-time activity director position for just a month. Their director was on maternity leave. They had been piecing together some activities with volunteers for a month now, but couldn't find anyone who wanted to work such a short stint and so few hours.

Jillian thought for a moment. Why not? It was only three days a week, five hours a day. She had always enjoyed her visits with the homebound when she had been a parish nurse. She was going to start right away Monday morning with an orientation and then work that afternoon, as it was bingo day.

She put away some of her things, but left others in the suitcase, not certain of her future plans. She couldn't wait to tell John about the job opportunity. This was something new for her—not just the type of job, but having someone to want to tell about it, other than her daughter. She went back to the house where John was just finishing up, drying his hands with a towel.

"I just got a job," she announced.

He put down the dish towel, and a strange look crossed his face. He was trying to act happy for her, but was having a difficult time masking his disappointment. "That's a good thing, right? Where is it?" he asked.

Jillian told him about the temporary position at the small nursing home. Then she asked him if he thought she should move to her friend, Karen's, house, after all.

"Is that what you would like?" he asked.

"Not necessarily, but I do feel a bit awkward living in the cottage without working here. Could I pay you some rent?"

"Not a chance," he said, walking toward her.

"But…"

"But nothing," he said, putting his hands on her shoulders. Again, Jillian felt like she was in a dream. "I don't think you understand, Jillian. I don't want you to leave." John wanted to tack on the word ever, but was afraid of scaring Jillian off again.

"But how can I repay you?" Jillian asked.

"Jillian, you have given me back my life. How can I repay you?"

Jillian was stunned by his words. She wanted to kiss him so badly, and finally she just said in a gentle voice, "You could kiss me."

John looked pleasantly surprised, and then looked at her lovingly. "I asked what could I do to repay you, not the other way around," he said softly. Then he took her face gently in his hands and kissed her. Now Jillian felt certain that she was dreaming, or perhaps had died and gone to heaven.

"I started thinking about kissing you from the very first time I saw you," John said, his forehead to hers.

"You mean in the kitchen, the day Lucy ran away from you?" Jillian asked. That was the first time they had seen each other face-to-face, months after Jillian had started working at the house. Had it not been for John's cat, they might have never seen each other in person.

"No, the day Jerry Mack dropped you off in my driveway thirteen months ago," he admitted.

That piece of information took Jillian by surprise. She looked at him, searching his face. "You were in the window, weren't you? I thought I saw someone," she said.

John just nodded.

Now it was Jillian's turn. "I started thinking about kissing you the day I found that dish of food in the garbage," Jillian confessed, remembering John's early act of defiance her first week on the job. She hadn't even admitted that to herself before, but now she knew that it was true.

They kissed once more, then held each other tightly. Jillian never wanted to let go.

"John, I think we should go buy you a bike and go pick up mine," Jillian said. She suddenly felt the need to take a good long ride.

John looked at her and said, "Good idea." She thought perhaps he was feeling that very same way.

Jillian called Karen to make arrangements to retrieve her bike. Karen and Robert were going to be gone that afternoon, but she said she would put the bike near her front door. Karen thought it would be safe if it wasn't out there too long unattended.

John and Jillian picked up her bike first, then Jillian directed John to the shop where she had purchased her bike. It had been her favorite of the three businesses she and Drew had visited when bike shopping the previous spring. It had a large inventory, with friendly, helpful, and knowledgeable employees.

There was a bright blue Giant that caught John's eye, but his last bike had been blue, and he didn't want any reminders of that bike or the accident he had while riding it. Instead, he decided on a Trek CrossRip LTD, a beautiful silver bike with orange trim. He selected a helmet, water bottle, and lock, and he was set.

Before they loaded up, Jillian took a photo of John posing with his new prized possession and, with his permission, sent it to his nephew, Tommy, with her phone. Tommy immediately responded, "Way to go, Zio." Zio—"uncle" in Italian—was what Tommy always called John. John decided that his next purchase would be a smartphone, which he had fought against two years ago, even before he had become so reclusive. And since he hadn't done any calling for the past two years, it had been a moot point until now.

They caught a bite to eat at Paco's on the way home. Jillian told John about how Pete had introduced her to this spot. Pete was one of her favorite people she had met since moving to L.A.—and ever. He was a personal trainer with a body that turned the heads of every female in Orange County, both young and old. Not only was he handsome, but he was as they say, beautiful on the inside, too.

Kathy J. Jacobson

Jillian and Pete had gone out a few times, but Jillian knew that he was still in love with his former fiancée, Kelly. And somewhere in the recesses of Jillian's mind, she knew she was in love with someone, too, but couldn't bear to come to terms with that idea.

"Is that the Mr. Universe guy I saw you with on a number of occasions?" John asked.

"Yes, Pete would fit that description, I believe." Jillian went on to tell him the story of how they met at the gym, then about Pete and Kelly, and then about their upcoming marriage the first weekend in March in San Francisco. John looked a bit relieved when she mentioned that fact.

John, you have nothing to be relieved about. Jillian was remembering how many times she was with Pete, or Drew, or anyone else, and could only think about John.

After the tacos, which John admitted were the best he'd had in the area, they went home to ride. They spent almost two hours biking, until Jillian thought John was looking a bit worn out.

Remember the man had a brain tumor removed a month ago, Jillian. It was amazing that he could be out riding a bike like he was. His recovery had been remarkable, some due to his otherwise great physical health prior to the procedure and much due to the use of the nasal approach. He was so fortunate that the tumor was in just the right location to be able to use that non-invasive procedure. That, along with a benign biopsy, had been very welcomed outcomes to a very frightening situation.

John and Jillian cooked a simple meal together that night, then spent the next few hours talking. They each continued to share their "story" with one another, making up for all the wasted time of the last year with barely a word between them.

Finally, Jillian was beginning to fade—again. She still wasn't completely recovered from the self-imposed ordeal of the last week. John again walked her back to the cottage, slipping his hand into hers once more. She could get used to this, she decided.

At the door he turned to her, and with a sparkle in his eyes, asked, "Could I repay you with a kiss again?"

She chuckled and said, "That would be nice." He kissed her, and she thought that each kiss from John was sweeter than the last. She could get used to that, too.

"What time is church tomorrow?" John asked, surprising her once more. "That is what you do on Sunday mornings, isn't it?"

Jillian nodded and told him the times of the services. "Would you like to come with me?" She had asked him on Christmas Eve, and he had hesitated, but declined her offer.

He nodded affirmatively. She thought they should start with the late service, which was a more blended service of worship—some traditional, the rest more contemporary. She always felt it was easier to follow than the early service, especially for guests.

"I'll drive," John said.

Jillian just looked at him, trying hard not to look so baffled by all of this. Lately this man was one surprise after another—all good ones.

Again, like the night before, he kissed her forehead, said good night, and walked back to the house.

Jillian went inside the cottage and watched him from the window. She had not wanted him to go. She turned away from the window, still in awe that John was going to go to church with her. She closed the blinds, then pulled down a built-in ironing board to press an outfit for the next morning.

She wondered what Drew's reaction would be to John accompanying her to worship. The two men had actually met on Christmas Day, but hadn't really had a chance to talk. She wasn't even certain that Drew knew who John was, or had given him a second thought. Drew had been anxious that day, wanting to put in his time serving at the community meal and get out of there as quickly as he could.

Kathy J. Jacobson

John, on the other hand, had stayed to help clean up. He had been full of surprises that day, too, first just by showing up, then by helping serve the meal. He had been so friendly with everyone as they went through the line, and after they ate with some of the street people, a little boy dropped his tray. The boy's father reacted angrily, calling him stupid. John dropped his tray on purpose to distract attention away from the boy's situation and also to make him feel better. Together, John, Jillian and the boy, Rick, cleaned up the messes. John had been so very kind.

Jillian messaged Marty and set up a video call time for the next evening, Jillian's time. She sometimes wished her daughter was back in the States. She would be by next Christmas, and Jillian was thrilled by the idea. If there were going to be so many wonderful and surprising things going on in Jillian's life, she needed her daughter closer, or in a place with better Internet service at the very least.

Jillian hung up her clothes and got ready for bed. She crawled into the comfortable bed and thanked God for an absolutely amazing twenty-four hours, then fell fast asleep.

Jillian had not considered the possibility that people would recognize John at church. It hadn't been an issue at the bike shop the day before, but it was clear in the church service that more than one person—primarily females—recognized him. Many people came up to her to say hello, which was not unusual, but there were a few that she had rarely spoken to who were suddenly very friendly. She was pretty sure that was because of John.

Drew recognized John, too—not from television but from serving together at the community Christmas dinner.

John extended his hand to Drew to shake it. "Drew, isn't it?" he asked.

"Yes, it is. I'm sorry, I can't recall your name," Drew replied.

"John," he said.

"Yes, nice to see you again," he lied. Jillian could always tell when Drew was not being completely truthful or sincere, and this was one of those occasions.

Luckily for Jillian, Drew had gone to the first service and was heading off to a meeting of the congregation's finance committee. Drew was an accountant, so it was a natural way for him to serve the church with his talents. Jillian was sincerely happy that she didn't have to sit in between the two men during the church service. On Christmas Day, she had stood for more than an hour between them while serving food. It was an unusual situation, to say the least.

Jillian knew that she was going to have to talk to Drew—soon. Things had definitely changed between her and John in the last two days. Drew, she thought, had finally given up on the idea of them being a couple, although every once in a while, it felt like he was testing her to see if she would reconsider. John or no John, Jillian knew that Drew was never going to be more than a friend to her.

Pastor Jim did a wonderful job delivering his message, as usual. He talked about Jesus healing a man possessed by demons and the new start he had been given, and that even the demons appeared to be freed and given a chance to reconsider their future paths. He pointed out St. Paul's words: "If anyone is in Christ, there is a new creation; everything old has passed away; see, everything has become new." It was very a thought-provoking message, and John listened intently. The songs were a perfect match for the theme of the day, and the piano and guitar players were excellent.

After the service, Pastor Jim hugged everyone on the way out, as was his usual practice. Jillian introduced Pastor Jim to John, who thanked him for his words, and Jillian noticed that John had folded up his service bulletin and put it in the pocket of his sport coat.

Nancy approached Jillian and hugged her. "And who is your friend, Jillian?"

"Nancy, this is John."

"Is this the John we prayed for last month?"

"This is the very one. As you can see, our prayers were answered the way we were hoping this time," Jillian answered. Nancy's own husband had died in his mid-thirties, leaving her with six children to raise. Many prayers had been offered up for Ed, but things did not have a happy ending, not in this life anyway. While Nancy was hurt and angry for a while after her loss, her faith and her faithful friends had helped her through. She was one of the strongest, most faithful, and nicest people that Jillian had ever met.

Nancy took John's hand in hers and said, "I am so happy that you are all right, John, and I am so happy that you are here with Jillian today." Nancy was as tall on sincerity and sweetness as she was short in stature.

"Thank you," John said, "and I'm very happy to be here with Jillian today, too, and to meet you, Nancy." Jillian could feel her face turning a shade or two redder.

They talked together for a few more minutes, then Jillian went to the music room to retrieve her guitar, as she wanted to use it at her new job. John and Jillian headed to John's vehicle. John opened the door for her, then put the guitar in the back. She felt like she was going home from church in Tanzania, her guitar in the back of a Land Rover and riding home with someone special.

"Church has really changed since the last time I attended," John said as they drove out of the parking lot.

"Good change, I hope?" Jillian asked.

"Very good change," he said.

"I like this church a lot, but I've been pretty lucky in that department. There are a wide variety of churches out there, but I was raised in one like this. It's the perfect balance of challenge and grace. I guess I need that."

"Most of us do," he said sincerely.

They were quiet the rest of the way home. John was thinking—processing again, she could tell. She liked how he did that, rather than just babbling on about things. He was such an intelligent man, and a real thinker, and she appreciated both of those qualities. She put her head back on the headrest, feeling relaxed and very thankful for a special morning.

"He went to *church* with you, Mom?" Marty asked in astonishment as she and Jillian talked over their laptop screens.

"Yes, and he was the one who brought it up. He asked me last night what time church was this morning, and then I asked him if he wanted to come with me, and he said 'yes.' I think he really liked it," Jillian said.

"I think that man really likes you. Sounds like he has it bad, Mom," Marty said.

"Do you really think so, Marty?"

Her daughter nodded her head affirmatively in an exaggerated way. "What do you think about him, Mom?"

"I'm pretty sure I have it bad, too," she admitted to her daughter.

Marty nodded her head again in the same way, which made Jillian laugh. They talked more about Marty and her week, made a plan for their next online "date," and then signed off.

Jillian got her things ready for the next day, a habit of hers since she was a little girl. She always liked to have everything ready the night before, especially if she had something important to do, and beginning a new job qualified as something that was very important in her eyes.

John had gone to the library to call Tommy at the same time that Jillian had gone to the cottage to talk to Marty. She had only been away from him for about an hour, and even when talking to her daughter, she couldn't help but think of him, wishing that they were together. She was not kidding when she told her daughter that she "had it bad," another one of her mother's old expressions.

That night, Jillian realized for the first time exactly what John had come to mean to her. She was completely and utterly in love with him. Jillian only hoped that her daughter was right, and that maybe, just maybe, he was in love with her, too.

Chapter Four

Jillian's first day on the job at the nursing facility was special. She had forgotten how much she enjoyed working with senior citizens.

The orientation felt easy and familiar. Many of the rules and regulations were similar to hospitals and nursing facilities in Wisconsin. She was given a tour of the tiny twenty-four-bed nursing home and met all the residents, except two who were sleeping and one who was sick that day.

The afternoon went quickly with rounds of bingo, a snack, and many conversations. Everyone wanted to meet Jillian, and she wanted to get to know them. This would be a fun situation for the next month, Jillian thought. She would still have plenty of time to work on her blog and begin the first chapter of her book. She had planned to have that started by now, but her near departure had derailed her temporarily.

Jillian couldn't believe that it was already the third day of February. Yesterday had been Groundhog Day. She had never even given it a thought. She figured that when you don't really have a winter, you don't pay much attention to Punxsutawney Phil out in Pennsylvania or Jimmy the Groundhog in Sun Prairie, Wisconsin. It's no big deal whether there are six more weeks of winter or not, because it was never really winter in Los Angeles, at least not to Jillian.

She went home that day thinking that she would have done this day for free. She hoped she would be able to come back and volunteer once in a while when her work assignment was over.

When Jillian returned to the house, John was all ears about her first day. He intently listened to her talk about the activities, the people, and some of their stories. John's listening skills were very well practiced. Jillian believed that was why he was such a talented and successful actor. He was always observing, thinking, and processing people and experiences, then applying what he learned to his craft. It was a real gift.

So as they sipped cups of coffee at the kitchen counter and discussed Jillian's work, she also said a silent prayer—that God would lead John back to his.

The next day Jillian wasn't scheduled at the nursing home, so she and John went smartphone shopping. They spent the morning exploring different products and their features, and Jillian learned more about her own phone in the process. After John chose one, the remainder of the day was spent experimenting with features and downloading apps, with a bike ride thrown into the mix before it got dark. Jillian thought that it had been a pretty expensive week for John, buying both a bike and a phone, but she knew that both would get a lot of use and he wouldn't regret the purchases.

One of the first things they had done upon arriving home was to enter Tommy's phone number, and then hers, into John's phone. Then John called Jillian, and she saved his number in her phone. Jillian sent him a text message with the photo she had taken of him on his new bike earlier that week, and John saved it as his contact photo. Jillian assured him that he would love having a phone with a good camera, to be able to capture special moments that too often get passed by.

"You mean like this?" John asked, snapping a photo of Jillian as she sat on the chair next to the pool.

Jillian walked over to him and bent over to have a look. "So, how did you do?" she asked, showing him how to check the photo. It was a candid shot rather than posed, and she liked that, but Jillian, like many people, really didn't like photos of herself. One thing she did notice when she looked at her face, however, was that she looked happy. It made her think of the night at restaurant when Leo told John that he looked different—happy.

"Well, the subject is a little suspect, but otherwise, nice job," Jillian said.

"Jillian, don't do that," John told her.

"Don't do what?"

"Put yourself down. You are beautiful."

Jillian always had trouble taking a compliment and also had a tendency to compare herself to others.

"John, I've seen the women you've dated in the past. *They* are beautiful."

He pulled her down next to him onto the bench where he was sitting. "Jillian, you are the most beautiful woman—no, more than that—you are the most beautiful person I know."

Jillian was speechless. She didn't know what to say to that. She started to shake her head "no," but John put his hand behind her head and gently pulled it toward him. He stopped and looked her straight in the eyes, shook his head up and down, and said, "Yes, you are," and then kissed her.

Jillian had a habit of asking God what she had ever done to deserve her beautiful daughter, Marty. Now she had a new question for God—what have I ever done to deserve this wonderful man?

Kathy J. Jacobson

Jillian was back at work the next day, this time with her guitar in tow. She was going to take a taxi, but John had insisted on giving her a ride and said he would pick her up later as well. She entered the facility and noticed a huge sign near the nurse's station that said: TODAY IS FEBRUARY 5, and one below it that said the next holiday would be VALENTINE'S DAY on February 14. She'd better get something for John—soon. She had one idea and would check it out during her break.

Music time was right after lunch. Jillian played the guitar and sang, and the residents sang along. Then Jillian sang a few songs for them. They clapped between each piece and were a very gracious audience.

Afterward, many of the residents stayed in the activity area to work some giant crossword puzzles. It was fun, and several of them were really good at them. She would have to find some harder ones for the next time.

Again, when she got in the car at the end of the day, John wanted to know about everything. Jillian told him, and he listened intently once more.

"John, if you would ever like to come in and volunteer for an activity, you are welcome. I think you would really like the residents," Jillian said.

"Let's plan something for Friday, unless the day is already set."

"Actually, we have a reading activity scheduled on Friday. Would you be our guest reader? That would be right up your alley, I do believe," Jillian said, smiling at him.

"Deal," he said, sounding excited.

Jillian smiled all the way home. She felt so happy, although she had to admit that from time to time she still felt frightened. It scared her how much she cared for the man sitting next to her, and she wondered what would happen if she ever were to lose him for any reason. She had made a resolution, however, that she would stop putting herself down and doubting, and just try to enjoy the moment and trust, and pray, that all would come out well in the end. She was determined to savor every minute that she had with John in her life.

During her break earlier that day, she had ordered a custom Northwestern football jersey for John for Valentine's Day. There were few material things that John needed, and she wanted to get something that would be different, and hopefully special to him in some way. It would say "Romano" on the top of the back, with the number 7 on both front and back, and it would be delivered just in time for Valentine's Day.

John had told her on New Year's Day that seven was his number when he was the quarterback for Northwestern, chosen because of his birthday on July 7. He had also picked it because it was supposed to be a lucky number. He said that one didn't pan out too well, as he had a career-ending knee injury at the end of his junior season. That reminded Jillian again that someday she was going to encourage him to see an orthopedic specialist.

That evening Jillian called Karen again, this time for a restaurant recommendation. She wanted to take John out for dinner and was looking for somewhere special. It needed to be somewhere she could afford, and preferably not part of the Hollywood scene. Karen gave her the name of her favorite place to go, not too far away.

"Jillian, I was going to ask you how you are doing, but I can tell by your voice. Are you really as happy as you sound?" Karen asked.

"Yes, I am, Karen. It's been a long time since I've been this happy. It's a little scary, but I'm going with it."

"That is great, Jillian. You deserve happiness."

They went on to talk about Karen's classes, which had just started up again for the new semester, and how things were going between Karen and Robert. Speaking of happiness, it appeared to be epidemic.

The call ended, and Jillian's phone immediately rang. It was Drew.

"Jillian, how are you?" he asked.

"I'm great, Drew. How about you?"

"Well, my fitness club just had a fire."

"Oh, no! I hope no one was hurt."

"No injuries. It happened during the night. Only the attendant and two others were there, and they got out right away. The owners have a couple other gyms, but they are so far away from my house. What was the name of that place you went to last summer, and what's the address?"

Jillian gave him the information. It wasn't as close to Drew's home as his own club, but more convenient than their satellites.

"Thanks. It will have to do."

"Make sure to make use of the personal trainers. Pete is great, but there are a lot of other good ones there, too, and you will probably get one free session like I did."

"Sure, maybe I will. So, want to catch a movie or dinner tonight?" Drew asked.

"Not tonight, Drew," Jillian said. She didn't know if she should say something about seeing someone or not, because she still was not completely sure what was happening with her and John. Were they "seeing each other"?

"Okay, maybe another time. I think I'll go and check out that health club, then."

"Good idea. If Pete is there, say hi to him for me," Jillian said.

"Will do," Drew said and hung up.

Jillian doubted he would. In fact, if Drew could remember Pete's name, she would be shocked. Drew had a very bad habit of not listening carefully to people, or at least not to Jillian. She supposed if he was talking to one of his accounting firm clients, he might pay better attention, but otherwise, he was pretty worthless in that area.

After the phone calls, Jillian took her black dress out of her suitcase to hang it out. She had purchased it last year to go to the Philharmonic with Drew. She was planning to wear it to dinner on Friday night, assuming they were actually going to go.

Later that night, she had the opportunity to ask John if she could take him out to dinner on Friday night. He accepted, and she told him the kind of place to expect, without the specifics. She was happy to be able to do something special for him, and with him.

On Friday afternoon, John came to the nursing home to read a very condensed version of Moby Dick, dressed in an old-fashioned white cotton sailor shirt and hat. Jillian wondered where he got them, but she figured that in his business he had plenty of connections to come up with a costume. He was amazing, and the people went crazy over his portrayal of Captain Ahab.

A few people recognized him from television, and once that happened, everyone wanted his autograph. He patiently signed one for each person, residents and staff alike, writing a personal note to each person. And with each one he signed, Jillian fell more and more in love with John D. Romano.

That evening Jillian drove up to the front door of John's house and rang the doorbell. She had borrowed Karen's car for twenty-four hours. Robert was gone on business and had left his vehicle, so Karen had loaned hers to Jillian for her dinner date.

Jillian was dressed in her black evening dress, with high heels

Kathy J. Jacobson

and her hair up. She couldn't even remember the last time she had worn her hair like that. John came to the door and opened it, being forewarned that she would pick him up there.

He just stared at Jillian. "And I thought you were beautiful before," he said quietly.

Jillian was determined to accept a compliment for once in her life. "Thank you. Are you ready to go to dinner, sir?" she asked, and extended her elbow to escort him to the car.

The restaurant was perfect—just the type of place that Jillian was hoping for. When she gave the host her name, he said, "Mrs. Wilson told me you would be coming," and proceeded to take them to a small, half-circle booth which was very intimate. *Thank you, Karen.*

John and Jillian sat next to one another on the soft leather seat. The table was covered in white linen, topped with fresh flowers in a clear crystal vase and candles, which the waiter began to light after they were seated.

They asked for a carafe of water and ordered a bottle of wine. John was so close to her that it was distracting. Jillian could smell his cologne and felt the warmth of his body next to hers. Then there were those gorgeous eyes of his. She wasn't sure she could stand it, but she made herself keep eye contact. So much for perusing the menu!

John looked so handsome in his dark sport coat, crisp white shirt, and solid-colored tie, and she could see a few people noticing him again. Jillian wondered how it felt to be a celebrity. If this was how he attracted attention now, after two years completely out of the limelight, she could only imagine what it had been like when he was at the height of stardom. She wondered what it would be like again in the future if—when—he returned to work. She was pretty certain, after what she had witnessed that afternoon, that this man could not stay away from the work he so clearly and dearly loved. She wondered how she would react if she was involved with him when that happened. *We'll cross that bridge when we come to it,* she thought.

John looked around the restaurant and then back at her. "This is a wonderful place, Jillian, but what's the occasion?" John asked.

She didn't plan to say it, but it just came out, "You."

For a moment, she thought he was going to kiss her right then and there, and she had to hold herself back from kissing him. Instead, he took her hand under the table and held it firmly. Now he was the one shaking his head "no," and she in turn, shook her head "yes." He smiled when she did that and then squeezed her hand.

Just then the waiter arrived at the table and asked if they were ready to order. Neither of them had really paid much attention to the available selections, so they asked for some suggestions, which turned out to be a great decision. Quite frankly, Jillian really didn't care what she ate. Her focus for the evening was John, and only John, if she was truthful.

The entire evening zipped by. The food was top tier, the service professional but friendly, and the company beyond compare. Jillian hadn't known that there was so much to talk about, but it seemed that one conversation led to another. John was an interesting person and had done so many things that Jillian had never done, and vice-versa.

At the end of the evening, John wanted to pay for dinner, but Jillian insisted that she was taking him out this time, and he acquiesced.

They walked out of the restaurant to the street. It was another beautiful evening, and it seemed too nice to just rush back into the car. The restaurant was across the street from a small park

Kathy J. Jacobson

with a huge fountain in the center of it, and they crossed the street toward it. Jillian imagined the park would have been filled with people had it been a summer night. Instead, they had the place almost to themselves. They walked around for close to an hour, letting their dinners digest and talking from time to time. Other times they were quiet, just enjoying each other's company and the fresh, evening air.

"We'd better get Karen's car back from the valet, I suppose," Jillian finally said.

They drove home, both quiet in their own thoughts. Jillian felt so many different feelings that night. She was comfortable with John, ridiculously attracted to him, and felt so much love for him. In the back of her mind, however, there was still that little bit of fear that this was just too good to be true. Her slight misgivings aside, Jillian couldn't remember ever feeling like this about anyone, anytime, during her life. If she had, it was so long ago that she wasn't able to recall it.

When they arrived at the house, John opened the garage door with the key pad. There was one empty space in the garage, and she drove Karen's car into it so that it would be safe for the night. Karen certainly was a wonderful friend, Jillian thought. She should take her out for a treat or something when she returned the car next afternoon, or maybe dinner since Robert was gone.

Jillian was starting to feel like she was monopolizing John's time. He didn't seem to mind, and she sure didn't, but she thought perhaps a little break in the action might be a good idea, especially with the way she was feeling toward him right then.

Thinking of Karen also made Jillian think about how she needed to get back to the book club, which met at Karen's house once a month. They had not met in December because of the holidays and Karen's final exams. In January, Jillian had been too busy with John's hospitalization, and subsequently, planning her "escape."

She had been an emotional wreck and had not read the book for that month or gone to the meeting. Yes, she needed to find out the title of the next book and read it before the third Wednesday of the month rolled around. Maybe John would want to go, too, she thought.

"What are you thinking about, Jillian?" John asked as he walked her back to the cottage, holding her hand as he had each night for the past week.

"About all the good people in my life right now," she said.

"I hope I made the list," he said, turning to her at the door, sounding and looking hopeful.

"The very top," she said in almost a whisper, and she kissed him with a passion that was a bit disconcerting to her. Her heart was racing, and she felt like she had just run around the block. "I've got to go, John," Jillian said breathlessly and unlocked her door.

She turned back toward him. "Good night," she said.

"It *was* a good night," John agreed, repeating the words she had said to him just one week before. He kissed her slowly and gently on the forehead and then they both reluctantly went their separate ways.

Kathy J. Jacobson

Chapter Five

The week preceding Valentine's Day passed even more quickly than the previous one. Jillian did indeed take Karen out for dinner the night after her dinner with John, which worked out well since Karen was lonely without Robert. Karen was happy that Robert would be home soon from his business trip and that the couple would be together on Valentine's Day. Apparently, Robert had something special planned for the occasion, and Karen was truly amazed. In all their years of marriage, he had never done anything like plan a Valentine's date.

The week for Jillian and the residents of the nursing home was filled with special activities. They read the story of St. Valentine—one version anyway. They made Valentines to give to each other and their family members who were invited for cake and ice cream on Saturday afternoon.

All week the residents kept asking when John was coming back, and what John and Jillian were going to do on Valentine's Day.

"What makes you think that we are doing something together on Valentine's Day?" Jillian asked. She had not introduced John as her boyfriend, just as a friend.

Edith, who was ninety-four, said, "You aren't fooling anyone, honey. No one looks at a friend like that, and I'm talking about the both of you!" Jillian could feel herself blushing, but was pleased that Edith thought that John had looked at her like someone who was more than a friend. Jillian smiled at Edith, then tactfully changed the subject. She had had a lot of practice doing that over the years.

A group of students from a church came to do a special Valentine's bingo party on Wednesday after school and sing some songs. Jillian decided that she would have to check if the youth group from Grace Lutheran would be willing to come and do a project sometime soon. She would ask their leader on Sunday morning.

Jillian also led a Bible study that week based on some of the "love passages" in the Bible, and they talked about the different ways God shows us love throughout our lives. Many people talked about their spouses, the majority of whom were no longer living. It was difficult, yet important, for them to remember how much love they had shared. Others talked about children, grandchildren, or best friends they had had throughout the years.

On Friday afternoon, a party was hosted by a women's service club, who brought homemade heart-shaped cookies, regular and sugar-free, party favors, and games to play. One woman brought her accordion and played love songs from the residents' era.

What a fun week it had been! Jillian could hardly believe that her time at the home was nearly half over. She would definitely be coming back to volunteer once her term was finished and was pretty sure her "guest reader" would make another appearance in the future, either before or after her official work assignment ended.

As Jillian walked out the door toward John's waiting vehicle on Friday afternoon, her cell phone rang. It was Drew. Jillian certainly hoped that he was not calling her for a last-minute date or party. She still hadn't found the right opportunity to tell him about John.

"Hi, Drew," she said. "Can I call you back in a little bit?"

"Sure, but I have to leave for a meeting in fifteen minutes, and I really need to talk to you." His voice sounded strange.

"Okay, I will try."

Jillian got into the car and looked at John apologetically. She explained the situation and then asked if he would mind if she called Drew back quickly. He had no objections.

"Hi, Drew," she said. He had picked up on the first ring. She hoped that everything was okay. The two of them might not be dating, but she did care about him.

"Jillian, have you met that Greta down at the gym?"

"No, I can't say that I have. She must be someone new. Why?" Jillian asked.

"She is the most annoying person I've ever met in my life. She is driving me crazy, Jillian. I signed up to have Pete as my personal trainer, but he is taking some time off to get ready for his wedding, so I got that Greta!"

Drew went on and on about this woman, how she would boss him around, tell him he was doing things wrong—both in the gym and in life in general—and argue with him over every little thing. His list of complaints went on and on.

"She even has her nose pierced, Jillian!" he continued. Jillian was not sure what the big deal was about that. She knew a lot of people in Madison with piercings of all sorts, and in Los Angeles, there were even more. She supposed that in Drew's more refined business and social worlds, piercings were not a common occurrence.

As Drew went on and on, Jillian wondered what he expected her to do or say about all this. Maybe he just needed to vent. She had never heard Drew sound so stirred up before, and then suddenly, it struck Jillian. Drew was attracted to "that Greta," and he didn't know what to do about it. That was the real problem, Jillian believed. Drew must have said Greta's name about twenty times in the last five minutes, and that was just not normal for Drew.

Jillian finally chimed in when there was a break in Drew's rantings. "I think you should take her out for a cup of coffee and have a chat. Tell her how the things she says make you feel. I think that might help."

"Take her out? You must be joking. I can't stand her, Jillian!" Drew said adamantly.

"I know you feel that way now, but if she knows how her words and actions are making you feel, maybe she'll change. I think it's only fair to honestly share your thoughts and feelings with her. Just a cup of coffee or tea, Drew—to talk things over," Jillian said with an impish smile.

"You really think so?" he asked.

"Yes, I really think so," Jillian remarked. "Do it—now." It reminded her of what she had said to Pete when he wasn't sure if he should contact the woman he would be marrying in a couple of weeks. Jillian had told him to go—right away—to ask for her forgiveness. He did, and he had never regretted it.

"Well, if this turns into a disaster, I'm holding you responsible," Drew said, sounding so serious.

"Okay, I'll take full blame if it blows up on you, Drew." Now she was grinning from ear to ear.

"Well, thanks, Jillian. I thought you might have some ideas. I hope this one works," he said, beginning to calm down.

"Me, too," she said, and meant it.

"Bye, Jillian."

"Bye, Drew."

John looked at her inquisitively. "What's up with Drew?"

"Oh, he's in love. He just doesn't know it yet," she said.

"You're certain of that, are you?" John asked, studying her.

She paused a moment. "Yes," she said and paused again. "I'm certain. It's love," she added, in a more serious tone. And she thought to herself, *I should know.*

John didn't have any response to her words. He just drove on, a thoughtful expression on his face.

Jillian's package for John arrived at Karen's house, just in time for Valentine's Day. Jillian wrapped it in plain purple paper with a white satin bow, and tied a red heart decoration onto the bow. She had thought about a card, but she could not find one that truly expressed her feelings. She would have to tell him how she felt instead, she decided, when they said good night tonight, on Valentine's Day. She would tell him that she loved him, whether it was a wise decision or not. She felt like she could not contain her feelings any longer.

John was taking her somewhere special tonight, but she wasn't sure what to expect. He said the dress she wore the other night would be fine, but she decided to buy a new one, one in a pretty shade of dark red, that she, and a wonderful young saleswoman who was most helpful, thought flattered her.

She decided to wear her hair down with the dress, and the woman had agreed. A trim at the beauty shop on Thursday made her hair lighter in weight, giving it some extra body, and a curling iron would give it the final touch.

John came to her cottage door that evening, a single red rose in his hand. When Jillian opened the door, she got a look similar to the one he had given her the week before. She would take that as a compliment.

"Jillian..." John said. He couldn't seem to finish his sentence. She would take that as another compliment. "Happy Valentine's Day," he said softly, and handed her the rose, then kissed her cheek. Jillian put the rose to her nose to smell its sweet scent.

"Thank you, John. It's beautiful." But not as wonderful as John looked to Jillian. He was so close that she needed to take a step back. "Come in while I put this in something."

He walked through the door and stood just inside the cottage.

"I have something for you, too, if we have just a minute," Jillian said over her shoulder as she went to the kitchen to retrieve a small vase from a cupboard. Her package for John was on the table between two overstuffed chairs. She carried the rose to the table, picked up the package, and handed it to John.

"Go ahead, open it," she said.

He untied the satin bow, tore off the paper, and lifted out the jersey. "How in the world did you find something like that?" he asked, an astonished look on his face.

"I had it made. A company in Wisconsin makes them. My friend had a Badger one made for her son. I just thought, even if you never wear it... it's more about the memories."

"You are so thoughtful, Jillian, and I will wear it, too. But I do like the memories part. Thank you," he said, seeming genuinely moved by her gift, and kissed her gently on the lips.

"We'd better go," Jillian said softly, feeling that would be a good decision.

"You're right." He took her hand and escorted her through the backyard to the house, dropping off his package in the kitchen on the way to the garage.

John drove them into the city. He was taking her to see Puccini's *La Boheme* at the Music Center. Between John's look, and the special outing to the opera, she was very glad that she had bought her new dress. The Center was impressive, and they were seated in a private box, which made the night seem even more surreal. The performance was *bravissimo*, and Jillian was sorry when it was over.

John had made a reservation for a late supper at a restaurant near the venue. They were seated immediately at a small table overlooking the city. After they ordered, they talked about the op-

Kathy J. Jacobson

era as they waited for their food, discussing the characters and their favorite arias. John helped her understand some parts of the performance she was not sure about, quoting some of the lines in Italian. *You're going to have to learn Italian, Jillian.* It was so romantic just hearing him speak it.

She remembered back to her date almost exactly one year ago when she accompanied Drew to the Philharmonic. He hadn't wanted to talk about the music or anything other than business, name-dropping, or what he or others were planning to buy in the future. This night with John had been the exact opposite of that experience.

John was animated as he spoke about the production, and she loved watching the passion pour out of him. And there was something else going on with him, too. Jillian just couldn't put her finger on it, but she thought she saw something in his eyes she had not seen before. They were sparkling, and darting back and forth, almost like they were dancing. It must be the opera, she thought. She just sat back and enjoyed the sight.

John just kept on surprising Jillian on a continual basis. She knew he was not a perfect person—there was no such thing—but she sure liked being with him. Correction: she loved being with him. And there was no getting around it anymore—she just plain loved him, pure and simple. Yes, she was going to have to tell him. Hopefully she would have the opportunity before the night was over.

On the way out of the restaurant, John took her hand in his as they walked back to the Land Rover. She was a bit surprised that he would do that in such a busy, public place. Again, she had seen people throughout the evening whispering to each other as they wondered if he was who they thought he was or someone who just looked like John D. Romano. Jillian's simple, ordinary life was perhaps not appreciated as much as it should be, she thought to herself.

They talked much of the way home. In the few quiet moments, Jillian was thinking about how best to bring up the subject that she was in love with him. She hoped she wasn't being foolish by planning to tell him.

They made it all the way home, and still she hadn't gotten the words out of her mouth. Maybe the car wasn't the best place anyway, she thought. They pulled into the garage and headed back toward the cottage, John holding her hand in their now accustomed manner.

He became very quiet as they walked together. Jillian thought perhaps the long evening was catching up with him. He still was not completely recovered, she knew that, and she hoped he was feeling all right.

They stopped at her door, and John looked at her strangely. Now she was really concerned. The last time he looked at her in an unusual way, he collapsed to the floor moments later, the result of his tumor. It had been six weeks now, and his recovery had been extraordinary, but still, she couldn't help but think about some sort of relapse or some other undetected health issue.

John took her hands in his and suddenly dropped down before her. Fear flashed through Jillian's body. "John! Are you okay?" she asked, panic starting to set in. But then she noticed that he was not crumpled in a heap like before, but was kneeling down on one knee.

He answered her, "I'll let you know the answer to your question in just a moment—after you answer mine." As he said this, he reached into his inner coat pocket, pulled out a magnificent diamond ring, and held it up toward her.

"I love you, Jillian, with all my heart. Will you marry me?"

Now Jillian thought she was the one who would end up in a heap on the ground, but she quickly composed herself.

"Are you sure, John? We haven't known each other very long..."

"Jillian, I feel like I've known you all of my life. It just took a lifetime to find you," he said.

Jillian nodded knowingly. "I completely understand what you are saying. I feel the same. I love you, too, John—so much—and I would love to marry you."

John smiled and stood up, then slipped the ring onto her finger. "May I kiss my fiancée?" John asked.

She nodded, and they kissed with a new intensity, and with something Jillian knew she had never experienced before—true love and real commitment. The combination was absolutely intoxicating.

Jillian felt like she was in a trance. John was kissing her again and again and saying something about Easter.

"Let's get married at Easter, Jillian," he said, kissing her neck gently between words. She was having a difficult enough time digesting all of this without him driving her crazy with his lips.

"Easter?" she said, starting to come back to her senses. "You mean the day before Easter?"

"No. Easter Sunday. In the afternoon or evening," he said, continuing to kiss her.

"Easter," she repeated. "That's the end of next month, John. I don't know if we can arrange for Marty to get home on such short notice..."

"Already taken care of," John said.

"What's already taken care of?"

"A ticket home is on hold for her for twenty-four hours, depending on the answer to my question. I'll call it in tonight."

Jillian looked at him, flabbergasted.

"You're not the only one who can do things behind the scenes," he said with his eyebrows arched. He was referring to some of her dealings with his nephew, Tommy, in the past. He continued to speak, "Marty said that Easter was a good time for her."

"You talked to my daughter?" Jillian asked in complete disbelief.

"Yes, we had a nice video chat the other day, when I asked her permission to marry you."

Now Jillian thought she had heard everything. She wasn't certain what was more amazing—that John, who had only gotten a smartphone about ten days before, was now doing video calls, or that he had thought to ask her daughter—her only living immediate family member—for her hand in marriage.

She was so in love at that moment that she thought her heart might explode. Jillian threw her arms around John and held him tightly, never wanting to let go. Finally, she pulled back and looked at him. "Easter it is. But how did you come up with that idea?"

"You once said that it was your favorite holiday—because it was all about new beginnings, new life and rebirth. That's what our wedding day will be, Jillian—a resurrection day—on Resurrection Day."

Jillian thought about something Tommy had said to her at the hospital after John's medical event. *You brought my uncle back from the dead.*

Jillian stood stunned for a moment, then tears came to her eyes. No one had ever said such precious, meaningful and loving words to her—ever. She would never forget that night, and how she felt at that moment, for the rest of her life.

They stood outside kissing and holding one another for a while longer. It took every ounce of self-control they had to say good night to one another that night, but soon—very soon—they wouldn't have to say good night anymore—not ever.

Jillian dropped into her bed that night in the cottage, as John went to the house to call in the plane ticket for Marty, and to text Tommy that she had said "yes." She had prayed so many times in the past year for God to give John whatever it was that he needed. Tonight, she said a prayer of thanks that she was the answer to that prayer.

The next morning, Jillian got up early for a video chat with Marty before church.

"So, what's new, Mom?" Marty asked, smiling mischievously at her mother on the computer screen.

"I think you already know the answer to that question, but in case there was any doubt in your mind, your plane ticket has been confirmed," Jillian said.

"How does it feel, Mom?" Marty asked.

"Well, I haven't been there yet, but I think this must be what it feels like to be in heaven," Jillian said, grinning from ear to ear. Then she got a more serious expression on her face. "Thank you for giving us your blessing, Marty."

"I'm so happy you feel like this, Mom. You deserve it. I really liked what I saw and heard when I talked to John, and I can't wait to meet him in person."

"I can't wait for the two most important people in my life to meet one another, too. You'll love him, Marty, and he will love you."

"I already love him, Mom. Anyone who makes you look and sound as happy as you do right now has got my vote," Marty said.

Jillian continued the conversation by filling Marty in on the evening at the opera and the proposal, including her moment of panic when she thought John was having another medical emergency. They set a time for later in the week when they both had more time to talk over some of the travel and wedding details. They were thrilled that they would actually be seeing one another for real, too, in just a short time. It would be a most blessed Easter indeed.

John and Jillian met with Pastor Jim after the late church service the next morning. John had already talked to him earlier in the week, but they wanted to make sure that he was really willing to do a wedding after the marathon Lenten season and the many services of Holy Week and Easter. Pastor Jim admitted that it was an unusual request, but said he had been so impressed with John's reasons for picking that day, that he couldn't say no to him.

Apparently John had practically quoted Pastor Jim's sermon back to him from the first Sunday John had gone to church with Jillian. The man's mind is amazing, Jillian thought as they sat in the pastor's study. John had proceeded to tell Pastor Jim about the new creation that he had become in the past year since knowing Jillian and how his life had been resurrected. Pastor Jim just couldn't refuse under the circumstances.

Their scripture reading would be 2 Corinthians 5:17: "So if anyone is in Christ, there is a new creation; everything old has passed away; see, everything has become new!"

John and Jillian wanted only immediate family in attendance and a very simple service. Pastor Jim seemed truly excited for them and planned to meet with them a few times before the wedding. He also gave them some material to read and discuss. John also asked how he could become a member of Grace. Pastor Jim didn't have any new member classes meeting right then, so he would work something out with John so he could officially join before the wedding. Jillian was once again surprised, in a good way.

That afternoon was unseasonably warm. John and Jillian sat at the small table next to the pool, huddled together and talking. Jillian couldn't keep her eyes off the ring on her finger, which was catching the rays of the sun. She couldn't believe that in forty days, she was going to be married. Forty days—very Biblical, she thought to herself. She wished it was forty minutes, not days, but if she could endure the past twenty-five years of her life waiting for the right person, she should be able to hold on for another forty days until her marriage to John.

Kathy J. Jacobson

John took her left hand in his. "I like seeing this on your finger," he said, looking at the ring. "Do you like it? If you want another style..."

"I wouldn't think of wearing any other ring than this one, John."

"I went to a number of stores, but the jeweler where I got this asked me all kinds of questions about you—what you looked like, your work, your hobbies, likes and dislikes, and just in general what kind of person you were. You know what he said to me when I was done describing you? He wanted to marry you, too." John smiled. "But I said you were spoken for, hopefully."

"Definitely," Jillian said. "Thank you for taking such care and time to look for a ring, John. It's perfect."

"It's a perfect fit, for the perfect fit for me." He rubbed his fingers over hers.

"I don't know if you would want one, but I'd really like to buy you a wedding ring," Jillian said.

"I would love to wear a ring you gave to me. And I want you to have a wedding ring, too. Should we look tomorrow after you're done at the nursing home?"

"Let's go to the place where you bought this ring. While we're there, maybe I should check out that jeweler, too, just to see what he has to offer," Jillian said teasingly to John.

John laughed and shook his head at her. "No way, Ms. Johnson, you are my fiancée, and don't forget it." He put his arm around her and pulled her close.

"I don't think there is any way in the world I could ever forget that, Mr. Romano," she said and kissed him gently.

That evening, they both participated in a video call on her laptop with Tommy and his family. Everyone was crazily excited. Tommy knew about John's proposal plans and had already been looking into flights. Everyone was going to come into LAX about four p.m. on Good Friday and leave late on the following Tuesday morning. John Anthony and Alison did not have school on Friday or Monday, so they would only miss one day of classes on Tuesday. They were both excellent students, so there were no concerns in that department.

It was a great call, especially since John Anthony also had some news to share. He had turned down several Division I football scholarship offers and would be committing to Northwestern University as a "preferred walk-on." He had also been accepted into Northwestern's prestigious musical theater program. John and Jillian were so happy for him, and John rushed upstairs to get the personalized Northwestern jersey that Jillian had given him as well as his old one that he must have dug out from who knows where, since Jillian had never seen it before.

"Cool," said John Anthony. "Uncle John, if I make the team, and it's available, would you mind if I used your number?"

Jillian watched John's face. He became very emotional, and had to clear his throat before answering. "I would be honored," John said. Jillian put her arms around him, feeling so happy for him, and feeling exceptionally blessed because of the beautiful family she was gaining.

After all the excitement of the call to the Romano family, Jillian decided to call Pete. His wedding was coming up in a little less than two weeks, and she had promised to be there. She was still planning on it, but she wanted to ask if she could bring a guest.

"Pete!"

"Jillian! How's it going?"

"It's going great, Pete, and you? Are you surviving the wedding preparations?"

"I had no idea that this wedding stuff was so complicated, Jillian. I'll be glad when the day is finally here."

"I totally understand, Pete. I feel the same way."

"You're not calling to say you can't come, are you?"

"No, but I do have a request. I know it's last minute, and I'll understand if you say no, but would it be okay if I brought someone?" she asked.

"Jillian. I can hear it in your voice. You're in love, aren't you?" Pete asked.

"Very much so," she said.

"I'm so happy for you, Jillian. You deserve it. And of course you can bring him. I will tell Kelly right now—she just came into the room with another project for me to do."

"Okay, I'll let you go. So, plan on two of us. I will make sure it's a 'go' and will call back by tonight if for some reason he isn't able to accompany me. I didn't want to ask if it wasn't going to work for you two."

"It will work—no problem, Jillian. I can't wait to see you, and meet..."

"John."

"Great. Jillian and John. It even sounds good together."

It does sound good together. "I cannot wait to see you, Pete, and meet the love of your life."

"Same here, Jillian. Same here," Pete said, putting his arm around Kelly's shoulders as he disconnected.

Chapter Six

Edith was the first one at the nursing home to notice Jillian's ring. "I *told* you," she said. Edith had assumed that John and Jillian were more than friends, surmising that from the way they both had looked at one another. Jillian hugged her, and they began a conversation about love and marriage. Edith and her husband, Ralph, had been married for seventy years when he died four years before.

"Any advice, Edith?" Jillian asked seriously.

Edith thought for a moment, then started speaking in a slow and steady voice. "The key to a good and long life is faith in God and hot milk. The key to a good and long marriage is faith in God and being both friends and lovers. It's not as hard as everyone seems to want to make it be these days. You set your mind to it, and you do it. You love each other and take care of each other when everything is good, and when everything is rotten. And you don't let other people or things get in the way—you stand up to 'em, and you stand up for the person you marry. You also have to stand up to him sometimes if he's having a stupid spell, and admit it when you are having one yourself," Edith said matter-of-factly.

Kathy J. Jacobson

One thing Jillian appreciated about working with older adults was that they would often "tell it like it is." Rarely were they concerned about being politically correct or being overly tactful. They just said what they thought in all honesty and sincerity. Jillian hugged Edith again and thanked her for what sounded like good, solid advice. In fact, Jillian wrote Edith's words down into a note on her phone right after their conversation, citing Edith and the time and date. She would share the words later with John, when he asked about her day.

John and Jillian found their wedding bands at the store where Jillian's engagement ring was purchased. The jeweler whom John had worked with, Ken, helped them choose the perfect set. He was an attractive gentleman who was very good at what he did for a living.

They were surprised to find, quite easily, ones that paired so well with Jillian's engagement ring. After they had chosen them, Ken asked if they wanted anything engraved inside.

"What do you think, Jillian?" John asked.

"I do have an idea. Would you want the same thing in both, or different?"

"Well, it depends on what your idea is."

"I was thinking that in yours, it should say, 'the right person.'"

John looked genuinely touched and squeezed her hand. "I like it. That could certainly be in both, because you are, too."

Jillian smiled at Ken, "I think that would work nicely then, for both rings."

They put down separate deposits on the rings. Jillian insisted that she was buying John's ring. They would pay the balances when the engraving was done, which Ken promised would be within the week. They started out the door, and John looked back and thanked Ken again. "My pleasure," Ken said, and under his breath, he added, "You're a very lucky man."

John heard him and said, "I know."

Jillian made several more important phone calls that evening. The first one was to her oldest friend and mentor, Carol, in Madison.

"Carol," Jillian said when her friend answered the call.

"Jillian, is that you?" Carol asked.

"It is. Don't you recognize my voice?" Jillian asked.

"The person I'm talking to right now sounds similar to my old friend, Jillian, but she sounds about one hundred times happier than I've ever heard her before," Carol said.

"You could tell that from one word?"

"I've known you since you were twenty years old, Jillian. I've seen you at your happiest and at your saddest, and everything in between. So, what is making you so happy today?... Wait, I know, it's the one... the one I knew you had met, but you wouldn't admit it to me, isn't it?"

This woman knew Jillian all too well. "It is, Carol. You knew it before I even knew it—or wanted to know it. His name is John, and we're... getting married at Easter." Jillian felt like she was telling her own mother and was suddenly getting choked up.

"I knew there was someone. Tell me more." Carol said, sincerely interested. Jillian told her the condensed version of the past year.

"Jillian, I don't think it was any coincidence that you ended up working at John's house in Los Angeles, do you?"

"There's no way this could be a coincidence, Carol. I was meant to come here, and we were meant to be together. I used to pray each night when I came here that God would give John whatever he needed—he wasn't a very happy man—and now it seems, it was me! And I needed him, too, more than I ever realized. He is a very

Kathy J. Jacobson

special person, and I hope that you can meet him sometime soon."

"So do I, Jillian. Is it okay if I let other people know about this?"

"Sure," Jillian said. "They probably won't believe it."

"It's not that they won't believe someone would want to marry you, Jillian, but that you actually gave somebody a chance. He must be something special, and I am so happy for you, dear," Carol said.

Again, Jillian felt like she was not only talking to a friend, but to family. "Thanks, Carol, I've never been this happy in all of my life," Jillian said truthfully.

Next Jillian called Karen. Karen was not at all surprised, and said that she and Robert would want Jillian and John to come over soon for an engagement dinner. Jillian thought that would be a lovely idea, and the reality of her upcoming marriage was beginning to really sink in.

Karen said at the end of the call, "Have you told Drew yet?"

"No, but I better do that as soon as we hang up. Even though we haven't really dated since New Year's Eve, and I'm not sure that really qualified as a date, I don't want him to hear it somewhere else. Thanks for the reminder," Jillian said.

"You're welcome. Check with John for some possible dinner dates, and I will coordinate with Robert and see if we can find a match. Again, Jillian, I am so happy for you. You deserve it," Karen said.

Jillian had heard that she "deserved it" several times in the past day or two, and she was finally starting to believe that perhaps she actually did. She blogged that night about all the happenings of the last few days, and her followers were ecstatic. They all told her to make sure to put her own story into the book—it didn't get any better than it did when it came to encouraging endings.

It was a little more difficult to push Drew's contact in her phone than it had been the others. She just wasn't sure what to expect when she reached him. The last time they had talked was the day that he called so upset about "that Greta," the personal trainer who was pushing all his buttons. Jillian thought he was falling in love with her, but she hadn't followed up to see how the plan to take Greta out for coffee had gone, or if it had even happened.

"Hi, Drew!" Jillian said.

"Jillian," he said. "Ah, I've been meaning to call you..." Jillian could hear a voice in the background, and he sounded like he was trying to speak to someone.

"How are you doing, Drew?" Jillian asked.

"Good... I'm good," and she heard him laugh a bit and talk in a muffled tone to someone again.

"Is this a bad time to talk?" Jillian asked.

"No, it's fine. I'm just driving back from Santa Monica. Greta and I just attended an indie concert at a coffee shop there."

"Sounds like fun, Drew," she said, but she was inwardly in shock. She was trying to imagine Drew at an indie concert anywhere—anytime—with anyone.

"Everything's all right then... with you and Greta?"

"It's more than all right, Jillian. Thanks for telling me to ask her out for coffee. We ah... worked everything out," he said, sounding happier than Jillian had ever heard him sound.

"That's wonderful, Drew."

"Are you okay with that, Jillian?"

Now Jillian wanted to laugh, but she held it together. "I think it's fantastic, Drew."

"Thanks, Jillian. Is there something you wanted to talk about?" he asked.

"Oh, another time. Again, I hope everything turns out great for you and Greta. You deserve to be happy," she said, echoing the words she had heard so many times lately.

"Thanks. So do you. Well, bye, Jillian," he said.

Kathy J. Jacobson

"Bye, Drew. See you at church and book club sometime. Bring Greta."

"I will."

Jillian couldn't stop smiling. She wasn't worried about Drew finding out about her upcoming marriage anymore. He would find out the next time she saw him or from someone else. She was sure he wouldn't be upset. She had thought she would tell him about the engagement during this call, but today she felt like it was his turn to share some good news, and she didn't want to steal his thunder. He sounded on top of the world.

Jillian did feel a bit concerned, though. She was trying to imagine Drew's family's reaction to all of this. Drew had been afraid to introduce her—a former nurse turned house-keeper and aspiring writer—to his family. She was trying to imagine them meeting "that Greta," who was a personal trainer with a pierced nose. But she guessed that would be Drew's worry, not hers. If he truly loved Greta, he would work it out.

As Edith had told her, you have to stand up for the one you love. Maybe she could share Edith's advice with Drew sometime soon. In the meantime, she decided she would start praying for them on a regular basis—that this would all work out well for everyone and that true love would prevail against the odds.

Suddenly it was the first weekend in March, and time for Kelly and Pete's wedding. John and Jillian booked two rooms at a bed and breakfast in San Francisco for the night before and after the service, planning to take advantage of what the beautiful area had to offer.

The marriage ceremony was at five o'clock at St. Joseph's, the church where Pete found Kelly the day he asked her to forgive him for his unfaithfulness. At that point, many years after the fact, he was beyond the idea that they would ever get back together. He had hurt her too badly, and too much time had passed, he had thought. He had asked for her forgiveness, if nothing else, so they could go on with their lives, and she gave it to him. From that moment on, they started to see each other again, and after seven agonizing years apart from one another, their wedding day was finally a reality.

Pete had been going up to San Francisco every weekend since that day. The couple had done pre-marriage counseling with Father Thomas at St. Joseph's during those trips. Pete had taken the last two weeks off to help Kelly get ready for the wedding. They would go on a week-long honeymoon after the ceremony. Then Pete would be back at the gym in Los Angeles, and Kelly would begin her new marketing position with a satellite office of her current company not far from the city.

The wedding was a very meaningful, well-planned service. Father Thomas did a nice job of challenging the couple, but also commending them for their perseverance and forgiveness. It made everyone in attendance feel hopeful, not only for the couple but for their own relationships.

A reception followed the service at a spot on Fisherman's Wharf. Jillian didn't know what business Kelly's parents were in, but she thought it must be something that made a good deal of money, as the entire restaurant, with its breathtaking views of the Bay, was theirs for the evening.

At the reception, Jillian finally got the chance to meet Kelly, and Pete got to meet John. Pete looked so incredibly handsome, and even happier than he did handsome, which was really saying something. Kelly was gorgeous. She was model height, with long, honey-colored hair, which was in an "up-do" on her wedding day. She had a stunning smile and her crystal blue eyes were sparkling, especially when she looked at Pete. Jillian was so happy

Kathy J. Jacobson

that Kelly had finally understood that Pete had had a stupid spell, as Edith would have called it, and had forgiven him. She wished them both much joy and a long, happy marriage, Edith and Ralph style, she thought to herself.

After the introductions and wishes, Jillian reached out her hands toward Kelly to hug her when Pete noticed her ring. "Jillian," he said, "you're *engaged*!"

"Yes, I am," she said, smiling from ear to ear.

Pete picked her up and whirled her around like she was as light as a feather. "That is fantastic!" He put her down, turned to John, and shook his hand rigorously. John was a good-sized man, six-foot-one-inch tall, and no stranger to the gym himself. But even John's quarterback hands seemed dwarfed in Pete's. "Outside of my wife, Jillian's the best! And this day wouldn't even be happening without her," he said, and Pete turned and hugged Jillian again.

Jillian and Kelly finally got their chance to hug, and Kelly congratulated Jillian and John, then whispered a very sincere thank you in Jillian's ear, for bringing Pete back into her life.

After an half hour of mingling with the guests, it was time for Pete and Kelly to take their places at the dais. Father Thomas said a table prayer, the best man spoke and proposed a toast, and then the maid of honor, Kelly's sister, followed suit.

Then Pete stood up to speak. "I just want to thank everyone for coming today and celebrating with us. I can't say how happy I am that I am standing here today, being given a chance—another chance—to live the rest of my life with my beautiful, sweet Kelly. I thank God every day that she is the kind of person that she is, so loving and so forgiving, and I plan to do whatever it takes to make each and every day, the happiest day of her life."

Jillian watched Kelly's eyes, which were filled with tears of joy and with love for her new husband.

Pete continued, "And I also just want to say thank you to a very good friend of mine—she knows who she is—for encouraging me to not give up. I wouldn't be standing here today if it were not for her. She recently found love herself, and I wish her and her fiancé the same happiness that Kelly and I are experiencing today."

Now it was Jillian's eyes that were misting, and John grasped her hand and squeezed it lovingly beneath the table.

Finally, Kelly's father stood up to speak. He talked about how he didn't think this day would ever come and was even a bit wary when he recently found out it was actually going to happen. But in the past months, he said he had seen two new people emerge in this world: Pete, who had grown into a wonderful and faithful man, and his daughter, Kelly, who, it seemed to him, had been reborn in the past few months. John looked at Jillian when Kelly's father said that. She knew he was thinking about their own situation and their wedding passage, which would have been a great one for this day as well.

"In honor of this wonderful, happy and holy event today, my wife and I would like to present Pete and Kelly with a special gift. Pete has always wanted to own his own health club, and we are going to help him make that a reality. So, here's to 'For Pete's Sake,' and for Pete's sake, everyone have a wonderful time tonight." Everyone chuckled at his words. "Pete and Kelly, we love you and wish you a long and blessed life together," and everyone toasted their glasses to them.

Jillian was so happy for Pete. He was having two of his biggest dreams come true all in one fell swoop. Jillian was very happy, too, that these dreams would most likely continue to unfold in Los Angeles, where they could all be together.

The next day John and Jillian ate more incredible seafood, then explored the Golden Gate Bridge area, enjoying a free walking

Kathy J. Jacobson

tour. An hour before closing, they decided it was time to head back, as it was a long ride home. They had made their way up to San Francisco slowly along the winding, scenic Pacific Coast Highway 1, but would drive home on the faster Interstate 5.

They stood back and looked at the bridge, then John took a "selfie" of them on his phone, with it in the background.

"It was neat to see a wonder of the world," Jillian said, looking at the bridge one last time before turning back to John. The bridge was often considered an architectural wonder by engineers.

"Yes, it is neat to look at a wonder of the world. It's even better to get to marry one," he said and pulled her into a kiss. As they parted, Jillian sighed with happiness. Easter could not come quickly enough.

Chapter Seven

One of the advantages of a last-minute wedding is its simplicity. Marty, Tommy, Maria, John Anthony, and Alison would be the only ones present at both the ceremony and the wedding dinner. Dinner would be at Leo's restaurant, the place that John and Jillian had gone that first night after John asked Jillian to stay.

Leo and his oldest son, Leonardo, would be the cooks and servers that evening, and a younger son, Danielo, would be the dishwasher. Jillian was concerned that they were giving up family time on Easter Day, but Leo insisted that John and Jillian were family, too, and that he wanted to be a part of this very special occasion.

In the midst of menu planning, Jillian also found out what Leo had whispered to John that first night as they were leaving the restaurant. Leo had hugged John and then spoken into his ear—"You're going to marry this woman?" John said it had sounded like both a question and a statement at the same time. Jillian had heard John's reply to Leo, "I hope so."

Leo's was the perfect place to have their wedding dinner, with people who cooked like family, and who felt like family. Jillian could not wait.

Since Jillian didn't have the luxury of dress shopping with her daughter, she invited Karen to go with her to the shop where she had gotten the dress for Valentine's Day. The young woman there had been so helpful, and from the look John had given Jillian that evening, it was obvious that the woman knew what she was doing in picking out a perfect dress.

The salesperson, Marianna, did not disappoint. Jillian found out that day that Marianna was a student in the bachelor of fine arts program in fashion design at the Art Institute of California in Santa Monica. She hoped to be a designer one day as well as have a shop and fashion line of her own. Jillian had no doubt she would succeed, as she not only had a keen eye but was bright and possessed wonderful people skills. Marianna was so excited to be helping Jillian find a dress for such a special day and found just the right one again. Jillian couldn't wait to wear it, and especially for John to see it.

Karen and Jillian finally coordinated a night for an engagement dinner at the Wilson's home. John suggested they take wine and flowers. Jillian put the wine in Robert's hands after hugging him, and then introduced them to John. John gave Karen the flowers and gave her a hug, and shook Robert's hand.

Karen had an unusual look on her face. "Jillian, why don't you help me put these in a vase and advise me on dinner." Jillian knew that Karen was an exceptional cook, and there was no way she needed any advice regarding food preparation, so Jillian was curious as she followed her friend into the kitchen. "We won't be long," Karen said over her shoulder.

The kitchen door shut behind them. "What's going on, Karen?" Jillian asked.

"You didn't tell me that John was John D. Romano, that's what's going on!" Karen said, sounding and looking star-struck.

"Oh, didn't I? I thought I told you that a long time ago, but maybe not. Is that okay?"

"It's more than okay. I always had a crush on him when he was on television, and my sister—well, my sister would absolutely die if she knew he was here in my house! We're just ordinary people; he's a famous actor."

"Believe me, you have nothing to worry about. John is one of the most down-to-earth, nicest people I know. I know you will like him, and vice-versa. Just be yourself."

"I'll try. I just needed a moment to compose myself. Oh, here's the vase I wanted," she said, grabbing one from a shelf in her pantry. She put the flowers in the crystal cylinder and filled it with water at the sink.

"The flowers were John's idea. He's very thoughtful." Jillian said.

"Not to mention gorgeous."

"That, too," Jillian said and smiled at her friend. "Come on, let's go."

Karen straightened her dress, then grabbed the vase of flowers. "Jillian, would you bring the appetizers out with you?" she asked, nodding at an impressive plate of her special creations. Jillian picked up the platter, and they both headed to the living room where John and Robert were now sitting and talking.

Again, Jillian was just beginning to understand what the life of a celebrity could be like, and she was soon going to be the wife of one. She could sense that it was definitely going to present its challenges.

Karen put the vase on a side table in the room. "Thank you for the flowers," she said to John as she approached the sofa. They

Kathy J. Jacobson

enjoyed a glass of wine with their appetizers. At first Karen seemed a bit nervous, but then she began to relax as she realized Jillian was telling the truth about John being a regular person.

Jillian was pretty certain Robert had no idea that John was anything special, so he talked to John like he would any guest in his home, mostly about work, what was in the news, sports, and his wife. Robert was really proud of Karen and told John how she had gone back to school.

Robert was a very intelligent man. He still worked a lot—probably too much—but was making a conscious effort to become more interested in other things since that first date with his wife to the Lakers game almost one year before. He said he was actually reading—and enjoying—the next book on the book club list and would try to make the meeting.

Robert suggested that they all go to a Lakers game together next season, as the current one was almost over. John said he would like that a lot. That led to talk about other sports. Robert was impressed that John had been a Division I football player in college. "Not very many people get the chance to do that," he said. "You didn't want to go pro?"

"I blew out my knee in the last game of my junior season."

"Oh, tough luck," Robert said sincerely.

"It wasn't good, but it led me in new directions that I wouldn't have tried if I had stayed in football, so I guess it all worked out in the end. Just like a lot of things often do," he said. He looked over at Jillian, which made her face feel warm.

The timer went off in the kitchen, signifying that dinner was ready. They moved to the dining room, where they enjoyed a feast of fresh snapper and wild live spot prawns with Karen's special sauce. Karen knew how much Jillian liked it. Karen really had outdone herself again, and topped off the menu with a new dessert— a blackberry mousse cake she had tried for the first time.

Karen had gradually become herself as the evening wore on, explaining to John all about her college program and plans for the future. John was genuinely impressed by her courage to go back to school and to work with disadvantaged students, and told her so.

By the end of the evening, Jillian felt like they all really could be good friends in the future and was happy about that. She did understand, however, that there would be others who would not be able to adjust to who John was and who he was going to become in the future. Jillian had a feeling that great things were right around the corner for John, not only in his personal life with their upcoming marriage, but professionally. And usually, when she got a feeling like that, it happened, sooner or later.

The forty days were almost up. Some days it felt like the wedding day would never arrive. Other days, time went more quickly, especially when Jillian was busy at work. At the nursing home, Jillian was helping the residents create a cookbook of their favorite recipes. It was a fun project, with about a hundred recipes collected in all. One of the best things about it was that it involved some of the residents' family members as they hunted for recipes or reminded their parents and grandparents of their favorites they had enjoyed. They also informed Jillian about the occasions for which each food item was usually made, and she wrote little notes after each recipe telling its "story." She was going to print one for every resident before she left, as a gift to them.

As the Lenten-Easter season was upon them, Jillian led a seasonal Bible study and helped residents create an Easter craft and dye eggs. A Purim celebration had been held a week prior, which had been the idea of a resident named Esther—who said it was her favorite holiday—and it had been a huge success. At Jillian's invitation, a rabbinic student had come in to talk to them about

Kathy J. Jacobson

the special day, and she would be coming back again to talk about Passover and explain the Seder as that festival approached. A pastor would also be joining her to speak about the Christian traditions related to the Passover.

Jillian was going to miss these people very much. But she knew it was time for their regular aide to come back. The aide had visited recently with her new baby. That had caused great excitement and helped Jillian "let go." She also knew it was time to move on with her own plans. First and foremost was the wedding. And then after that, she planned on writing the next chapter of her book. She had the first four chapters completely outlined, but the key was to actually get them written down.

Jillian's last day at the nursing home was the Wednesday before Easter. She walked in the door that day to the entire group of residents lined up in chairs and wheelchairs, shouting "surprise," and grinning from ear to ear. There was a cake with "Best wishes, Jillian and John" on the table, along with a stack of home-made wedding cards.

"It was Edith's idea," the administrator, Jenny, told Jillian. Jillian walked over to Edith and gave her a big hug. Ever since Edith had predicted that John and Jillian were more than friends, and later gave Jillian her precious advice on long-lasting relationships, the two had become particularly close.

The other residents had bought into the wedding shower idea completely. Some of the men didn't want to make a card, so they made a craft instead. There was an adorable door hanger and a candle made from a kit. Best of all was a carving made by a gentleman named Edgar, who was "sweet" on Edith, Jillian believed. He had carved two little birds perched together on a branch and pronounced them bluebirds of happiness. Edgar was obviously very talented, and

Jillian knew right where she would put them in the house.

Jillian couldn't really wrap her head around the idea that the house she used to clean each week was going to be her house in a couple of days. Although that fact was amazing, it seemed minor in comparison to the reality that she was marrying John. She loved him more and more each day, which she really didn't understand. Each day she was sure that there couldn't be any more love added to her heart, but it just kept coming.

That love doubled when John came bounding through the door. Everyone had wanted to see him one more time and celebrate with both of them, so the administrator had invited him and asked him to be in on the secret.

John walked over to Jillian with the biggest grin on his face.

"Surprise," he said, taking her hands.

"Yes, you are," she said, and then she kissed him to the hoots and hollers of the gathered crowd. By this time, the nurse, the janitor, and the nursing assistants had joined in as well. She was glad the nurse was there. With all this excitement, someone might need one, and Jillian wasn't fully licensed in the state yet!

Everyone had cake and ice cream, coffee and punch, with sugar-free alternatives for those who needed them. Then John and Jillian opened their cards, taking turns reading them out loud to the group. Everyone would clap at the end of each card or gift as it was opened. Jillian's heart was full, and she could tell that John was very moved by the entire experience, even if it wasn't a surprise for him.

After the cake, they took turns visiting with each resident. Jenny took a group photo and then individual ones of John and Jillian with each person. She promised everyone would get a copy of the group photo and their individual photos, and she would be making John and Jillian an album of the day's events.

Jillian just sat back at one point and watched her husband-to-be. John was so kind to the people. He had such a good heart, and Jillian's felt like hers was overflowing. She thought he was amazing, but he was only getting started that day.

As the staff began to clean up the tables, John gathered whoever wanted to listen to a short story into a circle off to the side of the room. He stood in front of them and began his tale. John had made up an original story, and every one of the residents in the nursing home was a character in it. When had he done this, Jillian wondered?

It was a funny and sweet story with a happy ending. The main characters were Edith and Edgar, who Jillian noticed looking at one another a few times throughout the performance. Jillian was so proud of John and thought she needed to make sure he knew that she was ready to support him whenever he was ready to begin his work again. No one with so much talent should be wasting it, and she could tell how much he loved to be in front of people telling stories.

The story ended to wild clapping and whistling, and John hugged or shook hands with everyone. Then the assistants started taking people back to their rooms for naps or to therapy, appointments, or whatever else they had on their dockets.

Edith was the last person to leave the room, and Jillian sat next to her wheelchair and held her hand. "Edith, thank you for everything—for thinking up this shower and especially for all your advice. I shared it with John, and we will both work hard to follow it."

Edith was teary-eyed as Jillian spoke. "You've got a real winner," she said.

Jillian eyes were misting as she hugged the woman. "I know. Thank you. That means a lot coming from you, because you ought to know." Jillian said, and Edith nodded in agreement. "And one more thing, Edith, you know that thing you told me about how people look at one another... well, I think that's true at any age,"

Jillian said, hinting at the way Edith and Edgar had been looking at one another during the story, and that friends didn't look at one another like that.

"No, no, no," she said, shaking her head.

"Yes, yes, yes," Jillian replied, nodding her head.

"Well, I dunno," Edith said.

"Well, I do," Jillian told her.

"Really?" Edith asked, trying hard to suppress a little smile.

"Really." And she hugged her one last time.

Edith wheeled herself out of the room, and Jenny came over and thanked them both profusely for making the day so special.

"We should be the ones thanking you," Jillian said, with John nodding his head in agreement, his arm around Jillian's waist.

Jenny said she had one more gift—Jillian could leave early. In fact, she suggested it might be easier on the residents if she did, so they didn't have to say goodbye a second time. Jillian agreed and thought it would be easier on her, too. She hugged Jenny, then she and John gathered their cards and gifts into a box and headed to the Land Rover.

Jillian felt happy and sad at the same time as she walked toward the vehicle. John opened the car door for her, then stopped to hold her a moment. Sometimes his sensitivity astounded her, along with the way he picked up on how she was feeling even when she didn't say a word.

"We'll come back to see them," he said gently, tightening his arms around her.

"You know, Edith told me I've got a real winner," Jillian said.

"Did she now?"

"She did, and I told her that she ought to know. So, I guess I'll take her word for it," Jillian said, trying to lighten up the moment with a little teasing.

John chuckled. "Edith's a pretty special woman. If it weren't for

Edgar...," he said, turning the teasing table back on Jillian.

"John..." Jillian couldn't finish her sentence.

He loosened his arms and looked at her. "Are you okay?"

"Sunday can't come soon enough," Jillian said, looking deeply into his eyes.

"Amen to that," John said and pulled her into a kiss.

Jillian was thankful for the busyness of the next two days. There were church services to attend, food to prepare, and rooms to ready for company. John did get a new household helper who would come in every Tuesday and Thursday to do cleaning, which helped with such a large house to maintain. Her name was Esperanza, a sweet young woman who was taking college courses at night and cleaning at John's and at another home during the day. She helped Jillian prepare some food for their guests, which was above and beyond her call of duty, but Esperanza wanted to do something for them in honor of their marriage, and they appreciated it very much.

Jillian also wrote as much as she could in her blog, which had expanded a lot since she started discussing the heartbreak that the elderly experience. There was so much loss—losses of homes, of freedom, of health, of beloved friends, relatives and spouses. So many people had been married for fifty or sixty years and then suddenly found themselves all alone. Some of her readers had this experience, or else had a parent going through this. They exchanged helpful ideas about how to respect and respond to these many losses. Others gave encouragement to those who were going through the hard but often necessary ordeal of having someone they love go into a care facility.

Her followers were also intrigued more and more by her own personal story. It was pretty amazing. Many told her she should put it into novel form. Jillian decided that someday she would do a story that somehow reflected the long road to happiness that both she and John had maneuvered, and encourage others to never give up hope.

Friday night was joyous as they watched their "family" arrive. John said that's how they should refer to them from now on. Amazingly, no one's flight was delayed more than an half hour, so their time at the airport was reasonable, the flights within an hour of each other.

Marty was the first to arrive. Jillian had not seen her daughter in the flesh in eighteen months. She watched as this beautiful young woman walked toward her. Marty had always been pretty—with thick, light blonde hair and that bright smile. She was a full inch taller than Jillian at five-foot nine and had always been physically fit. But now she was stunning.

Jillian and Marty just held each other for a minute. Neither could really speak—like mother, like daughter. Then they proceeded to laugh and cry at the same time, but then Jillian couldn't wait for Marty to meet John.

As soon as Jillian let go of Marty, Marty reached out to hug John. He looked pleasantly surprised by her gesture, but that was Marty. She had been passed around from person to person at church and the hospital as a baby and toddler, and was a "hit" with everyone in Tanzania and in Milwaukee. In Madison, she was a popular, involved girl in school with many friends. At church, she was a youth group leader and frequent servant trip participant. There wasn't really a shy bone in her body.

After the formal introduction, they claimed her luggage and headed to the gate to wait for Tommy and his crew. Another hug fest broke out when the Romano family stepped through the door.

Jillian didn't think she'd ever seen John so happy. She just want-

Kathy J. Jacobson

ed to stand to the side and watch, cherishing these special moments. It was getting harder and harder to remember how angry and sad he had been just a year before. Even months ago, he had been a different man. She had found herself thinking about that the evening before, during the church service. At the same service one year before, she had said a prayer for God to end his suffering, as that afternoon he had had a humiliating and scary bike accident and had come home with a bloodied body, a ruined bike, and a battered spirit. The transformation in one year's time was truly miraculous. Her prayers had been answered—way beyond expectation.

They gathered everyone's luggage and headed to the Land Rover. John had bought a new luggage rack for the back of the vehicle and used the rooftop racks for the first time ever. Jillian told Tommy to sit up front with John, and the rest of them filed into the back. It was going to be a tight squeeze. John kidded that everyone should hold their breath so they would all fit. It wasn't far from the truth.

Jillian and Marty looked at each other and started to giggle.

"Remind you of anything, Mom?" Marty asked Jillian, a huge smile on her face.

Jillian and Marty went on to explain how in Tanzania, and now in Senegal for Marty, there were "money buses" or "PMVs"—public motor vehicles—with people packed in like sardines. One might even be traveling with a chicken or a goat, to boot. Every ride on one of them was a new adventure.

"So, it could be worse. At least we don't have any livestock aboard," John kidded.

Maria, who was sitting next to Jillian, smiled and whispered to Jillian, "I've never heard him joke before. It's wonderful," she said. Jillian just smiled back at Maria, liking her immediately.

It was late when they all finally got unpacked and settled into their rooms. Jillian brought out the food that she and Esperanza had made the day before, and everyone dug right in. They sat in the kitchen at either the nook or the counter. It had been a long day of travel, but they happily visited about an hour or so, ending the night with some frozen yogurt sundaes.

Jillian was grateful that they had made a large amount of food. She had forgotten how much teenaged boys, especially male teen athletes, could eat. She never had one personally, but her friends had. Jillian had also witnessed some of the football players in the hospital order two or three trays full of food from the food service menu and easily put them away.

John Anthony was a unique mix of John and Tommy, Jillian thought. He was very handsome and smart, and filled them in about his plans at Northwestern and the musical theater program. Marty and he talked about their favorite musicals, and which ones they had performed in in high school. The musicals had been Jillian's favorite of Marty's school activities to attend.

Alison was in the orchestra at school and was an excellent violinist. Maria's passions were cooking and reading. She had just joined a book club, and she and Jillian talked about their latest "reads," and planned to share their respective book club reading lists.

Marty could have had her own room in the house, but chose to spend the next two nights with her mom in the cottage, then stay in it "solo" after the wedding. Jillian showed her to the cottage and introduced her to the "sunflower shower," which Marty planned to use before getting into bed. Jillian told her she would be back in a bit—she just wanted to say good night to John.

Jillian could hear John saying good night as he came down the stairs from escorting everyone to their rooms. His voice was strong and cheerful. He was still smiling when he walked into the kitchen, where Jillian was waiting for him. A house full of family, and

John's happy voice, made her smile, inside and out.

"You look happy," he said as he approached her.

"I could say the same thing about you," she said, moving closer to meet him.

"I've never been happier in my life. The only thing that will top this occurs in less than forty-eight hours, but who's counting?"

Jillian raised her hand like a child in a classroom in answer to John's question. John reached for it and took it in his, then brought it to his mouth and kissed it. "May I walk you to your door?"

"Of course. I should get back. Marty should be out of the shower soon."

"She's a beautiful girl, Jillian. Inside and out."

"I know. I'm not sure how that happened, but I am very blessed."

"I know how that happened. She looks and acts just like her mother," John said, brushing a strand of hair from Jillian's forehead.

Jillian started shaking her head no, but John grabbed it gently and made her nod up and down. "Yes, Jillian," he said. He kissed her, then as usual, reluctantly walked her to the cottage.

The family enjoyed Saturday at the house. Above-average temperatures made swimming a possibility, and everyone got in on the action. Marty was her typical self, making John Anthony and Alison feel comfortable and included in everything, even though they were both still in high school and she was a twenty-five-year-old doctor.

Maria and Jillian talked about Maria's idea for a small business, an Italian bakery/deli in Libertyville. She hoped to use some of John and Anthony's mother's recipes for bread, cannoli, gnocchi, and a few of her own family favorites. Jillian thought that sounded like a wonderful idea. She told Maria about the cannoli she had made for John for Christmas, and then about the recipe book she had helped the residents at the nursing home compile. They both agreed that there was something very special about recipes that are passed down from generation to generation.

John and Tommy spent a lot of time talking about a little bit of everything, catching up on events since his visit in January when John was hospitalized. That wasn't much of a visit, really. It had been a stressful time until John returned home, and by that time, Tommy had to leave to get back to work.

John and Tommy grilled some chicken breasts and hamburgers for lunch, the first time Jillian had ever seen the huge grill on the deck actually used. Jillian sat back for a moment to watch John cook, talk, and just plain be happy. She smiled as she watched him, and Maria noticed. She leaned over and quietly spoke to Jillian.

"I have never seen John like this before, Jillian, and I've known him for over twenty years," Maria said. "We are so happy that you came into his life."

"And I'm so happy he came into mine," she said, her voice full of love.

Even though he was too far away to hear what they had said, as if on cue, John turned around from the grill just then and looked at Jillian. It felt to her like they were the only two people on the planet at that moment. She couldn't take her eyes off his, nor he, hers. His look reminded her of the first time they had met face to face in the kitchen.

Noticing that John was distracted from his cooking duties, Tommy asked, "Zio, want me to take over for a few minutes?"

"Sure, go ahead. I've got to do something," John said, still focused on Jillian. He walked over to Jillian and Maria, who were seated in some wrought iron chairs around a table. John stepped behind Jillian and put his arms around her shoulders. Jillian crossed her hands over her chest and pulled him in close, wrapping herself in his arms. He kissed the side of her face, and she turned toward him.

"Hi," he said softly, crouching down next to her.

"Hi yourself," she said. "Did you resign from your job?" Her eyes darted for a moment to Tommy at the grill.

"No, I just needed a little break—to do this," he said and kissed her sweetly.

Jillian grabbed his hand tightly and kissed it before he walked back to Tommy. Maria asked, "Who was that masked man?" and shook her head in total amazement.

"Okay, I'm better now," John said to Tommy and took the spatula back from his nephew.

Tommy smiled and sent Alison into the house for a plate. She was a pretty girl, just starting to really look like a young woman. She was taller than her mom, with her mom's slender build and Maria's dark eyes, light brown hair, and sweet smile. She was going to be very beautiful in a year or two, Jillian thought.

Jillian listened to Marty's discussion with John Anthony about what to expect during the first year of college. Marty told him some of her thoughts on what to do, and what not to do, during one's first semester. She hadn't really had any major problems, but she had some friends who had learned some things the hard way.

The rest of the afternoon was filled with more swimming and sunbathing before they called a family meeting to talk over the logistics for the next day. The day would begin with the Easter service at eleven a.m., followed by an Easter brunch hosted by the church youth group. There would be a brief break at home to relax before getting ready for the big event. They needed to arrive at church by four p.m. for a photo session. Five o'clock was the ceremony, then off to Leo's for dinner.

At nine p.m., a limousine would pick up John and Jillian and take the two of them somewhere special for their wedding night. Tommy would drive the rest of the family home in the Land Rover. John and Jillian would return Monday afternoon to the house for one last evening with the family before they all departed on Tuesday.

After the meeting adjourned, everyone made certain their clothes were in order for church and the wedding, while others took a rest or headed for computers and cell phones. Jillian went back with Marty to the cottage to get their things ready and to pack her overnight bag for the next night.

That evening, John and Jillian cooked some of their favorite dishes for the family, and everyone wanted to help. John had asked Jillian to make some pilau. At first, she thought he was joking. This was the food that he had thrown, plate and all, into the trash the first week she had worked for him. But he assured her he was serious. Marty and Jillian made the pilau together, as they had many times in Tanzania.

When dinner was ready, they all said a table prayer. John offered a toast, then they enjoyed an eclectic feast of Californian, Italian, and Tanzanian delights. When Jillian brought the pilau to the table, she had to laugh.

"Okay, there must be a reason you're laughing, Jillian. What's the story?" Maria asked.

"May I, John?" she asked.

"Go ahead," he said and dramatically put his hands over his eyes.

Jillian proceeded to tell the story of her writing a note saying that she had left some food for him in the refrigerator, and that if he didn't care for the dish, he could throw it out. John had taken her words very literally and had thrown the entire dish of food, plate and all, into the trash receptacle, leaving a note that said he "didn't care for the 'dish.'"

"Zio, you didn't!" Tommy said.

"I did. I wasn't very happy back then. Not like I am now," he said and smiled at Jillian.

Jillian also told them how the next time she wrote a note about food she was leaving for him, she was certain not to put the word "dish" in it, which made them all laugh.

The new family talked the evening away. The older adults were getting tired, especially those who came from a different time zone, so Tommy and Maria were the first to go up to the guest suite.

Marty, John Anthony, and Alison decided that they were going to watch a movie in the theater room. They made some popcorn in the microwave, grabbed some water and soda pop, and headed off, discussing which movie they should watch.

John and Jillian watched them as they walked away, laughing and talking with one another. "We have a beautiful family, don't we?" John asked.

"The best," Jillian responded.

"May I walk you to your door?" John asked as he had that first evening when she decided to stay.

She nodded, and they took off through the kitchen door into a beautiful moonlit night, hand in hand. This was their nightly ritual, and in the last week it seemed to become more and more torturous for both of them.

John turned to her at her door and then kissed her. "This is the last time I have to say good night to you," he said, his head pressed to hers.

"What will we say to each other at the end of the day, then?" Jillian asked.

"How about 'I'll love you forever?'" John asked in a hushed tone.

"That sounds perfect to me," she said, and then she kissed him. John groaned slightly and said, "I've got to go. I think I understand about all that waiting of the Easter Vigil Pastor Jim was talking about. That's what I feel like."

"Well, don't stay up all night... tonight," Jillian said to him, thinking out loud.

"Jillian, you're not helping," he told her, pulling her close.

"I'm sorry, sweetheart. Good night, John," she said and turned toward her door. He walked away toward the house, and just as she was closing her door, she heard a big splash in the pool. Jillian ran to see what had happened and saw John in the pool, fully clothed.

"Are you okay?" she asked in a concerned tone, but then noticed his watch and wallet and shoes sitting on the deck.

"Just cooling off," he said. "Care to join me?"

She started to laugh. "Somehow, I think that might be counter-productive," she said.

John pulled himself up out of the pool. It reminded Jillian of her very first morning on the job, when she had awakened to a splash in the pool and later saw John standing in the light of early dawn after he climbed out.

She chuckled as he stood before her, sopping wet. "You are so funny," she said. "You make me laugh."

"Really?" he said, an unusual expression crossing his face. Perhaps he was remembering back, as was Jillian, to a reference in Monica Morgan's book. She had referred to John as a very serious, talented actor, and then went on to say how much she appreciated Ben, the man she married, who was funny and made her laugh every day.

"Really," she said, still giggling.

He hugged her, wet clothes and all, but Jillian didn't mind. "Should we practice?" he asked her.

Now it was her turn for an unusual expression. John could tell that Jillian was not certain to what he was referring. "Our new 'good night,' that is," he said, smiling.

She smiled back at him and said, "I'll love you forever."

He said the same back, kissed her quickly, grabbed his things off the deck, and scampered to the cabana at the back of the house.

Jillian thought back again to that first day, when she had seen him rise out of the pool, grab a towel, and walk slowly, shoulders slumped, toward that very cabana. He was not the same person anymore—and neither was she. As she walked back to the cottage, she thanked God for that.

Chapter Eight

Jillian woke up Easter morning with the sun streaming into the room and her precious daughter sleeping at her side. This would be Jillian's last morning waking up in this cottage. This would be her last morning waking up as a single woman. Tonight she and John would be staying somewhere special, unknown to Jillian. John wanted to surprise her. When they returned to the house on Monday, Jillian would sleep in John's room—their room—for the very first time. She still didn't completely believe it was all real.

It was another unusually warm day, but Jillian barely noticed the weather. It could have been one of those Midwestern Easters with six inches of snow, and she wouldn't have cared. The idea of an Easter wedding was making more sense to her with each passing moment. It seemed like the Easter message of resurrection had never been as powerful to her as it was that day, as she thought of how God had changed the world long ago on the first Easter, and how God had changed her world in the last year, bringing her to this day. Jillian felt like her life was just beginning.

Kathy J. Jacobson

The church service was packed, and the message and music absolutely joyful. Jillian sang with the choir on an anthem, and Marty, an excellent sight-reader, joined in as well. Nancy read the lessons and was excited to have all but one of her children and their families in attendance that day. Nancy, Pastor Jim, and his wife, Janet, were the only ones at church who knew what was happening later that day. Nancy couldn't stop smiling—nor could Jillian.

After worship, they enjoyed the Easter brunch hosted and served by the youth group and their parents. Marty and Jillian remembered back to the many Easter mornings when they got up extra early to cook and serve a similar meal back at their church in Madison. It was always the big fundraiser for the summer servant trip, as it was on this day as well.

"Some things never change, do they, Mom?" Marty asked as they watched the teens and their parents go in and out of the kitchen with dishes, pitchers, and thermal coffee carafes.

"No, and this is one of those things I hope never changes," Jillian said. She remembered fondly those summer excursions and how many lives were transformed during them—both the people who were served and the servants. Marty had gone several years as a youth participant, and Jillian had been an adult leader. The trips were some of their favorite times shared together during Marty's teen years, and Jillian and Marty told some of their favorite stories during the meal.

Jillian found it difficult, even in the midst of all the reminiscing and action of the day, to keep her mind and eyes off John. He had never looked more handsome, or desirable, to her. He must have been having similar thoughts, as they would often zone out from everything and everybody else around them, staring at one another until someone interrupted them or pulled them away to another task or conversation. Often Jillian would glance at her watch, wishing she could control time and make it five o'clock.

Jillian checked the time about every five minutes over the next few hours until it was finally time to head back to church. Jillian and John put their overnight bags into the Land Rover, and then the entire crew climbed in once again, glad that the church was not far away. No one wanted to ruin their nice clothes before the photo session and ceremony.

One of Nancy's grandsons was a photographer and agreed to meet them early. John was wearing a dark suit with a new white shirt and a tie Jillian had picked out with him. Jillian wore the dress that Marianna and Karen had helped her pick out. It was stunning. Marty was Jillian's maid of honor and had donned a dress she had tailored in Dakar especially for the day. She almost stole the show, but it is hard to outshine the radiance of a woman who was as in love with someone as Jillian was with John that day.

Nancy's grandson, David, took some photos outside and inside the church. And at five o'clock sharp, they gathered into a semicircle with Pastor Jim in the chancel area. Tommy, John's best man, stood next to him, and Marty next to Jillian.

Pastor Jim read their scripture passage from Second Corinthians. He then spoke about how John had approached him in early February, making a convincing case for an Easter wedding. John had said that he had become a new creation and felt like he had been resurrected in the past year since Jillian had come into his life.

Pastor Jim reminded them all that life, and especially marriage, needed to be like a thousand little resurrection days, always being renewed, always starting over, in good times and especially in not-so-good times. As usual, the good pastor hit the nail right on the head with his simple, but profound words, giving everyone the feeling that with God, everything was possible.

Pastor Jim had also asked each of them separately what they

Kathy J. Jacobson

liked and appreciated most about the other. John said he loved Jillian's ability to overlook flaws in others, to be patient and kind, and that she didn't give up on people. He loved her smile, the way she took care of people, and how she loved everyone—and especially how she loved him.

Jillian loved John's intelligence, his sensitivity and empathy, and the way he listened to people—especially her. He was kind and respectful of others. She loved how he kept on surprising her in good ways, and she appreciated the way John made her feel wanted, loved, and even more than that—cherished.

They exchanged their vows, then John put the ring with "the right person" engraved inside on Jillian's finger, repeating after Pastor Jim the words "I give you this ring as a sign of my love and faithfulness." Jillian did the same with his matching band.

Nancy's nephew snapped more photos as the new husband and wife kissed each other, then again as they were leaving the church hand in hand, huge smiles spread across both of their faces.

Jillian and John thanked Pastor Jim, who was now going to leave for a vacation with his wife and twin sons, and John gave him an extra-generous honorarium for doing the service for them on Easter.

The happy, and now "official," family climbed into the Land Rover, which this weekend actually seemed like a practical vehicle for the first time in its tenure, and headed off to Leo's.

Leo was waiting outside the restaurant with the biggest smile on his face. His son, Leonardo, was inside cooking. John had called Leo as soon as they left the church to give him an estimated time of arrival. Leo's younger son, Danielo, had set the tables beautifully and was ready for his assignment as busboy/dishwasher for the evening.

They sat down at a large round table, which on this occasion was covered with a white linen cloth and a generous number of tapered white candles. Leo brought out bottles of the wine that they had enjoyed so much the first night they had visited the restaurant together. He opened one and made a toast to the newlyweds.

Tommy followed with another toast, as did Marty. Then John surprised Jillian—again one of his good surprises—by saying a beautiful table prayer giving thanks for their family, friends, the food, and especially for her. She could hardly speak afterward. Instead she just looked at him and squeezed his hand, this time above the table, in the safe company of family.

Leonardo came out from the kitchen during the meal to see how they were enjoying the food. He was a gorgeous young man, with long, dark curls and beautiful dark eyes and eyelashes to match. Jillian saw her daughter and Leonardo noticing one another, and also recognized that this did not please John Anthony one bit. Alison was absolutely mesmerized by Danielo, who appeared to be about her age and was a younger version of Leonardo. Her eyes followed the young man's every move as he cleared dishes before the dessert.

It was one of those evenings when it felt like love was in the air. Tommy and Maria had been quite moved by the wedding ceremony. Jillian thought they looked very much in love this evening, like they were experiencing a little resurrection of their own.

But no one topped the bride and groom, who still couldn't keep their eyes off one another. As much as Jillian loved Leo's cooking, it took second place to her husband on this night, especially after that moving prayer. She had never felt as blessed in her entire life.

Leo's special tiramisu and hot coffee offerings topped off a perfect meal and evening. The limo arrived at nine sharp, and the driver took the bags from Tommy, who had retrieved them from the Land Rover. John took out his wallet to pay Leo, but Leo wouldn't accept anything. He said it was his wedding gift to his friends. After he and John had a friendly argument over the subject for about five minutes while the limo driver waited patiently, John finally gave in. He insisted on giving each of Leo's sons very large tips, however, which brought huge, grateful smiles to their faces.

John and Jillian slid into the backseat of the limousine. The only other time Jillian had been in one was for her junior prom in high school. Unlike John's life, there had been no luxury cars with drivers, red carpet arrivals, or cameras flashing in her past. She wondered for a moment if John didn't miss all of that. She briefly panicked, feeling that somehow she was getting in his way, but then realized that wasn't really the case. When, and if, he decided to return to acting, she would support him one hundred percent in whatever ways she could—because that's what spouses did for one another.

She was a spouse. She was someone's wife. John was her husband. Jillian sat quietly dumbfounded for a moment.

"What are you thinking about?" John asked, as he took her chin with his strong fingers.

"You," she said.

"What about me?" he asked.

"You're my husband," she said, still in awe of the idea. "I've never had a husband before. I've never been a wife before," a touch of amazement in her voice.

"I guess we're in the same boat, then, because I've never been a husband before, and I've never had a wife before."

"As long as we're both in the same boat, everything will be okay," Jillian replied, looking adoringly into John's face .

"It will be more than okay," John replied, moving closer to her and smiling.

She smiled back, then he kissed her tenderly.

The limo pulled up a short time later at a breathtaking beach house in Malibu. After their driver put the luggage into the house, John and Jillian checked out the view. The surf was roaring, and the rolling waves were shining in the moonlight as they stood on a huge deck that overlooked the beach and the ocean beyond it. The two gazed at the sight for a moment, but even the spectacular view couldn't compete with each other.

They made a plan to freshen up and meet back in the living room. Jillian thought she may have set a personal record for getting through the shower. The black marble bathroom had a soft, luxurious white robe hanging in it, and John informed Jillian it belonged to her.

She actually beat John to the living room, and noticed for the first time a vase of two dozen yellow roses on a tabletop. On a clear stake was a yellow sticky note, like the ones they had used to write notes to one another for much of the past year. On it John had written:

Jillian, I'll love you forever. John

Her eyes were misting again, as she felt John's arms wrap around her from behind, clothed in the sleeves of a matching white robe. He put his chin on her shoulder and his head next to hers, and she pulled his arms even more tightly around her. Then he kissed her gently on the neck.

Suddenly Jillian found herself trembling. It was a combination of feeling so overwhelmingly in love, and loved, and if she was truthful, being a bit nervous.

"Are you okay?" John asked, gently turning her around toward himself.

"I am," she said quietly. She hesitated a moment. "It's just that...

I've never really been made love to before."

John took in her words and processed them, a mixture of expressions crossing his face in a matter of seconds. "Well, come to think of it, I don't believe that I have been, either."

There was his incredible kindness showing itself, Jillian thought. Then again, perhaps there some truth to his statement.

John pulled her close and said, "I guess we have some catching up to do, then," and kissed her. When the kiss finally ended, he looked at her and said, "Oh, and before I forget, I'll love you forever."

"I'll love you forever, too, John."

Then John reached for her hand, and as they had for so many nights, they walked together hand in hand. But this time, they did not have to say good night.

Jillian would look back on that night for years to come and try to put it into words, but they all sounded so cliché. She finally gave up trying to describe it and just basked in the wonderfulness of it all.

She woke up to John's beautiful brown eyes gazing at her.

"Hi," she said.

"Hi, yourself," he answered.

She kissed him gently and caressed his face with her fingers. He put his hand to hers and held it against his face, then kissed it.

"You make me feel like I'm sixteen, instead of sixty," John said.

She smiled at him. "But John, if you are sixteen, what does that make me?"

"Oh, boy, then I'd really be robbing the cradle." Then his face turned serious. "Does our age difference bother you, Jillian?"

"No. Does it bother you?"

"No, but I just don't want you to get bored with me, when I get old sooner than you do," he said.

"I don't think it would be possible for me to get bored with you, John. And I've seen enough strange things over the years to know that anything can happen to anyone. Something could happen to me that could make me seem like the older one. And besides, I seem to remember us saying something yesterday about 'in sickness and in health, until death us do part.' All I know is that whatever time we have left on this earth, no matter what happens to either of us, I want to spend it together."

"Me, too," he said and kissed her. "I don't know what I ever did to deserve you, Jillian. I never knew I could love anyone this much."

"That makes two of us," she said and pulled him close.

The car returned for them at three o'clock that afternoon. If it wasn't for the fact that their family was waiting for them, they would have never left. They looked at the view one last time while the driver put their bags in the trunk and the vase of yellow roses on the floor of the front seat, having poured off the water.

They held each other close as they pulled away from the house. "How did you ever find that place?" Jillian asked.

"It belongs to a friend of mine. He winters out of the country and rents it out to people he trusts," John said.

"You must know him very well."

"I do. We used to be neighbors—I used to live a few houses down."

Everyone once in a while, Jillian would have to do a reality check and remind herself about all those years of John's life before she came into it. She remembered dusting his Emmy and Golden Globe Awards in his library, not fully grasping the life he had once led—ocean-side house, dating gorgeous actresses, and dealing

Kathy J. Jacobson

with the paparazzi. For a moment, she felt a bit intimidated by all those ghosts of the past, but then she remembered that John was who he was now, not then, and the same was true for herself.

She smiled at him and said, "It was a very special surprise."

"I'm glad... you liked it," he said, kissing her between words.

"I *loved* it," she said. Now Jillian was the one who felt like a sixteen-year-old as she kissed her sweetheart in the back seat of a car.

Jillian and John returned home to an excited crew. It was their final night together as a family, and they were going to cherish every moment. Marty, Maria, and Alison had done a bit of redecorating in John's room—correction—*their* room. They had asked for John's permission before the wedding ceremony, informing him that it looked like a boring bachelor pad.

The wedding photos had been posted by Nancy's grandson on a website. Tommy, Maria, and Marty had taken it upon themselves to make a small album and to enlarge two photos into eight by tens—one of the entire family in color, and another black and white candid shot that was taken as John and Jillian had come out of the church. It was a very romantic picture, which captured the faces of two people who looked incredibly happy and so in love with one another. It would be John and Jillian's favorite photo for many years to come.

On the table next to the photos were a box of gourmet chocolates, a bottle of red wine and two glasses, an iPod set up to play a song—"to dance to," Alison had informed them—as they hadn't had a dance after the wedding. There were several new candles adorning the space, and new sheets on the bed and towels in the bathroom with their names embroidered on them. Maria must have had this all planned out ahead of time. She had thought of everything. She was such a considerate woman.

John put their overnight bags on the floor of the huge walk-in closet, then came up behind Jillian as she gazed at the photos, putting his chin on her shoulder again. She loved it when he did that.

"I'm the luckiest person on the face of the earth," John said softly into her ear.

"Funny, I was just thinking the same thing," Jillian replied, hugging his arms, which were wrapped around hers. She felt like they were one entity, rather than two separate people. She ran her thumbs over his forearms. "I think we'd better join our family," she said in a soft voice.

"You are probably right," he said. He kissed her neck quickly, then took her hand as they headed downstairs where dinner preparations were in progress. A light rain had started to fall outside, so they ate in the dining room. The room had seen more action in the past few days than it had the rest of the time John had lived in the house.

Maria tried out one of her newest recipes—a northern Italian marsala, which she had prepared with Alison and Marty. After they couldn't eat another bite of the delicious fare, the men said it was their turn to wash the dishes and put away the food. The women did not argue. They sat and talked together, Jillian telling them about the house in Malibu. After a bit, Jillian noticed a straggler drinking glass and walked it back to the kitchen. She stopped just outside the door, loving the sound of the guys talking together.

"Uncle John," as John Anthony called his great-uncle, "you're quite a bit older than Aunt Jillian, aren't you?"

"John Anthony! That's an impolite question to ask," Tommy said to his son. Jillian didn't mind the question. She was too busy enjoying the sound of her new title of "aunt."

"Let him ask," John said calmly. "Yes, I'm twelve years her senior."

"Does it bother you?" The conversation reminded Jillian of their own earlier that day.

"No."

"Does it bother Aunt Jillian?"

"No, it doesn't appear to be a problem for either of us," John answered.

John Anthony continued, "Do older women sometimes marry younger men?"

"Sometimes. Not as often as the other way around it seems—I'm not exactly sure why that is—but it shouldn't really matter what your ages are if you're in love with one another."

"That's good to know," John Anthony said seriously.

It took a moment for the older men to realize what prompted these questions, but Jillian had sensed it the night before at the restaurant. John Anthony had a crush on Marty.

Tommy was drying a pan when a flash of understanding crossed his face. "You've got good taste, son, you've got good taste."

"It runs in the family," John added.

Jillian decided that this was her cue to enter the room. "What runs in the family?" she asked as she walked into the kitchen.

"Good looks," John said, his face stretching into that irresistible grin.

"Well, I can't argue with that," she said as she put the glass into the soapy water in the sink, then walked to her husband's side.

She didn't want to interrupt their conversation, so she gave John a peck on the cheek and headed back to Marty, Maria, and Alison. When she returned, she found they were in the process of moving into the living room. Marty found Jillian's new guitar and started strumming it, playing and singing a current song.

The men finished up in the kitchen and joined them, pleasantly surprised by the playing and singing going on in the house. When

Marty finished her song—with John Anthony entranced as she sang—she asked Jillian to sing a song with her.

"Let's do 'Tell Me Why,'" Jillian said, "for old time's sake." Jillian explained that the song had been taught to her as a child in her church's kids' choir. Jillian had taught her mom the melody, and she sang the counter-melody. It was one of their favorite "washing the dishes songs." Later, Jillian would often sing it as a lullaby to Marty, and when Marty was older, they sang it together while doing dishes, just as Jillian and her mother had done.

Tell me why the stars do shine
Tell me why the ivy twines
Tell me why the sky's so blue
and I will tell you just why I love you

Because God made the stars to shine
Because God made the ivy twine
Because God made the sky so blue
Because God made you, that's why I love you!

Jillian had always thought the song to be special, but on this night, singing it together with her daughter, and with John—her husband—listening and watching, it was elevated to a new level.

They sang another favorite song from Tanzania in Swahili, then set the guitar aside so they could all talk. Time seemed to go by at the speed of light, and soon it was late. Everyone had to be up early to go to the airport, and no one was packed yet.

The two teenagers still had plenty of energy, but Jillian could tell that Marty was getting tired, and most likely a bit melancholy about leaving. Maria and Tommy looked fatigued, perhaps for the same reason as Marty. She was quite certain that Tommy and Maria wished they could stay longer as well. Not counting the teens, John and Jillian seemed to be holding up quite well comparatively.

Jillian couldn't understand that, but decided that they must have been operating on pure adrenaline.

John walked upstairs with Tommy and his family, and Jillian walked with Marty back to the cottage. She helped her pack her bag and then hugged and kissed her good night. She was not relishing saying goodbye the next day.

After everyone was settled in for the night, John and Jillian met in the hallway outside of their room. John pulled her into a hug and just held her for a moment. Then before she knew it, she was being swept off her feet and carried through the doorway of the bedroom.

"That's what you're supposed to do, isn't it?" John asked.

"It works for me," she said, smiling.

John set her down gently and closed the door. They walked over to the "honeymoon table," as Jillian had come to think of it.

"So, let's hear what song we are supposed to dance to," she said, as she hit the remote to the iPod.

Michael Bublé's "You and I" came on. She put her hand in John's, he put his hand around her waist, and they danced their first dance together.

"I've imagined you in this room—so many times," John said as they slowly swayed to the music.

"Did you imagine us dancing?" Jillian asked.

"Not really, but I like it, and I'm not much of a dancer," he said.

"So, what did you imagine?"

"I did imagine you in my arms."

"Check," she said, tightening her grip on his shoulder and hand, and moving closer to him.

"And this," he added, pulling her into a deep kiss as the song ended.

"Let's save the wine and chocolates for another night," she said.

John nodded in agreement.

The buzz of the alarm was a most unwelcome sound the next morning. Not only were they exhausted, but neither of them was looking forward to the impending farewells. They ate a light breakfast with their family, gathered for a group "selfie" in front of the house, then packed the Land Rover.

They headed to LAX and made it to the airport in record time. There had been no major traffic backups that morning, which was very unusual for Los Angeles. John pulled into a parking stall, and they all poured out of the overstuffed vehicle. John and John Anthony unloaded the luggage, with planes roaring overhead and car doors and trunks slamming and echoing all around them.

An airport can be an emotional place, full of wonderful reunions and tearful goodbyes. Everyone's emotions were definitely running high as they headed toward the terminal. After a shower of kisses and hugs, they said goodbye to Tommy and his family first. They reassured each other that they would see each other again soon, as John and Jillian planned to stop in Chicago on their way to wherever they ended up taking a honeymoon.

Then it was Marty's turn. Jillian held her daughter for the longest time. For most of Jillian's adult life, Marty had been her one constant, the one main love in her life. Marty was the one who loved her unconditionally. Marty was her sounding board, her best friend, yet so much more than a best friend.

She stroked her daughter's silky, long hair. As usual, Marty's eyes shone, but this time there were tears in them as well. It had been a wonderful few days, and it was difficult to see it come to an end.

But Marty, being the type of person she was, didn't dwell on her departure. Instead, she focused on her mom.

"Mom, I'm so happy for you. John is wonderful, and he makes you so happy. And it's obvious you make him really happy, too. I

Kathy J. Jacobson

hope I find someone like him someday," she said.

"Your Grandma used tell me that someday there would be someone for me, out of the blue. It took a while to find the right person, but it happened. If it happened for me, I'm sure it will happen for you, at the right time," Jillian reassured her daughter.

"Thanks, Mom," she said, and they kissed and hugged each other goodbye.

Then Marty walked over to John, who had given them some space to say goodbye, another sign of his thoughtfulness. She hugged him and kissed him on the cheek. "Thank you for making my Mom so happy," she said to John.

"Thank you for sharing her with me, and for giving us your blessing, Marty," John said sincerely in response.

Then Jillian watched as Marty whispered something in John's ear. He pulled back, a surprised look on his face, and then looked to be fighting tears.

"I'd like that," he said softly, then hugged Marty and kissed her on the cheek.

"Okay, then," Marty said, picking up her bag and moving toward the gate. She looked back at Jillian. "Goodbye, Mom!" Then she turned back to John and said, "Goodbye, Dad," and was off to her terminal.

Now it was Jillian's turn to fight tears. She walked over to John and put her hand on his arm. They were both in a highly emotional state.

He looked at Jillian and said, "I've always wanted a daughter." He had said that out loud once to Jillian months before in the library without realizing it, after Jillian had told him how she used to read books out loud with her daughter.

"Well, now you've got one—a good one. Let's go home... Dad," Jillian said. John smiled, and they walked back through the airport and parking lot, hand in hand.

When they arrived home, there was yet another surprise waiting for Jillian. When the garage door opened and they pulled in, there was another vehicle in the space next to John's. It was a white Land Rover, not a fancy version like John's, but one a person might find in Tanzania. It was parked there with a large bow on it.

"I thought you might be tired of biking everywhere," John said as he watched Jillian walk around the vehicle.

"You are so very thoughtful, John," she said quietly. She didn't know if she could love a person any more than she loved John that day. Even her precious daughter loved him and asked if she could call him "Dad." The thought brought fresh tears back to her eyes. She grabbed John and held him as tightly as she could, like she was afraid that he might disappear at any moment.

"I love you so much, John," she said.

"I love you more than you could ever know, Jillian," he said and kissed her sweetly.

The house seemed so quiet when they went inside. But as much as Jillian would miss all the commotion and the people they loved, she also looked forward to some normalcy and, quite honestly, to having John to herself.

She and John walked together into the library, one of her favorite rooms since the moment she first saw the house. He sat down in his favorite chair and pulled her down gently onto his lap.

"So, we have some things to discuss," he said. "First of all, where do you want to go for our honeymoon?"

"Well, depending on how much time we have to travel, it would be great to stop for a while in Chicago, then a quick stop in

Kathy J. Jacobson

Wisconsin, then how about Italy? You still have family there, don't you? And then, I'd really like to show you..."

"Africa," John said.

"I want my friends in Tanzania to meet you and you to meet them, and for you to see the place where Marty and I left a part of our hearts. Before or after that, we could go to the other coast of the continent and see Marty in Senegal."

"So, it sounds like we need a good month," John said.

"When did you want to go?" Jillian asked.

"Well, that brings me to another subject. I had a call early on Friday from Alan, my agent. He wants me to audition for a few productions—a play, a guest star spot on an episode of a television program, and the other for a small role in a movie. I told him I'd get back to him soon—I had to discuss it first with my wife. What do you think, Jillian?"

"You should have told me," she said, so happy for him.

"I didn't want anything to take away from our special day, or our time with our family."

"You're right, but how could you keep something that exciting to yourself?"

"You think it sounds exciting?"

"I do! Don't you?"

"Actually, I *am* excited. I didn't even know how much I was missing acting, but you have awakened all kinds of things in me, Jillian. I am so grateful to you..." John said, his voice trailing off as he was overcome with emotion.

"Shhh," she said, putting her arms around his neck. "We both have awakened each other. We're good for one another, John. I know for a fact that you bring out the best in me." She put her forehead to his.

"I just want you to always be happy, and proud, that you married me," he said.

If he said anything else, she thought she would explode with happiness. All those years of heartbreak and disappointment were flying out of the window of her heart.

"John, I can't imagine that ever being an issue. And I hope that you know I will support you in whatever you want, or need, to do professionally—even if it means we have to wait a long time to travel. Whatever you want, I want."

He pulled her into an embrace and whispered in her ear, "I love you, Mrs. Romano."

"I love you, too, Mr. Romano," and she smiled as she remembered that was what she called John for much the last year. Never in her wildest dreams would she have imagined that things would turn out the way that they had.

"We'll decide on our travel dates after the auditions, then. Who knows? There's a good chance they'll be a 'no.' I'm not sure if I still even 'have it.'"

"Oh, believe me," Jillian said, "you still 'have it,'" and she kissed him, loving him with her whole heart.

Just then the house helper, Esperanza, walked into the room. They hadn't remembered that it was her day to clean the house.

"Oh, excuse me!" she said, surprised and embarrassed. "I can come back another time."

"It's okay, Esperanza, we were just leaving the room. Sorry that the place is such a mess after all our company the past few days. We hope you got our message about the bedrooms and cottage needing cleaning and linen changes, and the theater room probably needs to be checked," Jillian added.

"Yes, I did. The upstairs guest rooms are done already, and I was just checking to make sure this room was okay on my way to the theater room and then the cottage. It looks like everything is good in this room," she said with a shy smile.

"Oh, yes, it's very good," John said, smiling back at her and then at Jillian.

Esperanza wished them a good day, and they the same to her, then John kissed Jillian again.

"I suppose I should be calling Alan, but this is a lot more fun," he said.

"It is, but I think you should call Alan, and I'm going to do something I haven't done in a really long time. I'm going to take a nap."

"I'll call Alan, and I'll be up in a little bit. A nap sounds like a good idea."

Jillian kissed him on the cheek and headed up the stairs. With each step, she shook her head. She still couldn't believe that everything that had happened was for real, but smiled as she reached their room and realized it was indeed reality.

It had been an incredible couple of months. It had been an incredible couple of days. Now it was time to regenerate, and to get ready for what life had in store for them next.

Chapter Nine

Alan Abrams had been John's agent for almost thirty years, and was ecstatic—no—*shocked*, when John called him back and said "yes" to all three auditions. He even asked him a second time if he was sure about this. John reassured him, explaining to Alan that his wife not only approved but encouraged him to do the auditions.

Alan wondered if he was speaking to the right John Romano. He couldn't imagine John being so willing to audition. Even more so, he couldn't imagine John with a wife. He told John that he hoped to meet this wife of his sometime soon. John supposed that Alan might not have really believed that he had one.

"I'll talk to Jillian, and we will make a plan to have you over for lunch or dinner soon." Now Alan was in utter disbelief—an invitation to meet John's wife and to dine at his home. Both would be first-time events.

The first audition was just two days away. The others were on Saturday and Sunday, with callbacks possible in the days following. The first order of business was to research the play, then find a monologue for John that fit its genre. The Internet certainly made things a lot easier than in the earlier years of John's career, and Jillian helped him learn how to use it more efficiently to find what he needed.

They downloaded a copy of the play, and Jillian read lines with John, sharing her insights and discussing options of what the character might be like with him. Normally, John was not one to listen to anyone else's opinion but his own when it came to his craft, but for some reason, he was willing to consider what Jillian had to say. He even told her she wouldn't make a bad director. Coming from a man who had a reputation for arguing with directors, Jillian considered his words as quite the compliment.

No matter what would come of these auditions, Jillian was just happy that John was doing them. She knew it was a huge step for him, and she prayed hard that night that it would end up a positive experience.

The night before the first audition, Jillian could tell that John was on edge. He didn't really want to admit it, but he was nervous. It had been two-and-a-half years since his last audition, and his last experience on stage had not gone well.

He turned yet another way in the bed, trying to get comfortable, to no avail.

"Let me give you a good nurse's massage, John," Jillian suggested.

"I don't think that will really help, but it sounds good anyway," he said with a smile. "I'm sorry I'm not very fun tonight. I'm excited... and a little nervous," he finally confessed.

"I understand," she said, and really did. It reminded her of how she had felt just a few nights before on their wedding night, but John had easily dispelled her doubts and concerns.

"Do you have your alarm set yet?" she asked him.

"No, should I?" he asked.

"Well, this massage has a way of making people feel relaxed and sleepy fairly quickly—that's the idea—so you may want to make sure everything you want done, is done, before I start."

He reached over to the nightstand next to their bed and set the alarm on his phone. "Just in case this works, I'd better take care of the most important things first," and he pulled her lips to his.

"I'll love you forever," he said.

"I'll love you forever," Jillian replied, then told John to turn over onto his stomach. She would work his shoulders, neck, and upper back first, and go from there if needed.

Within ten minutes, John was sound asleep. Jillian snuggled up close to his body and just watched him breathe for a few minutes, still amazed that she was a married woman. She gently pulled the covers up over them both and drifted contently off to sleep.

They both awakened to the call of the alarm. John reached over and hit "snooze" on his phone, then turned to Jillian. "Wow, I should have married a nurse a long time ago," he said smiling. "I've never fallen asleep that fast the night before an audition."

"Well, I'm glad it helped, but I'm also glad you didn't marry some nurse a long time ago," she said, stroking his face. "Do you want me to go with you today?"

"That is nice of you to offer—maybe another time. It's a lot of just sitting around and waiting. I wouldn't want you to be there when I wait an hour for two minutes of someone's time, and possibly have to wait around even longer for a callback. And what if I flub it?"

"John, think positively. You are *not* flubbing anything today. Remember who you are, and what you are. You are John D. Romano, a very talented actor, and now, on top of that, you are a new creation, better than ever in every way. And best of all, you are *my* husband."

"Jillian, you are too good to me," he said softly and then kissed her.

Just then the snooze on the alarm sounded. John sighed. "I don't want to leave this bed."

"I don't want you to either, but being late would not be a *good* start to your *new* start. Break a leg, and make sure to text me when you are able with updates."

"I love you, Jillian," John said and kissed her lightly.

"I love you, too, John. Now go."

John swung his feet to the floor and made himself get up out of the bed. Jillian watched him head to the shower, then fell back asleep.

She was so tired that she didn't even hear John leave. Instead, she woke up to a text from him. "Waiting. Nervous. Director not one of my biggest fans."

She texted him back, "New creation."

He texted back a smile.

After breakfast, Jillian decided to make some phone calls. First on her list was Pete.

"Pete, Jillian," she said.

"Hi there, Mrs. Romano," he said.

"Say that again, Pete. I like the sound of that."

"Okay. Hi there, Mrs. Romano. How's married life treating you so far?"

"It's the best. I can't really describe it, but you probably know exactly what I'm talking about, don't you? How's Kelly?"

"She is great, Jillian, and yes, I know exactly what you are saying. It is indescribable. I've never been so happy."

"That makes two of us, Pete. I'm happy for both of us. So, any plans for the health club yet?"

"We are looking around for properties that are for sale and checking the demographics to see if there is an interested, but underserved area. We want to have the best possible chance of making it a 'go.'"

"I know that between you and Kelly, you will come up with the perfect place and plan. I can't wait to direct all my friends your way. And I know I have a fitness center in my house, but I might join just to help things get started. I once worked with this really great personal trainer..."

"Jillian, you're awesome. I can't thank you enough for everything. So, when are we all getting together?"

Jillian told him about John's auditions, and they decided they had better wait for the outcomes before they made a plan. Besides, Jillian and John had been married only a handful of days and were still honeymooning, even if they were just at home. Jillian was in no rush to get too busy, too quickly, even with people she adored like Pete and Kelly.

When Jillian ended the call, she noticed she had two text messages from John. She felt bad that she hadn't been available right away to answer them.

"New creation. Reading went well," the first message said. Then she hurried to see the next one. "Asked to read for another part, too."

Jillian was hoping that the other part was as good as the one John was thinking he might get. There were actually a number of male roles, all good ones, and then the lead role. John didn't think that he would be considered for that one, but Jillian wondered why he wouldn't. Maybe it was an age thing, but from what she had read, she didn't think that would be an issue. She decided to say a prayer that John would get a part, and the one that was the best for both him and the production.

She texted him back, "Excited. Go for it." That was what Jillian would often say to Marty whenever she tried out for a musical or solo at school.

She waited for about ten minutes, but no reply. She decided that John was back in doing another reading, so she called Karen.

"Hello, Mrs. Romano," said Karen. Jillian smiled at Karen's words. She was loving this.

The two friends hadn't realized how much news they had to share and talked for quite a while. Karen was nearing the end of her college semester, so she had a lot of papers to write and tests for which to prepare. But even with all the work of school, life was good. Karen was thrilled that she was getting so close to finishing her undergraduate degree. This was her last semester of regular classes, then she would student-teach in the fall and graduate in early December.

Karen would go on for her master's degree the very next semester at the same college, so she had a long road ahead. Even so, it was the sense of accomplishment of finishing a degree that Karen was most excited about—that, and getting out to work with the kids. She had already had a small taste of it in a practicum and was happy to find out that she was much more comfortable in the classroom than she had ever dreamed she would be.

After Karen finished her news, Jillian filled her in about the wedding and promised to send her photos soon. She would not be posting any photos on social media. She couldn't post any that included John, so she decided not to post any at all. She still kept her name the same on her page, as to not advertise the situation. It was sad that this was the way it had to be, but after seeing the articles on the Internet about John the year before, she knew how ridiculous and inaccurate they could be. She had no intention of starting up all kinds of new stories to be bent into more wild tales.

After Jillian ended the call to Karen, another message arrived from John.

"Waiting for callback list to come out at two. Sorry." It was already noon.

"No problem," Jillian texted back.

She made herself a sandwich and then went out for a bike ride, taking her phone with her. A little after two o'clock, John's message came. "Callbacks at 4:00 and 5:00."

"So proud. Break both legs. Love you."

"Love you, too."

Now Jillian was getting even more excited for John. Two callbacks. That meant that they were considering him for more than one part. She was ecstatic, and if nothing else came of it, John would know that he hadn't *flubbed* his audition. She smiled to herself, said another prayer for him, and then started thinking about what to make for dinner.

Jillian almost forgot that she had a car now. She supposed she should go down to the market and get some groceries. They had a few leftovers, but they and their guests had been hearty eaters, and with one of them a growing, teen athlete, their stock was running quite low.

She was sweaty from biking, so she took a quick shower, then took her inaugural drive in her wedding gift.

Jillian headed for the shopping carts in the front of the store. Now that she had a vehicle, she could buy more than a bag or two of groceries at a time and could actually use a cart. As she pulled one away from the long line, she was pleasantly surprised to run into Meredith, the young mother she used to see often when she went out for bike rides in the neighborhood. Jillian hadn't seen her for months and almost didn't recognize her or her son, Charlie. Charlie had been a very ill baby the year before at Easter, but now he was a healthy-looking toddler, strapped into the grocery cart child seat.

"Meredith!" Jillian exclaimed, "and Charlie, I presume?" The little boy turned his attention to Jillian at the sound of his name.

Kathy J. Jacobson

"Jillian! I haven't seen you for... forever!" Meredith said, a huge smile on her face.

They pulled their carts to the side to talk. Meredith told Jillian that she and her husband had decided to move to another neighborhood, not far away, but far *enough away* from her in-laws. Her husband's parents had been so controlling, and Meredith had not been a happy person. Now that they had moved, they finally had a life of their own life. "We even joined a church, Jillian!"

Jillian was happily surprised. When Jillian had mentioned at one of their earliest meetings on the street that she went to church, Meredith's response had been, "You go to church?" Her words had sounded like both a shocked question and an accusation.

"I got the idea from you," Meredith continued. "You seemed happy, and I knew you were kind. And you helped me when Charlie was sick. So, when we moved away, I told my husband that I wanted to go to a church. Charlie was just baptized on Easter Sunday!"

"That is so wonderful, Meredith. Easter is a great day for baptisms and other new beginnings." She almost thought about telling Meredith about her marriage, but she didn't want to take anything away from Meredith's excitement and good news. What a transformation! The first time she met the young woman, she had seemed frightened, lonely, sad, and she could barely look Jillian in the eye. Now she was vibrant, smiling, and full of hope. Her baby had been sickly, and now he was a rosy-cheeked, happy little boy, pointing at things and naming them.

Jillian decided that the trip to the store had been worth it just to see these two. She hugged Meredith goodbye, after exchanging cell phone numbers and social media contact information. That way, Jillian could follow Charlie as he continued to grow and change.

Jillian picked up a number of staples that she needed to replenish and a variety of foods for dinners and lunches. She was at a distinct advantage, as she knew her new husband's likes and dislikes in the food area from almost a year of cooking his dinners as his household helper.

Jillian's cart filled up quickly. She almost made it through the checkout when her phone rang. It never seemed to fail to happen in the most inconvenient of places. She looked at it and saw that it was John, so there was no way she was going to ignore it.

"Hi, honey," she said quietly.

"I like the sound of that," he said. "Well, I got the part."

"The one you thought you would get?"

"Not quite."

"Oh, I'm sorry. Are you disappointed?"

"Not exactly... I got the lead role, Jillian," he said, and she could hear the excitement, along with a bit of amazement, in his voice.

Why did these things always happen when she was checking out at a store? She wanted to shout at the top of her lungs.

"If I were not in the checkout line at the store, you would be hearing me scream wherever you are right now. Oh, John! That is so fantastic. You deserve it."

"I'm on my way home now. They are going to send the contract to Alan. He'll look it over, and I'll sign it later tomorrow. Will you be home soon?"

"In about ten minutes. How about you?"

"I'll be right behind you. Jillian, I..." Jillian could tell he was getting emotional.

"John, drive carefully and tell me all about it when you get home. I am so proud of you." She added that last statement because just a couple of days before, John had made a comment that he hoped that Jillian would always be proud that she had married him.

She apologized to the checker, who was waiting for her to put her PIN number into the debit machine, and to the person in line behind her. She headed out to her Land Rover with her bounty of goods, incredibly happy that she was not biking home this time.

Kathy J. Jacobson

Most of all, she was glad she would be home in half the time of her bike route and would be there when John arrived.

She pulled into the garage, made two trips into the house with the groceries, and just finished putting them away when John walked into the kitchen from the garage entryway.

He didn't say a word. He just walked over to her, picked her up and swung her around. Then he kissed her passionately.

"John, I think you should do auditions more often," she said, smiling and taking a deep breath. "So, tell me what happened."

John described how they had called him back for two parts. He wasn't even certain what the other one was until he got into the room. He auditioned for the director, the one whom John had mentioned in his text had not been his biggest fan in the past.

"Wiley asked me what happened to me. I told him I had had some health issues, which were now over, and that I had been out of commission during that time. Then he said that wasn't what he meant. He told me I was *different*—in a positive way. I told him that I just got married, for one thing. Then he said it must agree with me," John said, moving his face just inches from hers, "and believe me, it does." Then he kissed Jillian with even more fervor than before.

"We should celebrate," she said.

"Exactly what I was thinking," he told her.

"I suppose we should get some dinner sometime tonight," John said later as he held Jillian, her head on his chest. She could feel his heart beat, and felt safe and so loved in his arms.

"In or out?" she asked. "We're restocked now."

"Should we just order something in? I don't feel like cooking, and I don't want you to have to, either," he said, stroking her arm.

"Deal," she replied and kissed him. If it wasn't for the fact that her stomach was beginning to growl, she wouldn't have moved for anything.

John called in an order, and Jillian threw on her new white robe. They ordered from an Asian restaurant not far away, and the food was there in no time. John answered the door when it was delivered.

Jillian turned on the gas fireplace in the bedroom suite and spread a spare blanket over the area rug in front of it. "Let's have a picnic," she said when John asked her where she wanted to eat.

John grabbed some plates and utensils, and brought them upstairs. He decided that Jillian looked pretty comfy in her robe and changed into his matching one. They both sat cross-legged in front of the fire. Opening the bottle of wine that Maria, Marty, and Alison had left for them, they toasted in celebration of John's new job. Rehearsals would begin in two weeks, and the show would run for a month at the Santa Monica Playhouse. Jillian was thrilled that he wasn't going away to work so shortly after the wedding.

"Sorry we're spending our wedding week with all these auditions instead of doing something special," John said.

"This is something special. I've never had a picnic on the floor of my bedroom with my husband before," Jillian said sincerely.

"You are awfully easy on me," John said. He looked thoughtful for a moment, thinking back to the high-maintenance relationship he had once had with Monica Morgan. Rarely could he please her, no matter how hard he tried.

Snapping back to the present, John asked, "What would you like to do tomorrow?"

"Don't you need to prepare for your auditions?"

"I think I'll have plenty of time to get ready, especially with your help, and still do something with you tomorrow. So, what do you think?"

"It's supposed to be a nice day. You'll probably think I'm being silly, but I'd really like to go to Disneyland." She explained how

Kathy J. Jacobson

she, Marty and her parents had enjoyed a memorable trip to Disney World long ago. She had asked Drew to go with her to the original Disney park, but he had told her that it was for kids. She didn't share that bit of information with John, but she couldn't help remembering it.

"I've never been there," he said, "so, let's do it."

"Are you sure?"

"If you're going to be with me, I don't really care where I go," he said.

Jillian's eyes smarted. "That's one of the nicest things anyone has ever said to me."

"You deserve someone to say nice things to you," he said, pulling her closer.

Jillian held him tightly, closing her eyes and saying a prayer of thanks to God for bringing this person into her life.

True to form, the "Magic Kingdom" was once again magical. It was especially nice that John and Jillian were there on a weekday, even though there were some children off for spring break.

John wore sunglasses and a baseball cap, which she had never seen him wear before. Jillian hadn't considered that the amusement park was an awfully public place for him to spend an entire day. She noticed some people staring at him from time to time, but his disguise seemed to do the trick—or at least it kept them guessing.

John was like a big kid. He loved the rides and having their picture taken with the characters. He bought himself a souvenir T-shirt, and Jillian bought a coffee mug.

"Think about how this all started with the imagination of one person," Jillian said as they left the park that night after the parade. They hadn't planned on staying that late, but after they had dinner at one of the nicer restaurants, they decided they might as well stay for the grand finale.

"It really is impressive," John said.

Jillian stopped near the park gate and looked at John. "Not as impressive as my husband, though. Thanks for coming here with me," she said and kissed him. Just as she did, some fireworks went off over the castle like they were choreographed to go along with their kiss.

"How's that for timing?" Jillian asked when the kiss ended.

"Let's see if it works again," he said, pulling her into another kiss, with fireworks exploding overhead again.

They laughed as they headed back to the car. It had been the perfect ending to a perfect day. One of many more to come.

Chapter Ten

Jillian had no idea how fortunate they were that they had gone to Disneyland when they did, as John's good fortune in the audition arena continued. Soon he wouldn't have much free time, and later, he would be even more recognizable, and a baseball cap and sunglasses wouldn't be much help.

Next up was the audition for a guest star role on a popular medical show. His agent thought that he would be a natural at that one, having played chief of surgery for six years on *O.R.*

However, the audition was for the role of a patient this time. John kidded that he should know how to do that one pretty well after his recent hospitalization. Seriously, he had learned to appreciate what it felt like to be in a hospital bed facing a scary, significant medical issue. He had also gained insight into what real doctors go through. And as far as nurses were concerned, he had his own resident expert in that area at his ready disposal.

They had worked on some lines together and watched a couple of recent episodes of the show on an Internet site, so that John could honestly say he had seen the show. Jillian would not accompany him to this audition, either. She didn't ask, and decided that if, and when, John ever wanted her to go with him, he would let her know. She had no intention of forcing the issue.

While John was auditioning, Jillian was going to do some writing, baking, and biking and would finally make a call to Drew. Ever since Disneyland, Drew had been on her mind. She couldn't wait to hear the latest about "that Greta," and she also needed to tell him she was a married woman.

"Drew!" Jillian said when he answered.

"Hi, Jillian," he said, sounding happy, which made her happy. "What's up?"

"I just called to see how you were doing. I haven't seen much of you lately and didn't get to wish you a Happy Easter. I hope it was a good one."

"Yes, it was a great one. Sorry I wasn't able to be at church. I went to Greta's parents' home in Encino for Easter dinner. Her mom and stepdad made a great vegetarian meal. At first I didn't think I could live without an Easter ham, but I really enjoyed the food. There were all kinds of dishes I've never tried before."

"That's sounds really neat, Drew. I'm happy for you, and Greta."

"You're not upset, are you, Jillian? I know that this came up pretty fast."

Drew obviously had still not heard about John and Jillian, which was good, because that meant it wasn't common knowledge yet. She wondered how long they could keep it quiet and out of the tabloids.

"No, it's fine, Drew, really."

"Thanks, Jillian. So, what did you do for Easter?"

"Well, my daughter was home from Senegal, so that was special. We went to church, then to the brunch the youth put on... and then at five o'clock that evening, I got married."

"That's nice... wait, what did you say?"

Jillian didn't know what it was about her conversations with

Drew, but he just never really paid attention to what she said, and she often needed to repeat herself. His lack of listening to her was one of the main things that made their relationship a 'no go.' "

"I said, I got married."

"To Jim?" he asked.

"John."

"Oh, yes, I knew it began with a J. He seems like a nice guy."

"He is a nice guy—very nice."

"That's wonderful, Jillian. Congratulations to the both of you. We should celebrate sometime."

"You know, that's not a bad idea, Drew. I'll talk to John, and perhaps we will have a little celebration at our house with just our closest friends. We had a wonderful wedding dinner with Marty and John's nephew and his family, but no one else. I'll ask him when he gets home later. He's out trying to get a job right now."

"Oh, well, good luck to him. It's a tough market out there. If you ever need any help, Jillian, I could loan..."

"That's not necessary, Drew, but thank you for the offer. We might need an accountant sometime, though. One never knows. You'll be the first person we call if we do."

"Whatever I can do, please don't hesitate to call. I owe you a lot, Jillian. I still keep thinking about you telling me to take Greta out for a cup of coffee. If that hadn't happened... I hate to think about it."

Drew's words made Jillian think about something Marty had said about John a while back—that he "had it bad." Jillian smiled to herself and thought Drew "had it bad," and she was so very happy for him.

"You are welcome, Drew. I'll let you know if, and when, we are going to have a celebration. Oh, I have a call coming in from John, I'll call again sometime soon. Don't be a stranger."

"I won't. I can't wait for you to meet Greta," he said.

"Me, too. Bye, Drew," she said and immediately hit the accept button on her phone. She was a bit nervous. If John was calling this early, it most likely had not gone well.

"Jillian," John said. "I'm glad you picked up."

"Hi, honey," she answered.

"I really do like the sound of that," he said.

"Me, too, but you are killing me. What's up?"

"Oh, not much. I just wondered what you were doing for dinner tonight?"

"Dinner? I haven't really been thinking much about dinner, John. There are a few more important things on my mind."

"Oh, such as?"

"You are a tease, John!"

"Oh, okay, I just wanted to ask if I could take you out to celebrate another 'yes' to an audition?"

"Already? I thought this would be an all day or more process," she said.

"Me, too, but they wanted me. I also heard for the second time this week that I was different," he said, "and I know who is responsible for that."

"I do, too. New creation, John, new creation," she replied.

"I love you, Jillian," he said.

"I love you, too, John—so much. I am so happy for you, and I can't wait to hear all the details."

"I'll be home in a couple of hours. I need to stop by Alan's office. He might have a heart attack when he finds out I have two jobs."

"Let's hope not, but I'm happy for him, too," she said. Even though she had never met Alan, she was grateful that he hadn't abandoned John, even when John would not work for two years straight. She thought he was more than an agent. He was a faithful friend. She would be sure to add him and his wife, if he had one, to the guest list if they had a party.

John and Jillian enjoyed a romantic dinner at a seaside restaurant, at a very private table by the window. Jillian figured John must have pulled some strings for that one. Jillian brought up the idea of some sort of celebration of their marriage, and John completely agreed. They made a list of those they would invite—Karen and Robert, Alan and his wife, Beverly, Drew and Greta, Pete and Kelly, Nancy from church and her guest, Pastor Jim and his wife, Janet—perfect.

When they returned home, they took a stroll around the neighborhood, walking hand in hand.

"Jillian, would you go with me to my audition tomorrow?" John asked when they returned to the house.

"Of course," she said and hugged him. "I will do whatever works best for you."

"You work best for me," he said. He pulled her gently into an embrace and put his face close to hers. "Tomorrow is a special day."

"It is. It's an important audition, isn't it?"

"It is, but I was referring to our one-week wedding anniversary."

Jillian was always surprised by John's sensitive nature and the way he noticed and thought about things many others did not.

"In some ways, I can't believe it's been a week. In other ways, it seems like we have been together forever," she said, looking into his deep brown eyes.

"I am so glad you agreed to marry me," he said softly.

"I am so glad you asked me to marry you," she replied and kissed him.

Jillian was the one who was nervous the next afternoon, but she didn't dare say so and pretended that it was no big deal. She didn't want to add any pressure to the situation for John. They stood off in a corner together, talking in low voices about anything and everything, and then heard John's name called.

"May I have a kiss?" John asked, surprising her.

She answered him with her lips.

He gently pulled away and smiled at her. "I'll be back soon," he said.

"Take your time. Show them who you are. New creation," she answered.

He nodded his head and headed into the audition room.

Jillian prayed for him as the door closed to the room. Most of the actors before John seemed to be in their auditions for anywhere from ten minutes to twenty minutes, one only for five. John was in the room over a half hour when she checked her watch. Jillian was pretty certain that that was a good sign.

It got to be forty-five minutes before he emerged from the audition. He came out and took her by the hand, leading her to the outside of the building.

He pulled her into a huge kiss. "Never in my life have I had a week like the one I've had with you, Jillian," John said.

"I take it things went well," she said, smiling.

"They liked my first reading, for the part I thought I was auditioning for. Then they asked me to read for the part of Mack."

Jillian had helped him run lines in the script and knew that "Mack" was a much bigger role than the one he hoped to get. In fact, it was the supporting role to the lead male role in the movie.

"Wow! That's fantastic, John," she said. "When will you know more?"

"I'm not sure, but they said they would be in touch soon. That's usually a pretty good sign that they are at least considering you. It just felt so good to be back doing this again, and I never would be doing any of it if you hadn't landed at my house last year. You've changed my entire life, Jillian."

"And you've changed mine, so we are even."

He held her. "I want to do something with you, but I need to be able to hear my phone. Any suggestions?"

"Let's go home and watch basketball. We can keep it down low; we don't need the commentary," she said.

"Again, you are so easy on me, Jillian."

"Like you said the other night about going to Disneyland, 'If you're going to be with me, I don't really care where I go.' Or what I do. I just want to be with you," she said and gave him a huge hug.

During half time of an exciting NCAA tournament matchup, John's phone went off. It was Alan.

"I don't believe it. They want you to come in for a screen test on Wednesday at the studio. What is going on with you?" Alan asked.

"Married life, I guess," he said.

"You should have gotten married years ago," Alan told him.

"Only if I could have married the woman I'm married to now. I can't wait for you to meet her," John said.

"I'm looking forward to meeting her, too. She must be extraordinary."

"That would be a fitting description," John said.

The screen test was on Wednesday afternoon. Jillian gave John another neck and shoulder "nurse-style" massage the night before, and a "refresher" just before they left for the studio. John wanted her to come along again, and she went willingly. She took her laptop so she could write while she waited.

The test was at Universal Studios. Jillian again felt nervous, but again would in no way let on that she was. Shortly before he was called, John kissed her.

"Warming up?" Jillian said.

"I guess you could say that. You know, I may have to kiss someone in the screen test. Are you okay with that?"

"As long you don't like it as much as you like kissing me," she said.

"There's no way that could possibly happen," he replied sincerely.

"Then we're okay. I will have to learn to live with it—because John, I think this is only the beginning."

"You really think so?"

"I do, and when I get a feeling about things like that, they have a habit of coming true."

"Thanks, Jillian. You make me feel like I can do anything," he said.

"You can, John. I know you can."

He hugged her, and then they heard his name called.

Jillian again said a prayer for him as he walked through the huge, heavy doors.

One of the things Jillian liked best about writing was that time just flew by when she was at it. She felt lost in the words and didn't even notice that almost two hours had gone by when John finally emerged from the filming studio.

"Sorry it took so long," he said.

"No problem, I've got lots of work to do," she replied. "So?"

"I think it went well. I read again for both parts, with several different people. I think it will depend on what other actors they choose. They need to get the right combination, so that's what really takes time right now. They will look at the tests and see who goes best in what role with which actors. They said they would be in touch soon, which again, I think is a good sign. Right now, I just want to go home with my wife," John said.

"Deal," Jillian answered. She closed her laptop, then took John's hand as he moved it toward her.

Driving in the slow, congested afternoon traffic of Los Angeles is not usually considered a good time, but Jillian enjoyed every moment of John's animated explanation of his screen tests. Seeing him so happy and excited made her heart dance with joy. It reminded her of how she felt when something special happened in her daughter's life, which in turn reminded her that she and Marty had a video chat date coming up soon. Jillian had a lot of news to tell Marty and hoped they knew the results of the screen test by that time, one way or the other.

John showered when he got home and changed into jeans and the long-sleeved shirt Jillian loved so much, the one he was wearing the first time she met him in person.

"I'm cooking tonight," he announced as he uncorked a bottle of wine. He had ordered some baguettes earlier that day, and they were sitting on the counter along with a loaf of the multigrain bread Jillian had enjoyed since day one of her time at John's house.

John started pulling pots and pans out of the cupboards and drawers, along with the fixings for something Jillian guessed was an authentic Italian recipe.

"Is there anything I can do?" Jillian asked.

"You could, but I don't want you to do anything," he said, looking like a man on a mission. Whatever it was he was going to make, he must have made it many times, considering the ease with which he maneuvered the ingredients and utensils.

Jillian decided she would work on making a wedding announcement and an invitation to their celebration, which would be similar to one another. One would be sent to people she wanted to know about her marriage but were far away, and another to those invited to the celebration at their home. Making her list in each category, she wondered if she should invite Carol, her long-time friend and mentor, who still lived in Madison. Jillian returned to the kitchen to ask John what he thought about that idea.

"Would you mind if I invited my friend, Carol, from Wisconsin, to our celebration?" she asked as he worked on a dough of some sort.

"I want you to have whoever you want, Jillian," he said.

"I think I'll go call her to see if that even makes any sense. Otherwise, I'll just send her an announcement."

"Good idea. This will take a while, but it will be worth it. I promise," he said with a smile.

Jillian figured the adrenaline from his screen test was still in his system for him to have the energy to cook after such a long day. She wasn't complaining. Rarely had anyone cooked for her in her adult life, so this was a real treat.

Jillian plopped herself down into John's favorite chair in the library to make the call to Carol. She was most likely just getting off from her day of teaching and supervising nursing students, which she had done now for almost thirty years.

"Carol!" Jillian said when she heard her friend answer.

"Jillian, how are you, girl?" Carol had a way of making her feel like a young student again.

"I am the best I have ever been, I believe," Jillian said sincerely.

Carol listened intently as Jillian filled her in on the wedding, the celebration plans, John's acting prospects, and Jillian's blog and book, which was now beginning to really gel.

"That sounds like a whole lot of happiness, Jillian," she said. "It couldn't happen to a more special person."

"Thank you, Carol. You're the best. I don't suppose you could come out here for a weekend, or even longer? We would love to have you at our celebration." Jillian told her the available dates. Drew and Greta were available any time, and the dates she chose were ones when Robert was not gone on business. Nancy said anytime was good for her, too. Alan had few commitments outside of work, so he and his wife were very flexible. Pete and Kelly were ready and waiting for the date.

"I think that sounds wonderful, Jillian. I have some vacation coming. Could I call you back tomorrow night, after I do some checking? It would have to be for just a long weekend."

"We will take anything we can get with you. You can stay in the guest cottage. It's wonderful—I lived in it for over a year."

"This is sounding better by the minute," she said, excitement growing in her voice.

They hung up, and Jillian finished her designs for her invitation and announcement. She was using the photo Nancy's grandson had taken of them shortly after they had come out of the church, the one that Marty and the others had had enlarged for them, the black and white romantic shot. There was so much love in their expressions, and Jillian never tired of gazing at it. The only thing better than the photo was actually looking into her husband's very own face.

She posted in her blog and then headed toward the kitchen to see if John had changed his mind about wanting help. When she got there, the room looked like a tornado had hit it, and John was nowhere in sight. He came in moments later from the dining room.

"Dinner is served," he said, extending his hand to hers.

The chandelier was dimmed, and candlelight glowed on the table where a fresh salad, a baguette, and something that looked and smelled absolutely amazing on a platter, were awaiting them.

"It's gnocchi," he said, "the way my mother taught me." He smiled, but she could always sense a hint of sadness when John spoke of his mother. They had been very close, and she died way too young.

John pulled out a chair for her, very close to his. "I didn't want you too far away from me," he said. "I hope you don't mind."

Jillian often felt that she couldn't get close enough to John and was happy that she was not on the other end of the very long table. "This is perfect, John. I don't want to be far from you, either," she said, wanting to kiss him, but figured she shouldn't start that, after all the work he had put into dinner.

Jillian had only had gnocchi a few times and had liked it, but this was very special. Most likely, she loved it because it was a family recipe, her husband made it for her, and it had that special ingredient—love.

She hadn't realized how hungry she was until she was finished with her meal. She could have eaten another helping, but exercised her willpower. "So, John, if you decide to give up acting, you could always market this gnocchi," she said after blotting her mouth with her napkin.

"I'm glad you liked it, Jillian. I just wanted to do something for you after all you have done for me," he said, putting his hand on hers, his eyes filled with love.

"I don't know what I've done to merit this, but I sure do appreciate it," she said.

"And I appreciate your support, Jillian. It is so nice to know someone really cares about me and what I do—if I get a part or don't, if I am happy or not. I haven't had that in my life... well, I don't think I've had that in my life—with the exception of Tommy, but he's always been living far away—since my mother was alive. I guess that's why I wanted to make you her specialty dish."

Jillian felt like crying and could feel the pressure behind her eyes. "You are too good to me, John," she said emotionally.

"There is no such thing," he said and reached over and kissed her tenderly. "Dessert?" he asked in a soft voice.

"Uh-huh," she said nodding and then kissed him.

Jillian was happy she had her writing to keep her mind occupied the next day. She didn't know how actors could take all the waiting and all the rejections that they so often experienced. The acting profession was not for the faint of heart. She had seen how many people there were at the auditions. There were only a few parts, and many more people than parts trying for them. She imagined one got pretty tough-skinned after a while, but she thought there must be limits, too, to how many times one could hear the word "no."

The call from Alan came two days later while Jillian was preparing a salad for dinner.

"They want you to be Mack," he told John, "and I have a contract with your name on it sitting on my desk. The studio should be calling you sometime shortly. Congratulations, John. You hit a triple this past week. Unbelievable!"

John's eyes lit up as he listened to Alan, and Jillian knew that there was some kind of good news on the other end, she just didn't know how good. The part of Mack was an amazing part, and beyond John's expectations. The call ended, and John just looked at her.

"Good news?" she asked, knowing that it was.

"*Great* news... I'm Mack," he said, in a tone of disbelief.

"Don't sound so surprised. I knew you could do it," she said. "Details, please."

John filled her in on the information that he knew of at this point. They would not begin filming until July 7, which happened to be John's birthday, but they would have some meetings the week before. One of the best things was that he should have about five weeks off between the end of the first two projects and the movie meetings. Now they could start planning their honeymoon.

What a week of fantastic news! All the auditions were a success, Carol was flying out for their celebration the next weekend, and everyone else was able to come as well. Nancy was planning to bring a friend, she said, and Karen's favorite caterers were doing the food and some simple decorations. Jillian had thought about hiring Karen to do the cooking, but she wanted her friend and her husband to simply enjoy their time. Jillian couldn't wait to see Kelly and Pete, and was very curious about Greta, with whom Drew was obviously very much taken. It would be a great way to usher out the special time she and John had spent together, as he would begin a new chapter of his career the Monday following their party.

John came around the island in the kitchen toward Jillian, as she wiped her hands dry on a towel. He didn't speak, but threw his arms around her and held her for the longest time, holding her so tightly she could barely breathe. When he finally let go, Jillian could see that his eyes were shiny. She had known that this had meant a lot to him, but she just didn't know how much until that moment.

When he was finally able to speak, he said, "How did I ever get so lucky?"

Jillian responded, "It wasn't luck John, it was talent and hard work."

"I wasn't talking about the part," he said with an adoring look.

"Oh," she said, just before his lips met hers.

Kathy J. Jacobson

Chapter Eleven

Jillian was excited. Her book was really beginning to take shape. Her blog readers often advised her as to which stories they found most helpful, and she made careful notes. A visit to her friends at the nursing home also gave her a new idea. Certain that nearly every one of these people had had experiences with heartbreak, she thought that they could shed some wisdom only people with such life experience might have. Their stories and advice could be a great way to wrap up the book.

She was smiling to herself as she worked on her laptop at the kitchen counter, thinking of one of the stories that Edith had shared with her that afternoon. She was so engrossed that she didn't even notice that John had come into the room. He was watching her not far from the spot where he had stood the very first time she saw him face-to-face.

Finally she looked up, and she smiled widely at him.

"I'm sorry, I'm interrupting you," he said.

"It's a *pleasant* interruption," she answered.

"It looks like it's some *pleasant* work you are doing. You were smiling," he said, walking over to her and moving just behind her.

His strong hands massaged her shoulders gently, and she gave out a sigh of pleasure.

"It is. I guess this is what I was hoping for when I retired from nursing, that I would enjoy the work of writing. I may never sell a book, but I will have treasured the process."

"I know how good it feels to do something you love," he said. "I'm glad you are loving it. And what makes you think you won't sell a book?"

"Oh, I'll probably sell some to my blog followers, but when you self-publish, you're lucky if you break even. Getting an 'in' with a publishing company is very difficult, and you usually need an agent for them to even look at your manuscript. I guess I could try that route, but I may just do this one on my own and see what happens. If all else fails, I could always go back to my previous profession. It's not that I didn't like it anymore, but I wanted to give this a shot when I felt I could."

"Well, just don't give up too quickly. The writing business sounds a lot like acting—lots of tryouts, lots of rejections, but when you finally get a 'yes,' it's worth it."

"You're right, John," Jillian said. She grabbed one of his hands that was on her shoulder, pressed her cheek to it, and then kissed it. She turned around in her chair and faced him. "I love you, Mr. Romano."

"I love you, too, Mrs. Romano," he replied and kissed her gently on the lips. "How much more do you have to write?"

"Oh, about fifteen chapters," she said.

"Let me rephrase that. When do you think you might be done today?"

"I just want to get the story Edith told me today down before I forget some of the finer nuances. She really is a special person, and I appreciate her views. But to answer your question, I should be done in about an hour. What are you up to?"

"Memorizing lines," he said.

"Great. I'll help you when I get done, or I could stop this now and work on it another time."

"No, you finish up. We'll have plenty of time to run lines later. Oh, and I almost forgot why I came in here in the first place. Alan called. He said his wife made a big mistake and forgot that her brother is coming down from Stanford this weekend. He thought maybe they should stay home from our party, but I told him I thought he should just bring his brother-in-law along to our gathering. He said he would only do that if I checked with you—so, I'm checking with you."

"Actually, that would be perfect. We had an odd number with Carol coming. Call him back and tell him we would love to have his brother-in-law come."

"That's what I thought you would say," he said, then kissed her.

"John, don't start that, or nothing is going to get done," she said.

"Okay, okay. I'm out of here to call Alan. I'll see you in an hour or so," he said, reluctantly letting go of his wife.

Carol arrived at LAX the next evening, miraculously on time. Jillian was giddy with excitement as she watched her come through the airport gate. Carol was like family and friend rolled into one.

They both called out each other's names at the same time and practically ran to one another. It had been over a year since they had seen each other.

Carol looked fantastic. "What have you done with my old friend, Carol?" Jillian asked, standing back and admiring her friend.

"Oh, she just got fed up with everything and made some changes. First, I started going to a gym about six months ago. Your stories about Pete inspired me, I think," and she winked at Jillian. "Then I cut my hair. Then I told Joe that I was thinking of dating other men, and it didn't even phase him. That's when I realized for certain that we really had no future beyond friendship. So, outside of bowling together in our winter league, I don't see him anymore."

Joe was Carol's longtime "boyfriend." They had begun dating about five years after Carol's husband had died in a work accident. Apparently, there had been talk of marriage at some point, but it just never seemed to happen. Jillian always thought that Carol should consider some other options in that department and never felt Joe really appreciated her friend the way she deserved to be appreciated.

"Well, your decisions must have been good ones. You look wonderful," Jillian said.

"And so do you, Jillian. You are absolutely glowing. Marriage obviously was the right choice for you."

"Thank you, Carol. I can't wait for you to meet John. I love him so much I can hardly stand it."

"Incredible. I didn't think I'd ever hear words like that from your mouth, Jillian."

"Neither did I," Jillian said.

They walked through the bustling terminal. Carol had only a carry-on and a backpack, so they didn't have to go to the baggage claim. John was driving around the airport grounds and would loop back and get them. Jillian texted him the spot to meet them.

The women only had to wait a few minutes before he arrived. It was warm outside by Wisconsin standards, so Carol didn't mind waiting. In fact, she was enjoying it. She was a workaholic who rarely took time off, even now that her kids were out of the house. Her youngest, Mark, had lived at home until two years ago, when he finally graduated from technical college at the age of thirty. He had given Carol quite a "run for her money" as a teen and young twenty-something, but he had finally settled down, gotten his degree, and had a great job as a plumber. Her daughter, Carrie, was thirty-four and lived in Minneapolis with her husband and two dogs, which Carol said would probably be as close as she would come to having grandkids.

John pulled the Land Rover over into the pick-up lane and jumped out. He came over to Carol and gave her a hug. "I've heard a lot of wonderful things about you, Carol," he said.

"And I about you, John." John took her luggage and put it in the back of the Rover. Carol gave Jillian an approving look and mouthed a single word to her—"wow." Jillian smiled back at her and opened the door to the backseat for her to climb in.

"Do you two want to sit in the back seat together so you can talk more easily?" John asked.

"Oh, that's not necessary," Carol said.

"Actually, that's a really thoughtful idea, John. Are you sure you don't mind?" Jillian asked.

"No, I'll just take notes on the experience, in case I ever get a role as a chauffeur," he said with that grin of his.

Jillian kissed his cheek, then climbed into the seat next to her best friend. Carol gave her another smile and nodded her head affirmatively.

There was not a moment in the car ride home that was silent. Even John got in on some of the conversation. At one point, when Carol was in conversation with John, she mentioned that perhaps she should have sat up front with him, which made them all laugh. Jillian had forgotten how engaging Carol could be. She was so intelligent, but also very kind, patient, had a good sense of humor, and was an amazing teacher and mentor in the nursing school. The most important and useful things Jillian had ever learned about nursing, she had learned from Carol.

The traffic was terrible, so John suggested that they get off the freeway and go to a restaurant for dinner, which was a wise choice during rush hour.

When they finally arrived at the house, Carol's eyes looked a lot like Jillian's had the first time she had seen the neighborhood and been driven up the circle drive. With the exception of some of the homes around Lake Mendota, there were not too many areas or houses like this one in Madison.

John carried her bags to the cottage with Carol and Jillian walking behind. "So, would I make a good chauffeur or not?" he asked.

"The best, dear," Jillian said.

"I'd hire you anytime, John," Carol said.

"That's good to know, in case the career doesn't work out," he said.

He left the two so Jillian could show Carol around and get her settled in. Afterward, they would meet at the table by the pool and enjoy the fresh air. John turned an outdoor heater on as he walked back to the house.

The door to the cottage closed and Carol looked at Jillian. "Wow, again, Jillian," she said after a moment. "I understand why you are so crazy about that man—handsome, sweet, and funny. Know any more like him?"

"No, he's one in a million. But you would never believe what he was like when I first arrived. He's not that person anymore, and I'm not the same, either."

"I can see that—in a good way," Carol said, unpacking and hanging up her dress for the next afternoon.

Jillian and John decided that they would wear what they wore for the wedding for their little gathering, since no one else had seen them except for Pastor Jim. It would make it feel like a true wedding reception.

Nancy's grandson was coming over for a brief time to take some photos. He had done such a good job at the ceremony, they wanted him for their reception as well. Jillian was certain he had a bright future ahead of him as a photographer, if he would so

Kathy J. Jacobson

choose. They would certainly give him a glowing recommendation. Jillian was happy that he would be the one to document the celebration of their marriage with their special friends. It would be a day to remember.

Because it was only early April, they decided to have the reception in the afternoon, during the warmer time of day. The forecast was seventy-eight degrees for a high that day—perfect. They had plans B and C in place just in case of bad weather, but they were grateful it didn't come to that.

Alan had given them the gift of a string quartet, who would play background music and also some dance numbers if they wished. They had told people not to give gifts, but Alan was so thrilled with John's three new job assignments that he said he couldn't help himself.

The reception was from three to six, with a meal to be served around four-thirty. Pete and Kelly were the first ones to arrive. Pete, who was a gorgeous man naturally, looked better than ever, his happiness enhancing his whole persona, inside and out.

Jillian hugged him. "Pete, you look amazing," she said. "Obviously, life is good."

"I've never been so happy, Jillian, and I can tell that you feel the same way, too. You look stunning."

"Thank you, Pete. It's amazing how love can change everything, isn't it?"

"You've got that right," he said and squeezed her hand.

Speaking of stunning, Jillian thought Kelly looked uncommonly beautiful and wondered to herself if perhaps she might be pregnant. Jillian had seen that supernatural glow from time to time in new mothers-to-be.

Next to arrive were Drew and Greta. Greta was a pretty, young woman, most likely in her late twenties or early thirties, Jillian guessed. There seemed to be about the same age difference between Greta and Drew as between herself and John. Greta's haircut was sassy, Jillian thought. She had auburn hair that looked natural, but a streak of black in it that was definitely dyed. It looked good on her and fit her personality. Greta's eyes were a fierce green, and there was a black gemstone stud in her pierced nose. She wore a unique ensemble with a long, multicolored skirt that was very attractive on her. Best of all, there was a certain strength and energy about her.

Jillian liked her right away, and the two quickly struck up a conversation. Drew was actually a bit jealous that Greta wasn't paying as much attention to him and kept trying to interrupt. "Chill, Drew," Greta finally said to him. "I see you all the time. I'm talking to the bride right now." Jillian loved it. This was exactly what Drew needed, she thought.

"Okay, I'm going to get a drink," Drew said reluctantly and walked over to a small bar that was set up on the patio, where he ordered an iced tea.

Karen and Robert walked in, looking so happy together. Just a year ago, Jillian had wondered if their marriage would make it. Things had certainly changed for them, for the better.

Nancy arrived with her guest. His name was Buck, and he wore an off-white western style suit with a matching cowboy hat, which he took off as he greeted them. He was a tall, strong man, who towered above Nancy, but neither of them seemed to mind. Jillian couldn't wait to get the story out of her friend about this gentleman.

Pastor Jim and Janet arrived next. "Sorry it took us so long. We have a new babysitter, so we had to give more instructions than usual. Thank you for having us. It's nice to get out once in a while without the kids," Janet said. Their twin boys were adorable, but also very active. Jillian remembered how nice it was to have her mom and dad, or later one of the women at church, watch Marty every once in a while so she could do something with another adult from time to time.

"We are so happy you are here, Janet, and so appreciative that Jim performed our ceremony on Easter Sunday evening. We will never forget that special Easter," Jillian said.

"Jim said it was the best wedding he has ever officiated," Janet said. "He said it was all about your marriage and the beginning of your new life together instead of just some kind of show." John and Jillian smiled and nodded.

Last to arrive was Alan, along with his wife and brother-in-law. "Sorry we're late," Alan said quietly to John. "I had a little bit of convincing to do, as Jerry was quite hesitant to come along," referring to his brother-in-law.

John and Jillian made sure to make Jerry feel welcomed after hearing that. He was about John's height, six-foot-one, an attractive, distinguished-looking man, but Jillian noticed some kind of sadness in his eyes. Later she was to learn that he was a widower, losing his wife four years before. Jillian remembered her own mother after her father's death. She had never been the same. Even Jillian and Marty were not enough to pull her out of her grief, despite their best efforts.

Jillian motioned for Carol to join them. She had been talking with Pete and Kelly, telling them how she had been inspired to join a gym after Jillian's experience with Pete as her personal trainer. They were telling Carol that they just bought some property and were just a step away from beginning to remodel it into a gym. Hopefully, they would open sometime during the summer, "smog season" as Jillian had called it, or early fall at the latest.

Carol excused herself and began walking toward John, Jillian, Alan, Bev, and Jerry. Halfway across the patio, she noticed Jerry for the first time. She actually halted in her steps for a brief moment, then continued on.

Jillian thought her friend looked a bit flustered and flushed as she joined them, which was not like Carol. Jerry, too, seemed different from just the moment before. He stood up straighter and extended his hand to Carol.

"Jerry," he said.

"Carol," she replied after a moment of hesitation, and then she took his hand. Jillian wondered if her friend was having trouble remembering her own name. It reminded Jillian of the time she had extended her hand to John after serving the community Christmas dinner together. His touch had sent shivers down her spine, and she was pretty sure something similar was happening to her good friend at that very moment. She and Carol knew each other very well and were often in tune with one another's feelings. When Jillian was in love with John before she would ever admit it, Carol had sensed that Jillian had met someone special, just by the sound of her voice.

Alan and Beverly were introduced to Carol next, but Carol's and Jerry's eyes kept gravitating toward each other's. Jillian was finding this situation rather enjoyable, but wished that the two did not live two thousand miles apart from one another. At least they would be able to enjoy an afternoon together, she thought to herself.

It turned out that Jerry was Dr. Jerry Stein, who taught in Stanford's medical school. Jerry was pleasantly surprised to hear that Carol was a nursing supervisor for students at the University of Wisconsin. They ended up sitting down at a table to "talk shop," as Jillian's father, Martin, would have said.

Beverly watched her brother talking and laughing with Carol at the table, and remarked to Jillian that she hadn't seen him smile like that in four years. She thanked Jillian for letting him come to the reception. Jillian thanked her for bringing him and mentioned that they were happy that he could join them. Jillian didn't

Kathy J. Jacobson

mention it, but she was equally excited to see her good friend having such a wonderful time with Jerry.

Everyone else mingled and moved around, talking about all sorts of goings-on. Then Nancy's grandson appeared with his camera. He took photos of everyone—candid shots, group shots, and couples together. He arrived at the table where Carol and Jerry were seated and announced, "You're next."

Carol said, "Sorry, we're not a couple."

"Oh, I'm sorry, you look like one," he said, which made Carol start to blush.

"It's okay, Carol," Jerry said standing up, "I wouldn't mind a photo with you—if you don't mind."

Carol looked pleasantly surprised and said, "I don't," and stood up next to him for the shot.

Nancy's grandson gave them his card and told them to go onto his website under "John and Jillian" to access the photos. The password was written on the back of his card.

Just then it was announced that the quartet would be playing some dance numbers. John and Jillian led the way, then the others joined in, couple by couple.

"Well, since we're an officially photographed couple, may I have this dance?" Jerry asked Carol.

She nodded, dumbstruck. Carol put her hand in his and her other one on his chest as he put his other hand on her waist. Her heart began to race. She looked over at Jillian, who was looking at her and smiling. She mouthed a little "wow" of her own to her friend when Jerry's back was to her. Carol smiled a nervous smile, but smiled nonetheless.

"Looks like love is in the air," John said to Jillian.

"It sure is," she said and put her head on his shoulder. "I always wondered what it would be like to dance at my own wedding," she added softly.

"Is it everything you imagined?" he asked.

"No, it's better," she said and kissed him. For a moment, it felt like they were the only ones there, until a whistle from Drew brought them back into reality. The song ended along with their kiss.

John looked at her with love and longing in his eyes. "Hold that thought," she whispered to him.

Jillian walked over to thank Alan and Bev for their musical gift. The group was very talented and just right for the occasion. Bev thanked Jillian for inviting Carol to the wedding and thought she was witnessing an absolute miracle happening with her brother. Jillian just hoped that he didn't get even more hurt in all of this and sent up a silent prayer to that effect.

A meal was served right on schedule, topped off with tiramisu that they commissioned Leo to make for the occasion, and served with cappuccino, coffee, and tea. Afterward, John and Jillian made sure to talk with each one of their guests, thanking them for their love and support and for celebrating this special occasion with them.

"Pete," Jillian said when she had a moment alone with him, "I am so happy that things are going so well. You both look wonderful, and Kelly, well—she has a very special glow. Is there something you're not telling me?"

Pete looked surprised, then excited, by her question. "Do you think so, Jillian? You would know, wouldn't you, being a nurse and all? We've been trying ever since our wedding. If I wouldn't have goofed everything up seven years ago..."

"Pete, don't go there again. And it doesn't take a nurse to notice something like that. I hope that the glow is what I think it is, and if it isn't, I'll start praying for you both."

"Thanks, Jillian, you are a great friend."

"So are you, Pete. Thank you so much for coming. It means to world to me... to us," she said with a smile as John came to her side. He and Pete shook hands, and then Pete and Kelly headed home—or to the nearest drugstore for a pregnancy test, Jillian thought to herself.

Jillian had a moment to talk to Drew alone, too. "Drew, I love Greta," she said.

"You do? Great, because I love her, too," he said honestly.

"I can tell. In fact, I thought that when you called me that first day. I felt the reason she was annoying you so much was because you were attracted to her, and I don't think you wanted to be."

"Really? You could tell then?"

Jillian nodded her head. "Greta is very special."

Drew nodded in agreement. "Jillian, how long do you think someone has to know someone before they ask them to marry them?" he asked.

"I don't think it's the same for everyone, Drew. You're both mature people. Your hearts will tell you when it's the right time."

"Thanks, that's what I was hoping you would say," he said and gave her a hug. Greta came over to them, and Jillian hugged her, too.

"Let's do coffee sometime soon, Greta," Jillian said.

"Yes, that would be great, Jillian. Thank you for the invitation to your celebration, too. This was cool."

"I'm glad you came, and that you had a good time."

Next to leave were Karen and Robert. Karen hugged her and told her she would see her at the next book club meeting. The month after that, there would be none, as Karen and Robert were taking a ten-day Alaskan cruise. Jillian was so happy for them both and how they had learned to find time for one another—and along with it, a new spark in their relationship and marriage.

Pastor Jim and Janet reluctantly left to relieve the babysitter from "the twin terrors," as Janet called them. They were not bad children—just healthy, busy young boys. Nancy and Buck were next. Jillian really liked Buck, who seemed to be quite a gentleman, and who, they learned that afternoon, owned a ranch east of Los Angeles. Jillian couldn't wait to get the scoop on how they met, but that would have to be another time, maybe even the next morning at church.

Last to get ready to go were Alan, Bev, and Jerry. The caterers and musicians were packing up as they approached John and Jillian. Jillian had asked the caterers to make some sandwiches for the musical group, and they handed them out to them, along with a beverage, before they completely closed up shop. Jillian couldn't believe how efficient they were. No wonder Karen had recommended them. She would have to thank her friend again for such good advice.

The six of them moved into the kitchen to get out of everyone's way. They talked a while longer, then called it a day. Jillian could tell that Carol and Jerry did not want to say goodbye, but perhaps it was for the best. They shook hands again, this time a more lingering handshake.

John, Jillian, and Carol decided to change into more comfortable clothes, so John and Jillian headed upstairs and Carol to the cottage. They met back in the house and decided to take Carol to the beach to watch the sunset.

Looking out over the Pacific, Carol said, "I can see how one could get used to this pretty quick," and looked dreamily out over the sunlight shimmering on the water, the sound of crashing waves pounding in their ears. John hugged Jillian from behind, as they watched the sun appear to drop into the ocean.

It had been a very special day, Jillian thought. She wished that Carol could stay longer, though. As the sky darkened, they climbed into the Rover and drove downtown briefly, just to give Carol a little taste of the city before going back home.

"I'm coming back here—soon," Carol remarked as they pulled into the garage.

"I sure hope so," Jillian said. "I thought you would like it."

"And you say it's just a little cooler than this in January, but not much?"

"Yes, no snow, unless you go up into the mountains, and green all year."

"I think you might be on to something, Jillian," she said.

They retired for the night, especially since Carol was still operating on Central Standard Time.

Jillian walked Carol back to the cottage and hugged her good night. "Thank you coming out here, Carol. It would not have been the same without you. You made this day so very special."

"Thank you, Jillian. I haven't had this much fun in... I can't remember the last time I had this much fun," she said seriously.

They hugged again and made plans for the morning. They would have a light breakfast early in the kitchen, then go to church, then to their favorite place for brunch, and lastly do a little more sightseeing on their way to the airport.

Jillian stepped into the kitchen where John was waiting for her, an expectant look on his face. "What are you up to?" Jillian asked him as she approached him. She put her hands on his shoulders and looked into his sparkling brown eyes.

"I'm just holding that thought," he said, repeating her words from their dance that afternoon.

"Oh, I thought maybe you forgot," she said teasingly.

"Not a chance," he said and pulled her into a kiss.

A moment later, Jillian's cell phone told her she had a text message. She was going to ignore it, but something told her to look when their kiss ended. "Do you mind if I see who that is?"

"Go ahead," John said, moving behind her and kissing her neck gently as she checked her message.

"Yes!" Jillian exclaimed, and turned back toward John.

"Good news?" he asked.

"It's from Pete. I told him today that I thought Kelly looked like a woman who was pregnant. He told me they've been trying ever since the wedding, and they stopped on the way home to get a test. It was positive!"

"Wonderful! I'm happy for them," he said sincerely.

"Me, too," Jillian said smiling, but a then a brief flicker of sadness crossed her face.

John picked up on it immediately. "But... ?"

"Oh, nothing," she said.

"You don't look like it's 'nothing.'"

"How do you know me so well already?" She hesitated a moment. "It's just that sometimes I wish I was younger than I am right now..."

"So you could have another baby?" he asked, intuitively.

She hesitated again. "So I could have *your* baby."

John put his hands on her waist and pulled her close. "That might be the nicest thing anyone has ever said to me," he said in a gentle, loving tone, and held her for a long moment. He let go and looked into her eyes, his look from the dance that afternoon back on his face, and gave her a kiss that Jillian was sure would elicit another "wow" from Carol.

It was the perfect ending to another perfect day. To be honest, Jillian thought that since marrying John, every day seemed to be just that.

Chapter Twelve

John's return to the stage was much more successful than he could have ever hoped. His role was a difficult one to pull off, according to the critics, and needed someone who was just right. And also according to the critics, John D. Romano was just right. Comments like "we don't know what he's been up to for the past two years, but whatever it was, other actors should follow suit." Another called his work "poignant and convincing," and another said that John D. Romano was "back—and better than ever."

John was modest about the reviews, but Jillian could tell that he was pleased with them, and also very relieved. After such a long time away from his work, he just wasn't certain what would come out of his mouth on stage. The last time he had been on one, he could not find a word, the result of the brain tumor. The experience had propelled him into a life of doubt, depression, and seclusion, convinced that he had Alzheimer's disease like his older brother had battled.

The television spot was shot shortly after the play opened, when John was free during the daytime hours once again. It didn't take many days to shoot, and it went well, although at times the story reminded John a bit too much of reality and his own brush with serious illness at the New Year. He told Jillian he didn't need to act, as much as to remember. The director had been thrilled with his realistic portrayal, and even more thrilled with how easy he was to work with this time around. The director, who had locked horns with John on a project years before, had been prepared to deal with a "difficult" actor, but didn't encounter one.

John and Jillian were finally at a point where they could hop on a plane and begin their month-long travels. John had worked diligently to learn his lines for the movie. Jillian had always been impressed with the way he could spit things she said right back at her, and he memorized lines just as easily. He had an incredible mind, and most of the time when they ran lines, he already had them memorized, so he experimented with different ways of relaying them. They enjoyed discussing what might be going through the character's mind, and what kind of person "Mack" might be. Of course, the director might have another entirely different idea in his head as well. Jillian found acting to be a fascinating profession and enjoyed that John had invited her be a part of his world.

Carol was done with her semester of teaching at the University of Wisconsin and volunteered to house-sit for them while they were gone. She was going to stay in the cottage, but would also keep an eye on the rest of the property. Esperanza was going to take two weeks off while they were gone, so it worked out great that Carol could be there. Jillian was pretty certain that there might be some ulterior motives in this situation, but Carol had not offered any information as of yet. She knew that Carol and Jerry had been emailing one another ever since they met, but they had both been incredibly busy at the end of their respective college semesters, so it had been impossible to do much more than that.

Kathy J. Jacobson

At least they both understood each other's crazy life.

Carol arrived the day before John and Jillian left, and they gave her all the instructions about the house, the alarm system, Esperanza's schedule once she returned from her vacation, the numbers for the lawn and garden maintenance, and the pool. Just in case there were any other issues, they gave her Karen and Robert's and Alan and Bev's numbers as well. Jillian gave her keys to both Land Rovers and answered any questions she had about the vehicles. After Carol's "lessons," they took her out to dinner at Leo's. She proclaimed it the best Italian food she had ever tasted. There appeared to be a consensus on that.

The next day, Carol bravely dared to drop them off at the airport. They each gave her a big hug, then John and Jillian held hands as they headed toward the gate, their excitement building with each step. They would stop in Chicago first, to see Tommy and his family. Seeing them and Marty were going to be highlights of their trip.

Jillian put her head on John's shoulder after they settled into their seats on the plane, and he put his head close to hers. "Here we go, Mrs. Romano," he said softly, taking her hand. She smiled and gave his hand a squeeze.

Tommy, Maria, John Anthony, and Alison were all waiting for them when they arrived, smiling and waving as they emerged from the gate. Jillian thought John Anthony had grown another inch or two since she last saw him, which was only two months ago. He confirmed that he had indeed grown three-quarters of an inch, as his graduation gown was a bit shorter than expected when he tried it on. He was also more handsome than ever. Jillian wanted to see a photo of John at that age and compare it sometime. Alison kept getting prettier and prettier, and looked more like a young woman than a teenaged girl now. It was always miraculous to watch teens grow and change, and it was even more noticeable to those who didn't see them every day.

They stopped for some Chicago-style hot dogs on the way home, which was perfect since it was getting late. The next night, Maria would cook for them the family favorites. Jillian was really looking forward to that, having sampled some of her cooking when they had come for the wedding. Maria's business was getting closer and closer to becoming a reality, so this would be a big test for her, Maria said. If John liked the food—most of the dishes were his mother's recipes—then she would feel like she was ready to make a "go" of it.

Tommy's house was large and comfortable, with the feeling of a family home rather than a showcase, even though it was a very nicely constructed brick home, well-decorated, and in an upscale neighborhood. Jillian got the "tour," and especially enjoyed seeing all of John Anthony's awards and newspaper clippings, which were being assembled for a display (his "shrine," he called it) for his high school graduation party. John and Jillian hoped to attend the celebration on their way home, barring travel delays or flight cancellations.

They had a wonderful few days of visiting. They took in one of John Anthony's baseball games—he even hit a home run. Next, they attended the year-end concert of Alison's orchestra, in which she played a beautiful solo on the violin. They spent a lazy afternoon walking around the Lincoln Park Zoo in absolutely gorgeous weather. The next day, Maria took John and Jillian down to the little place that she hoped to rent by the fall and turn into her Italian specialties shop. She said that every day she thought of another item to add to her offerings. Maria's excitement was contagious, and Jillian was happy and thrilled for her.

Sometimes Jillian wished they didn't live so far away from the

Romanos, because she really enjoyed Maria as a person. If they lived closer, she was certain that they would spend a lot of time together and become good friends. And Tommy—he had felt like family the moment she had met him, and she had appreciated his love and concern for John even before that.

Time flew by, and they were glad that they were stopping back in Chicago on the way home, or it would have been even tougher to leave. Since Carol was in California, they decided Wisconsin could wait until another trip, so Tommy dropped them off at O'Hare, and they were on their way to Rome, the "city of love."

Jillian and Marty had done a nice tour of the major cities of Italy years ago, and it had been one of their favorite vacations. Jillian remembered thinking when she was there how wonderful it would be to experience it with someone with whom she was in love. Fifteen years later, it was a reality. Better late than never, Jillian thought to herself.

She must have been smiling, because John asked her what she was thinking about, and she told him. He kissed her hand, and then put his head next to hers. He fell asleep after a while, so Jillian watched a movie on the screen in front of her, an earphone plugged in her one free ear, as John was leaning against the other. But she wasn't complaining. She was on her honeymoon, something she never dreamed would happen in her lifetime.

Jillian had remembered Rome as beautiful and the food as spectacular, but it took on an entire new dimension with John at her side. It was especially fun to be with someone who spoke the language. She didn't know what it was about Italian, but she could see why it was termed a "romance language." Whenever John spoke it, it made him seem, as her mom would have said, "dreamy." Her mother had felt the same way every time she listened to a Dean

Martin record, especially when he sang in Italian. It seemed to put Jillian into a trance whenever John spoke it. If he would have started singing, she wasn't sure what would happen to her.

The two of them sat on the edge of the Trevi fountain and threw coins into it with the other tourists. One was supposed to make a wish, but Jillian felt that she already had everything she had ever wanted, and more. But she decided finally on a wish that was more of a prayer, that she and John would have many happy years together.

They toured many of the sites and ended their days eating fresh pasta or pizza al fresco in the moonlight. They ate more gelato than they should have—the dark chocolate was her favorite—and drank the rich, thick, dark coffee they both loved. Each night they toasted each other with smooth Italian wines, which Jillian deemed her favorites in the world. California wines came in a close second, especially as the vineyards became older in the Napa Valley, but these wines were special, or perhaps it was just where she was, and who was with her, that made them seem that way.

One of Jillian's favorite things was just walking hand in hand on the narrow, winding stone streets, looking in shop windows, stopping to watch some food item being made from scratch or a piece of art taking shape before their eyes. They rented bikes one morning and, on their final night in the city, enjoyed a moonlight cruise on the Tiber.

They were renting a car the next day and driving down to a small town outside of Naples, where John had a relative from his mother's side of the family. He had never met him, but used to write to him over the years, with the exception of the past two. The man, Pietro, had been thrilled when John had contacted him by phone and said he would like to meet him and his family, and was bringing his wife with him. Jillian had been able to hear the

Kathy J. Jacobson

loud exclamations emanating from the phone all the way on the other side of the room when John had mentioned that piece of information.

Pietro had invited them to stay at his home. Pietro's mother, Emma, and John's mother, Amelia, were cousins. They had started writing to each other as very young girls, Emma sending her letters from Italy, Amelia from the United States, and had written faithfully to one another until Amelia's death. They met in person only once, when Amelia and her mother, Isabel, had gone to visit Emma's family in the very house John and Jillian were headed to. The girls had been just teens, but it solidified their relationship for good. They were as close to each other as their mothers, who were sisters.

It was a long drive down to Pietro's home, but a beautiful one. Pietro met them at the gate to the property, and squeezed in with them in the little rented Fiat as they drove up the winding gravel road lined with lemon and olive trees. The home was two stories and made of stone, with large wooden shutters on the wide-open windows. Pietro's wife, Caterina, met them at the door, and hugged and kissed them both on both cheeks.

Caterina had been busy in the kitchen. She had made her own bread, and the smells made one's mouth water. She was serving fresh fish and seafood caught that day, homemade pasta and sauce, salad, and of course, a local wine. There was also a beautiful cake sitting on the counter, decorated with fresh flowers on top. Jillian was certain that if she didn't keep walking several miles every day, she would gain a couple of pounds on this trip.

One by one, people kept coming to the house—Pietro and Caterina's daughter and her husband, their son and his two little boys, another cousin, and then some neighbors who remembered John's and Pietro's grandmothers, and their mothers. Others were good friends of Pietro's grandmother and Emma.

Apparently they were throwing John and Jillian a little wedding celebration, as they brought little gifts for them.

"I told them to make sure to bring something small, as you were traveling," Pietro said, very proud of the celebration and proud to have his family from America in the house.

John and Jillian had to tell their story of how they met, and also had to fill them in on Tommy and his family. Jillian showed them some of the photos she had taken on her phone, happy that she had signed up for an international plan before they left. They oohed at the photos of the handsome John Anthony and were impressed with his plans for the future. They aahed at the beautiful Alison. But the best stories of the evening were the ones about John's grandma and mother, and Emma and her mother. Everyone laughed, and sometimes they cried, as they reminisced together.

The gifts were precious—an ornate wooden spoon carved by a friend of Pietro's son, some small hand-painted dipping bowls, and an embroidered dishtowel one neighbor had crafted. But best of all was a small package from Pietro. In it was a square black and white photograph in a small frame. In the photo were John's mother and father holding their children—John, who was about one and in his mother's arms, and three-year-old Anthony, who was in his father's arms. Everyone was smiling, and his father and mother were looking at each other with such love in their eyes.

Jillian could tell that John was very moved by the photo.

"Your mother sent that to my mother," Pietro said. "It was my mother's favorite photo. I made a copy of it for myself, but this is the one that came in the mail. Oh, how my mother loved the letters from your mother!" he said, sounding very emotional. His mother had died four years ago, outliving John's mother by many years. She had missed Amelia and her letters so much after Amelia's death.

"And there's one more thing," he said, unfolding a handkerchief. From it, he pulled out a beautiful gold cross necklace.

Jillian could see a look of recognition on John's face. "How... ? John began to ask, but stopped, his voice choking with emotion.

"When your mother died, my mother was so very sad. Your father knew that. He knew that my mother was like a sister to your mother, so he sent it to her—I think to make her feel better. It did. She wore it to the day she died. And now, I give it back to you."

John took the necklace in his hand and just looked at it. He couldn't seem to speak.

Pietro sensed this and said, "Let's have some cake! It is Caterina's almond cake. You will love it!"

And they did love it. The cake was moist and flavorful, and served along with strong coffee, it gave them a second wind after their long day of travel and evening of food and wine. The room was filled with chatter, laughter, and the love of newfound family and friends until the wee hours.

At the end of the evening, they closed the door to their little room, deposited most of their gifts onto the dresser, then sat down on the bed next to one another. The gifts from Pietro were still in John's hands. He stared at the photograph, his eyes watery.

"I never saw my father look at my mother like that," he said softly.

"It's nice to find out something unexpectedly good about someone, isn't it?" she said and put her arm around his shoulder.

"Yes, but I sure wish I could have witnessed something like this, at least when I was old enough to understand, anyway. My father was always so cold, so distant at home," he said and paused for a moment. "The last couple of years, I was afraid that I was becoming just like him—and my brother—until you came along and unlocked my heart."

His words were making her melt inside. "Well, you are not your father, nor your brother. You are you, and if you take after anyone in the family, it sounds like it was your mother." Jillian said.

"I wish you could have met my mother, and she, you. She would have loved you, Jillian. You're a lot like her in so many ways—warm, kind, loving."

"Well, I know one thing we have in common for certain. We both love her youngest son—tremendously."

John put down the photograph and opened his other hand, which held the necklace. "I didn't think I would ever see this again. My mother never took it off. I thought perhaps it had been buried with her, but now I find out my father gave it to Emma. That was actually a thoughtful thing for him to do, as she and my mother were so close and she was so sad," he said, shaking his head in disbelief.

"Again, it's nice to find out something good about someone. You know, maybe your father just didn't know how to show the things he really felt," Jillian said.

"You really are like my mother, Jillian. That's sounds like something she would have said," he said. He looked into her eyes, then looked at the necklace in the palm of his hand. "Would you wear this?" he asked, lifting up the necklace.

"Are you sure, John?" Jillian asked, both surprised and honored by his question.

"I want to see it on you—my wife—the woman I love," he said.

Jillian found it hard to speak, so she just gently turned away from him, lifting her hair so that he could put the necklace around her neck.

He clasped the necklace and kissed her neck gently, then moved his lips to her bare shoulder, next to the strap of her sundress. Then he said, "So, let's see."

Kathy J. Jacobson

Jillian turned back toward him, the gold of the necklace shining against her tanned skin.

"Beautiful," he said. "The necklace, too," and moving closer to her, he kissed her like there was no tomorrow.

The next day they spent at one of the many beautiful beaches for which the area is famous with Pietro and his family. They brought along a picnic lunch that would be hard to top in the future. Breads, fruit, cheeses, meats, and lemonade made from freshly squeezed lemons from the family trees were spread out on a huge beach blanket. They swam in the warm water, threw a ball around, and made sand castles. It reminded Jillian of the time she and Pete had made a sand castle together, and she smiled as she thought of the expecting couple. They would be finding out soon whether the baby was a boy or a girl. Pete said he wanted a girl, and Kelly wanted a boy, but most of all, they just wanted a baby.

Pietro's son and daughter and their families went home at the end of the long afternoon. John and Jillian wanted to take Pietro and Caterina for a nice dinner, so they went back to the house to wash up and change. It took some talking, but they finally convinced their hosts that they really did want to treat them, and to a place they would consider special. Pietro listed a few of the better places in the area. Caterina's eyes lit up at the name of one of them, and John noticed.

"Let's go to that one," John said. Caterina tried to control herself, but she was clearly excited. They called for reservations at eight—early by Italian standards—but Jillian never liked eating too late in the evening. It was the only drawback of European dining in her mind.

Again, Jillian admired her thoughtful husband as they put on the nicer clothes they had brought. Jillian had bought a new dress in Rome, and she decided to wear it on this final evening in Italia.

John watched her as she straightened the dress in the mirror. "You really shouldn't wear that dress, Jillian," he said.

"You don't think it would be appropriate, or you don't like it?" she asked, thinking it wasn't like John to say something like that.

"That's not the problem," he said, coming up beside her. "I like it—too much." He put his hands on her hips and turned her to face him. She put her hands on his chest.

"Enjoy it while you can. Once we get to Africa, it will be long skirts or slacks, and very little "skin"—definitely the opposite of this dress," she said.

Just then there was a knock on the door. "Sorry to interrupt, but I think we should go," Pietro said.

"Saved by the knock," John whispered to Jillian.

Pietro drove them into a neighboring village to a beautiful little restaurant with an inner courtyard where a white, linen-covered table awaited them. There were fresh flowers and candles on the table, and the waiters wore white coats and black bow ties. It was just the kind of place they had envisioned for their final night with their family.

They were at the restaurant, Pace, pronounced "PAH-chay," which means peace, for three hours, not uncommon in that part of the world. They really got a chance to just talk to their hosts, and invited them to come to the United States sometime. Jillian was not certain that was something that Pietro could afford, but she thought that if things kept going well for John, and perhaps with her book, maybe they could help make that a reality in the future.

It was a very enjoyable evening, and Jillian was so glad that they had taken time during their trip to meet family. As someone

Kathy J. Jacobson

who was an adopted child, she always thought that having family, and getting to know them, was something of extraordinary value in life. She felt at that moment that she was very correct in that assumption.

It was a tearful goodbye the next day. They headed out early in the morning in the Fiat, which was packed to the hilt. They all promised to email one another, but also to write letters. They had learned over the years the value of a handwritten letter, so they would not let that family tradition die. They hugged and kissed one another, and the newlyweds were on their way.

John and Jillian were returning their rental car and flying out of Rome to Kilimanjaro International Airport. Jillian's long-time friend, Loi Godwin, would be picking them up with a borrowed van and taking them to the guest house in Arusha, where they would stay for much of their time. They could have gone to a nice hotel, but John said he wanted a different kind of experience. She was certain that he was in for one and prayed that he would enjoy it, at least on some level.

Chapter Thirteen

The customs worker at Kilimanjaro was the same man as the last time she had passed through these gates. Jillian and he had come to an "understanding" long ago. Jillian would not be gouged unfairly, but would tip him generously for his fair assessment of what she was bringing into the country. She really didn't want any delays today, because she could see Loi and his family anxiously waiting for them across the large, open room.

After she and John tipped the man in the uniform and cap, they were on their way with their bags and heading toward a group of happy people who were now jumping up and down, waving and shouting. "*Karibu, karibu!*" were the welcoming cries of Loi and his family.

By the time they crossed the room Jillian was crying. She loved these people with all of her heart. Loi gave her a huge bear hug. He was a tall, strong African with eyes as black as coal and skin the color of mahogany.

"*Habari*, my friend," Jillian somehow managed to squeak out, asking her friend how he was.

"*Mzuri sanna*," Loi responded. "Jillian, you look so happy!"

"How can you tell that when I'm crying, Loi?" she asked, holding onto his tree trunk-like arms and looking into his smiling face.

"I can tell—I can tell. And this must be Romano," he said, calling John by his last name as many of the men called one another in this place. Loi extended his hand to John.

Jillian had taught John the traditional handshake, and Loi was surprised and pleased when John shook his hand in that manner. "Good man, good man," he said and slapped John on the shoulder to affirm that.

They proceeded to be greeted by the rest of the family.

"This cannot be James!" Jillian exclaimed, as she looked at a young man even taller than Loi, muscle-bound and strikingly handsome.

"Mama Marty, it is me," he said, smiling. The smile was the same, but little else. James was the same age as Marty, and they used to play together all the time. Jillian was pretty certain that his heart was broken when they left, as she thought he was developing a crush on her daughter as they headed into their teens.

She hugged the others, his daughter, Elieshi, who was twenty-two and was holding her two-year-old daughter, Ruth, and Loi's other son, Samuel, who was now twenty-one. Loi was a widower of many years, his wife dying in childbirth upon Samuel's birth. He had never remarried, saying that he would only do that if the Lord sent him another wife like Zawadi. So far, that had not happened for him, but Jillian knew that if she could find true love, Loi might be able to as well.

When she had lived in Tanzania, some people tried to get Loi and Jillian together, but he was not ready for that kind of relationship after his heartbreaking loss. Instead, they had a close friendship, and he had become like a big, protective brother to Jillian. Rarely was anyone disrespectful, but if anyone ever said anything other than a positive word to or about Jillian or Marty, they had to answer to Loi.

They piled into the old mini-bus, one person per seat. Loi had a driver with him, so he could visit on the way instead of driving. The road was a bit better than Jillian had remembered, but once one got off the main highway, they were back to the familiar mud and ruts, which would have been dust if it were the dry season.

For whatever reason, baby Ruth just loved John and had to sit on his lap. Jillian snapped a photo when he wasn't looking, so they could cherish the moment in the future. They talked all the way to Arusha, sometimes slipping into Swahili or KiMeru, a local dialect. Realizing from time to time that they were not being polite, they would switch back to English. Jillian was happy that the language came back so easily. She wasn't really sure what to expect, and with all the hubbub surrounding the wedding and writing, she had not had time to refresh her skills.

The house looked better than she remembered it, and the landscaping outside had really developed in the passing years, with trees, bushes, and flowers of all types reaching mature states. Even in the semi-dark, it was an impressive display, and Jillian couldn't wait to see it better during the daylight.

They made plans for the next day before stepping out of the bus. Loi's family needed to be dropped off at their homes, and the mini-bus needed to get back to where it belonged. They would have dinner the next evening at Loi's home near Usa River. He would send someone to get them in the late afternoon.

"We will let you get settled in now," Loi said. He hugged Jillian again, and he and John shook hands again, as did the other men with John. Ruth started to cry when John had to give her back to her mother.

"I've never seen her like that with anyone," Elieshi said. "That is a good sign. Jillian found a good man to marry."

Jillian smiled and nodded her head in affirmation of that, as John hugged Elieshi and Ruth goodbye. Then they waved goodbye.

Kathy J. Jacobson

Jillian gave John the tour of the small, ranch-style home. In addition to their room with a double bed, there was another room with three twin beds and another with three sets of bunk beds. A living/dining area, a small bathroom with a shower, a small kitchen, and a storage closet for luggage filled out the rest of the small but comfortable house. The floor was still the same—polished cement. There was a small fireplace with some wood sitting nearby, as it was winter in the southern hemisphere. Even though it did not get very cold, it was definitely cooler than the summer months. People had to wear light coats or sweaters from time to time, especially after the sun went down, and there was no central heat in the house—thus, the fireplace. A cook/housekeeper would be by in the morning to make them some food if they wanted, or else just to clean.

John and Jillian took their things into the room and unpacked their clothes into a closet and a small dresser. All of a sudden, there was music outside. It sounded like a choir. Jillian knew there was a school across the street, and that at this time of the year, there were competitions in many activities. Luckily for them, singing must have been one of them. The group was most likely practicing its song for an upcoming event, singing in harmony to the beat of a single drum.

They stood still and listened. Jillian smiled as she caught some of the words.

"What are they saying, Jillian?" John asked.

"That God is good. God made the world and everything in it, the earth and all its creatures. I think it's a song based on Psalm Twenty-four."

"It's so beautiful," John said.

Jillian found the sound of Tanzanian music to be both mesmerizing and moving. It also made her feel so thankful to be back. She and Marty had always said that they left part of their hearts in this country, and they were not kidding.

When the music stopped, the weary travelers got ready for bed. It had been a long day. Jillian filled John in about using bottled water for teeth-brushing and drinking, and to not get water from the faucet in his eyes or mouth.

They crawled into bed, and Jillian was about to doze off in John's arms when a shrill cry pierced the air. "What was that?" John asked, a bit startled.

"A komba! A bushbaby! Do you want to go see?"

"Sure," he said, jumping to his feet like a kid heading for presents under a Christmas tree.

Jillian grabbed a flashlight from the nightstand. One was never without a "torch," as the electricity was often unpredictable.

"They are nocturnal, part of the monkey family. They have huge eyes and ears, and love to come out to play at night. They are pretty noisy, until you get used to the sound," Jillian informed John.

They stepped outside into the yard and listened for another cry. When they heard it, Jillian turned the flashlight on and shined it on the tree where the sound came from. There were two of them on a branch, staring at them with their huge eyes and ears to match, and soft, tawny fur. One of them jumped to another branch when the light hit them, but the other one looked right at them like he or she was posing. Perhaps they were getting used to visitors coming out to see them at night, Jillian thought.

It was getting chilly, so they went back inside. They jumped back into bed and snuggled up to one another. "Sorry, there's no heat," Jillian said.

"That's okay, we'll just have to keep each other warm," John said smiling. "Jillian, thank you for bringing me here," he continued sincerely, gently brushing her hair back from her face.

"Thank you for coming here with me," she said and kissed him, suddenly not so tired anymore.

Kathy J. Jacobson

❖

They awakened to someone singing in the kitchen. They peeked out the door of the room to see a plump and pleasant woman with skin like ebony, whose name they later learned was Naomi. John showered while Jillian greeted her and told her that they would have some ugali, a corn-meal dish not unlike grits, along with eggs and toast for breakfast. Usually they didn't eat that heavily in the morning, but it had been a long time since their last meal, and Jillian's stomach was protesting. Naomi started cooking, and Jillian jumped into the shower while John got dressed.

She and John cleaned their plates. They would not be eating dinner at the house that evening, but they did order a vegetable pie for the next evening. Jillian was very happy to see that there was a small microwave in the kitchen for heating things up, in case they didn't make it back when the pie came out of the oven the next day. She told Naomi to cover it and leave it in the refrigerator if they were not back before she had to leave.

They headed to town, walking down Ilboru Road toward the downtown area of Arusha. Along the roadside were little *dukas*, tiny shops that sold coffee, tea, soda pop, and a few other items. Next to them were many small homes, some made of handmade bricks, some of sticks. Some people sat outside playing the game Mancala on homemade boards, with pebbles for playing pieces.

Children swept yards with small brooms and looked up and smiled at them as they went past. One said, *wazungu*—white people—under his breath, although whites were not as uncommon in the area as they once were.

The walk to town was a couple of miles, but it felt great after all the sitting of their travels the day before. Jillian wanted John to see the Clock Tower and the area commonly referred to as "carver's row." She also wanted to visit the church that she and Marty had sometimes attended in town, as well as a stop next door to it at the Arusha Lutheran Medical Centre. The center was completed in 2004, a year after Jillian and Marty had returned to the United States. It was the best medical facility in the area by far. Jillian had given input into the planning of it, but never got to work there. She had worked at the clinic it replaced at times, but mostly she made her rounds out in the small rural hospitals and "dispensaries"—small clinics that served the people in remote, rural areas.

"Miss Jillian, is that you?" asked an older woman seated at a desk inside the church.

"It is!" Jillian said, rushing to the woman's side. It was Rosalie, the church secretary, a life-long resident of Arusha, which was not that common in this particular church. The church had members from all over the world and from many faith backgrounds. It was like going to worship at the United Nations.

Jillian was hoping to meet the new pastor, but he was out. After introducing John to Rosalie, she showed them the sanctuary and the new organ in it, and a new Sunday School classroom.

"We are growing, and needed it," Rosalie said proudly.

"It is wonderful to hear that, Rosalie. And you and your family are well?"

Rosalie went on to tell her how her son had graduated from college and was studying now in London. But her daughter, she said, had gotten AIDS and died six years ago. Rosalie was now raising her granddaughter.

"I am so sorry, Rosalie. Neema was a beautiful girl," she said and hugged her.

Rosalie wiped away a tear, and then the office phone rang. She took the call and put the person on hold, saying she really needed to take the call unfortunately. Jillian told her that they needed to be on their way as well, so she hugged her goodbye and said that she may be back, depending on how the week developed.

Kathy J. Jacobson

They walked next door to the medical center. It was beautiful, especially the stained glass inside of it. There was a photo of the bishop of the Arusha Diocese and the lead doctor of the facility dedicating it. She had known the bishop fairly well, even though she had primarily worked with the bishop from the Meru Diocese of the Evangelical Lutheran Church in Tanzania. She had also worked with the doctor in the photo on occasion.

Jillian was surprised by all the new faces, forgetting how long she had been gone. One nurse who was on her break gave them a quick tour around after Jillian explained who she was and that she had worked at the former facility on the site. The building and equipment were wonderful improvements, and Jillian was very happy for the people of the area. She felt grateful that all the hard work put into the planning of the hospital had paid off.

After their tour, they stopped at the Naz Hotel and bought lunch at the counter. John had *ndizi nyama*, bananas with beef. Bananas come in many varieties, and these were not the sweet ones, but more like a potato in flavor. Jillian had a samosa and a salad. There were many Indian-Tanzanians in Arusha, which influenced the food selections that were offered.

After lunch, they went to watch the wood carvers and barter with them if they found the right piece to buy. The carvers assumed they were just tourists, and spoke to one another in Swahili and some in KiMeru as they walked by, not realizing that Jillian could understand them.

They saw many wonderful items, but decided to buy from a man who was very kind and respectful and did beautiful work. His prices were very reasonable, and John was ready to buy the whole lot, but Jillian reminded him that they had to go to Senegal yet. They settled on a few nice carvings and decided that they could come back in a few days if they wanted to get some more.

After they paid for their purchases, Jillian said some farewell greetings to the other astonished carvers in Swahili and KiMeru, then hailed a taxi to take them back up the hill. They and their carvings bounced their way up the bumpy road back to the guest house.

They unloaded their treasures and freshened up for their trip to Loi's. Someone was supposed to pick them up in an hour, but it could be two hours or more, Jillian knew. Time had an entirely different meaning in Tanzania.

They put their feet up and relaxed until they heard a knock at the door. Surprisingly, their ride was only a half hour late, by American standards. Outside sat a white Land Rover, much older than Jillian's new one, but otherwise very much the same. They jumped in, John sitting in front with the driver so he could see more. The first part of the ride was smooth, but once they turned off the main highway, Highway 104, it was a different story. Luckily, it was not muddy, but the deep, hardened ruts in the road jostled them from one side of the vehicle to the other as they drove along.

It took a short hour to reach Loi's home near Usa River. Many people were gathered outside the small robin's egg blue, wooden house to greet them. The neighbors, Jillian told John, were there to help make dinner. Making food for company was a communal effort. Many hands made the work lighter, and many contributors made feeding guests possible for hosts with limited resources.

Loi took John on a quick tour of the house and grounds, show-ing him his two cows, the patch of elephant grass that fed them, the chickens, and the small field of maize growing in back. He then invited John to join the other men for some chai and to talk.

Jillian got ready to help Elieshi and the other women cook. A young girl asked if she could braid Jillian's hair, so she let her braid a lock on the front right side that kept falling in her face. Then someone handed her a kanga, and she wrapped the color-ful cloth over the skirt she had worn. She looked, and felt, more

Kathy J. Jacobson

like her old self with each passing moment, and was beginning to experience déjà vu.

They all sang together as they snapped beans, boiled rice, and ground spices for pilau, a rare treat for the Tanzanians. They plucked two chickens and put them on a grate high above a wood fire to cook. They kneaded dough for *chapati*, a type of fried bread, and one of Jillian's favorite treats. It was a good thing they had done a lot of walking earlier in the day, Jillian thought.

Almost two hours later, she joined Loi, John, James, and Elieshi for dinner at the small dining table in the house. The others ate in the backyard, the men together in one spot, the women and children in another. Some things had not changed, although there would have been a day when no man and woman would eat together, so it was better than it once had been.

John looked at home as he approached the table with Loi and James. He was happy to see Jillian again, though. He smiled at her, and his grin widened when he noticed her new braid and the African wrap around her waist.

The neighbor women took turns serving them each of the dishes. When the pilau was served, John's face turned a bit red, only enough that Jillian would notice. She could tell he was upset, and she planned to talk to him later about it.

Jillian made certain to bring up a topic that would take his mind off the currently served dish. They talked about the medical center and then asked Loi how things were going out in the rural areas. Loi said that they might be able to hire the same driver who was waiting for them and eating with the men currently to go out to the countryside the next day. That sounded like a great idea to them, and John's smile returned.

They talked and ate, and talked and ate. It was quite a feast that had been thrown together. John remarked about it, and Loi said to thank the many good friends that he, and Jillian, had accumulated over the years. They had all pitched in together to make it happen.

At the end of the night, they hugged everyone goodbye and thanked Loi and all those who were still around. They bumped their way back to Arusha and did indeed hire their driver for the next day. They gave him a good tip when they got back to the guest house and headed in the door with a flashlight that Jillian luckily remembered to take with her at the last minute.

They stepped inside the house, and John hugged her. "What an amazing place," he said.

"It is, isn't it? Did you enjoy dinner tonight?" she asked.

"It was delicious, and the way everyone helped cook it and brought something to contribute to it..." He stopped speaking suddenly, and she noticed his upset face returning. "I can't believe..."

"John..." Jillian said softly, cutting him off mid-sentence.

"I can't believe what I did last year. I threw that food in the garbage. Food that people here would..."

"John, it was a tough time for you. You are a new person now, so don't beat yourself up. Our entire nation has problems with wastefulness. You know, I heard once that every day we throw away enough food to feed all of Europe. We need to learn, and we need to change."

"Well, I'm learning very quickly," he said.

"I know you are, because you are a wonderful, sensitive, and caring person. I wouldn't have married you if you weren't," she said.

"I know I've said this before, but I'll say it again. You are way too easy on me, Jillian," he said, pulling her closer.

"And you are way too *hard* on yourself, John," she said, meaning it.

He looked like he was carefully considering her words after that statement. He started to shake his head "no," but Jillian gave him an affirmative nod, so he stopped. Then he pulled her into a grateful embrace.

Kathy J. Jacobson

The next day the hired driver drove them out to see the little house that Jillian and Marty had shared, as well as some of the hospitals and dispensaries she used to visit on rotation. Their final two stops were at an orphanage and an elementary school that was in session.

At the school, the teacher was having students read a story. It was amazing to Jillian that each of them had a copy of the reading book, a big sign of improvement. One boy named Omar did not like the story and was being a bit of a pain. It didn't help that the teacher was making the lesson about as boring as one could possibly make it. John asked the teacher if he could make a suggestion, and she agreed. He thought they should act out the story. There were a lot of characters in it, so many in the class could take part. The others could be the audience, he explained, and told them they were important, too, as actors usually perform better for good audiences.

They gave it a try, and what do you know, little Omar was quite the actor. He enjoyed being the center of attention, and because he appeared to be bright, he was given the leading role, which made him even happier. He was an excellent reader, which one would never have guessed several minutes before when he was slogging through his oral reading. John gave him some direction from time to time, having him repeat a line a different way. It was really fun to watch, and the teacher was very grateful. She said she would try doing this more often, since it had gone so well.

As they drove home, Jillian just watched her husband. She would have loved to kiss him, but public displays of that kind between men and women were not favored in this society, not even between husband and wife. John was like a kid in a candy store in Tanzania, trying every new thing, and absorbing and noticing everything in his usual, observant way. She was so grateful to be able to share such a special place she loved with someone whom she loved.

The next day, they walked back into the city with backpacks on their backs. They were going to hire someone to take them out to the animal parks for a day or two. This time they would stay at a lodge one night and camp out another.

They found two gentlemen with a Land Rover standing outside of a safari company. One said he was the driver, the other the cook. They negotiated a trip with them and headed out to Lake Manyara National Park first, then to the Serengeti. The next day it would be on to the Ngorogoro Crater, the Great Rift Valley, and Olduvai Gorge.

The animals were active, especially the zebra and giraffes, at Lake Manyara. It was supposed to be a good place to see an elephant, but after a half day had gone by, they saw none. They were feeling a bit disappointed, when suddenly the driver told them to look behind them.

They turned around in their seats. A line of elephants was coming down the road behind them. As the elephants neared the Land Rover, they turned to their right and headed into a wooded area—all except the final one. For whatever reason, he kept walking toward them. The driver whispered to them to be very still.

Jillian held her breath. The window next to her was open a few inches. Had she wanted to, she could have reached her hand through it and touched the gigantic animal as it lumbered past. Her heart was pounding. Earlier, the driver had mentioned that they should get no closer than thirty meters to an elephant. The ones coming up behind them had been closer than that, and that had been a bit unnerving, but this one was right on top of them.

Kathy J. Jacobson

Their eyes followed the elephant as he passed the front of the vehicle. Jillian was hoping he would turn right into the woods like the rest of the herd, but instead, he hesitated, turned to his left and rotated completely around, and faced them squarely.

They were not experts, but both John and Jillian knew that this wasn't good. The driver turned off the engine and sat frozen in the front seat. John gently and slowly reached for Jillian's hand and held it tightly.

All Jillian could think about was that she had just had the most wonderful honeymoon and had been so happy to be in Tanzania with John, and now they were going to be attacked and seriously injured—or worse. She had known victims of elephant attacks, and had even treated some of the people. Some were maimed for life, others did not survive given the level of care available.

The animal stared at them, its huge, wrinkly ears flapping, its head, trunk, and large tusks swinging side to side. Jillian felt like crying, but even her tears seemed frozen. Behind their vehicle, a double-decker bus of tourists pulled up. The driver cut his engine, too. Seeing the elephant ahead of them, some of the people from the bottom climbed out the side windows and onto the top of the bus, which was not at all reassuring.

Jillian gripped John's hand even more tightly and prayed fervently. It seemed like a lifetime, but a few minutes later, the elephant gave up his stance, and turned and went into the woods. The driver started up the Land Rover, and they slowly proceeded forward.

John and Jillian both let out huge sighs and hugged each other.

"I'll never complain about not seeing an elephant again," Jillian said.

"Same here," John said. "Wow, that was pretty amazing, though, wasn't it?"

"I don't know. I think I need a little more time before I can put it in the *amazing* category. *Scary* is where I'm at right now," she said.

John took her hand again, then put his other one on top of it for added reassurance. He didn't let go until they were far out of the park.

The next stop was just inside the Serengeti. The two hired men jumped out and immediately set up camp. John and Jillian's tent was up in no time at all. The driver gave them some safety instructions, as there were baboons in the trees nearby and hyenas who liked to come sniffing around during the night. Then he joined the cook to help make dinner, a simple fare of carrot soup, chapati, and some fruit.

The evening was beautiful. The sun was just setting as they sat on small folding stools and ate in the fresh air. Jillian finished all her food in record time.

"You must like carrot soup," the cook commented.

"It was delicious," Jillian said. Then, quietly she added to John after the cook walked away, "It's amazing how hungry the fear of death can make you," only half-jokingly.

They sat and talked while the men cleaned up and put their tent up in the semi-darkness. It was clear that they had done that many times, with the ease of their feat.

Finally, they called it a night and headed into their tent. It was an interesting night, filled with sounds that not even Jillian had heard before—lions roaring, zebras warning each other of danger, and hyenas laughing. It was warm in the tent, but John held Jillian close. She was happy to be in his arms with all that wildness going on outside of their tent, even if it was a distance away.

After a breakfast cooked over a fire the next morning, they were off to the Rift Valley and Olduvai Gorge, where the bones of "Lucy," the oldest human found to date, had been discovered. They stopped and talked to some Masai boys, who let them take their photo for some sticks of gum. Masai men were herding some goats

Kathy J. Jacobson

nearby, while women sat on blankets on the ground and worked on their weaving and beading.

The Rift was always amazing to Jillian. It made her feel like the earth might crack apart at any moment, and one half of the world would just disappear. The two tectonic plates were in actuality slowly splitting apart, and someday, far in the future, that might just become a reality.

They were fortunate to have another good weather day as they headed into the Crater. They would stay at the Lodge there that night, one of the nicest hotels in the country. The cook would get the night meal and breakfast off, as John and Jillian would have an incredible buffet at the Lodge that night and breakfast in the morning, and both the driver and cook were happy to get to stay at the accommodations the hotel provided for them.

On the way back to Arusha the next day, they stopped for a few more photos, including one of a huge and beautiful herd of zebra, with a few wildebeests mingled in. They had seen pretty much every animal they had hoped to see, with the exception of a rhino, which was getting more and more difficult to spot as poaching was decimating their numbers to near extinction. Jillian had hoped to see one, but didn't dare say so. She was afraid the same thing might happen with a rhino as with the elephant, so she held her peace.

They arrived back in Arusha, tipping their guide and cook well, especially since they had gone out of their way to drop them off at the guest house. It had been a perfect safari, even with the "elephant incident," as they often referred to it in the future.

Laundry needed to be done, and they took their dirty clothes out of their backpacks and suitcases and made a pile. Naomi could be hired to wash clothes, and she would do their laundry for them the next day in the backyard. The wet clothes would need a day to dry, and they needed clean clothes for church on Sunday and then for Senegal.

Jillian was getting excited at the thought of seeing her daughter in only a few days. She had thought of Marty so many times that week in Tanzania and hoped that perhaps Marty could get there before she headed back to the States. True, it was the wrong direction, but that was okay. It would be worth it to see this place, and especially the people, once more.

Jillian and John invited Loi and his family to join them on Saturday night at a nice restaurant in Arusha. It was something Loi and his family never had the opportunity to do, so it was a special treat for some special people. Earlier that day, they had gone back to the area where Jillian and Marty had lived to see if they could see the inside of their little house. They had called *hodi,* announcing themselves, outside the house several times, but there was no answer, which meant either no one was home or they had come at an inconvenient time and should try again. They were happy that this time the owners were home and invited them in. They also hoped to make a few other stops along the way.

On Sunday morning, they attended the early worship service in Arusha. It was wonderful to see all the people from everywhere at the downtown church. But their next stop, the country church, was by far the best part of the entire trip. Their driver waited for them in Arusha and took them to the little church near Loi's home.

As they approached the cinder-block building, with its wooden altar and cross, and long wooden backless benches, they were mobbed by many people who knew Jillian. They were ecstatic to see her again and to meet her husband.

Jillian was asked to say a few words during the sermon time, and she also translated the service for John. Loi still had the guitar Jillian had left with him and invited her to sing with him, one of their favorite hymns, and then to help lead the Lord's Prayer, "Baba Yetu." Tears filled both Jillian's and Loi's eyes on that one.

After the service, the congregation filed out into the churchyard for the auction. People who had no money to put into the offering plate had brought items for the auction—sugar cane, milk in a jar, a bundle of firewood, a bunch of bananas, even a live chicken. They were auctioned off to those who did have money, which was then given to the church treasury to pay for the pastor, maintenance, and an evangelist who traveled out to the most remote areas. Some of the people there that day had walked miles to get to the service and would have to walk miles home again. It was certainly a different situation than in Los Angeles, where everyone seemed to drive everywhere.

John, Jillian, and Loi had lunch at the pastor's house with his wife and youngest son, who was still in secondary school, the equivalent of an American high school. He had just been a toddler when Jillian and Marty had left. They reminisced together. Jillian told them how they had been able to visit the little house the day before. It hadn't changed very much at all, and she had taken photos of the house and the people who lived in it now to show Marty. They had also gone to a farm, seeing the maize fields and someone grinding it into meal, coffee growing, and coffee beans drying in the sun.

Their next stop had been at a small cheese factory owned by a local woman, which had been a project of a man who had visited from Wisconsin and taught her the process. They asked Jillian if she knew the man, but he was from the other side of the state, and she did not, unfortunately.

One of their last stops had been at the Mwangaza Partnership for Education Centre, where they learned about the latest programs to improve the skills of teachers across the country. The center had a wonderful *binti-mama* (daughter-mother) program, which promoted education for females, taught about women's health issues, and encouraged female entrepreneurship.

It was a wonderful afternoon of visiting, but before they knew it, it was time to say goodbye to everyone, not something that Jillian was relishing at all.

"*Tutaona kila mmoja*," Jillian said to Loi as he set their luggage down inside the airport terminal. The phrase means "we will see each other again," and Jillian liked that better than goodbye, even though she knew deep down that the chances of them seeing each other again in this lifetime were pretty slim. She tried not to think about that as she hugged him.

"I am so happy for you, Jillian. Maybe God will send me someone special, like God sent Romano to you," Loi said.

"I hope so, Loi. I will pray for it," she said, so pleased that Loi approved of John.

Jillian watched the two living men she admired and loved the most on the planet shake hands and embrace.

"You are a good man," Loi said to him. "And a lucky one, too."

"Yes, I am lucky indeed," he said, looking at his wife. "Thank you for everything, Loi. Thank you for watching out for Jillian and Marty all those years, too."

"It was my pleasure. They are family," he said.

Jillian needed to get on the plane—now—or she was going to lose it. John could sense that she needed to go, so he gave Loi one more handshake, and they were on their way to security.

Jillian was unusually quiet as they settled into their seats on the plane. John could tell that she was very sad to be leaving a place, and people, that had such a special place in her heart. In his kind way, he was just there for her, gently putting his hand on hers. After they took off, Jillian put her head on his shoulder, and tears

Kathy J. Jacobson

gently rolled down her cheek. Not saying a word, he tightened his grip on her hand and with his other brushed away her tears, then very gently kissed her forehead.

Jillian grasped his hand that held hers even tighter, so thankful for this special person, as Loi put it, that God had sent to her.

Chapter Fourteen

Jillian rarely slept on a plane, but this time she drifted off quickly—and thankfully—into a deep sleep. She didn't wake up until the announcement to prepare for landing. Poor John, she thought. She had been terrible company on this flight.

"Hi, sweetheart," he said gently, as she came to.

"Did I really sleep all the way to Dakar?" she asked in disbelief.

"You did. You must have needed to," he said kindly.

"As someone once said to me, you are way too easy on me," she said, squeezing his hand.

He smiled at her—that smile that always made her heart do flips—and she smiled back in appreciation.

Her understanding husband, and her nap, had definitely improved her mood. And the thought that in just a short few minutes she would see her—their—daughter, lifted Jillian out of her previous funk.

They were greeted by Marty's luminous smile as they stepped through the gate. "Mom! Dad!" she yelled to them. If there was any

Kathy J. Jacobson

sadness left in Jillian, it flew right out the window at that moment.

A group hug ensued, followed by kisses. Marty seemed exceptionally happy, Jillian thought, more than just the happiness of having her parents come to visit. She would have to find out what was going on with her daughter. Marty could read her mother like a book, and Jillian was equally good at reading her daughter, and something was definitely "up."

A taxi took them to a hotel located between the small house Marty shared with three other interns and the hospital where she worked. Dakar seemed huge and bustling compared to Arusha and the countryside they had just visited in Tanzania.

The taxi driver was friendly. He spoke to them in French and something Jillian could not comprehend. French and Wolof were the primary languages of Senegal, and Marty had told her that sometimes people used a combination of both. Marty was fluent in French and had once mentioned her concern that she was developing a bad habit of mixing the two languages like the locals. Both John and Jillian had studied French, so they caught about half of what the driver was saying to them. They had to rely on Marty for the rest.

Once they arrived in their room, they literally threw their luggage inside and headed out with Marty to meet some of her friends at a nearby restaurant. One of them was "on call," so they needed to be close to the hospital. There were two other doctors from Harvard, Jackie and Edward, and then another who had recently joined them for a special project, a young man named Michael, who was in a similar program of study at Stanford.

Jillian asked Michael if he knew of Dr. Jerry Stein, and indeed, he had taken a course with him. Jillian and John explained how they had met him at their wedding reception, and also his relation to John's agent. Jillian would have to ask Carol to ask Jerry about Michael, because if she was reading her daughter correctly, he was the reason for her extra shot of happiness.

John and Jillian briefly filled Marty in on everyone in Tanzania and showed her a few photos on their phones. Not wanting to be rude, they soon turned the conversation to learning more about the other interns. Jackie was a native of Massachusetts, growing up not far from Boston in Hopkinton, home of the start of the Boston Marathon. Jackie had dreamed of going to Harvard ever since she was a little girl.

Edward was from Terre Haute, Indiana, and had wanted to be an astronaut until he realized he was afraid of heights and suffered from motion sickness, neither of which worked well for space travel. He was very good in science and math, and after his uncle became ill while visiting a developing nation, Edward became fascinated with the diseases that affect people around the world and decided he would study them.

Michael was from South Dakota—at least, that was where he spent his formative years. His parents had worked with a church organization serving the people of the Pine Ridge Reservation. Marty and Jillian had gone on a servant trip with the church's youth group to Pine Ridge. That connection had jump-started a conversation between Marty and Michael when they first met, and Jillian thought, judging by the way her daughter lit up when he had entered the room, it had also jump-started a relationship that had either begun, or was soon to begin.

They were just about to order dessert when Michael's pager went off. "I'm so sorry. I've got to go," he said. He looked very disappointed to be leaving, and so did Marty, which furthered confirmed Jillian's suspicions.

"I hope to see you again," he said to Jillian and John, and shook their hands.

I'm sure we will, Jillian thought to herself.

The five of them finished their meals. Jackie and Edward went home to get some sleep. John, Jillian, and Marty walked around the area for an hour, then they walked Marty home, as she had to work in the morning. Luckily, she could spend the next evening and the entire day after that with them. They hugged good night, then Jillian and John headed back to their hotel, tired again by this time.

Jillian crawled in between the comfy sheets, a definite upgrade from their last accommodations. John was readying for bed in the bathroom, so Jillian called Carol quickly back in L.A. She had been checking every three or four days to make sure there were no problems. This time, she wanted Carol to inquire about Michael the next time she had an opportunity to speak with Jerry.

"I'll ask him," Carol said when Jillian asked. "He's sitting across the table from me at Leo's restaurant. He drove down today after I told him I would take him out for the best Italian food anywhere."

Jillian smiled to herself as Carol talked to Jerry. Jillian was so happy and excited for her friend.

Carol came back on the line. "He says he remembers him. Brilliant and humble—an unusual combination, he says," Carol reported as Jerry dictated to her.

"Marty is working with him here in Senegal. We just had dinner with them and two other interns until Michael's pager went off. Anyway, everything is well?"

"Everything is wonderful," Carol said.

"I'll want the full report when I get home, Carol—and I'm not talking about the house."

"Yes, I will be sure to do that."

Jillian could hear the happiness in her friend's voice and smiled. They said goodbye just as John slipped into bed, throwing his head back into the fluffy pillow. Jillian laid on her side and studied him for a moment. He looked tired, but happy.

"I think our daughter is in love," Jillian said, putting her hand on his chest.

"Michael," he said.

"Uh-huh."

"He seems like a nice guy," John said, turning toward her.

"Takes one to know one," Jillian replied and moved her hand up to his cheek to caress it. "I was just talking with Carol. She was with Jerry, and he remembers Michael as 'brilliant and humble, an unusual combination.' That sounds good to me."

"Yes, it does," he said.

She was quiet a moment. "John, thank you for being so nice to me today—when I was feeling so down," she said.

"I didn't really do anything. I just wanted to make you feel better."

"You did, just by being there—and letting me cry all over your shoulder," she said, propping her head up with her hand, gazing lovingly down at him. "Have I told you lately how much I love you?"

"I'm not sure. Refresh my memory," he said, putting his fingers under her chin.

"I love you more than life itself, John Romano."

Marty gave them a tour of the hospital the next day after her shift ended. It was an older building, but the equipment was more updated than the newer hospital in Arusha. It was a much larger city, so that made sense.

They met more of Marty's friends as they toured around. Everyone seemed to know and love Marty—from the doctors to the nurses to the patients to the janitors and the cooks in the cafeteria. She always treated everyone with such respect and kindness, and it paid off in the admiration of just about everyone she met.

Marty was thrilled to be able to introduce all these people to her family, and Jillian could tell that John was enjoying it every time Marty would say, "I'd like you to meet my parents..."

They took her out to dinner afterward, happy to have her all to themselves. They talked about Rome, John's family in Naples, more about their time in Tanzania, and of course, about Chicago and Tommy's family. So much had transpired since the wedding.

Marty couldn't wait to hear the details about the wedding reception and John's acting jobs. She asked John if he had been nervous the first time he stepped back onto the stage or in front of a camera. He admitted that the first time he stepped on stage was pretty nerve-racking, but after a few minutes, it all seemed to come back to him. He said he had forgotten how much he loved it and was very excited for his next venture—the movie. Jillian reveled at the sound of joy in John's voice.

The next day, Marty took them to Goree Island, where they took "The Door of No Return" tour. It was heart-wrenching. In the afternoon, they headed to the beach. It was beautiful, but the sickening thought of the people who had been taken by ship from these shores and forced into slavery was in the back of their minds, even as they relaxed on the sand.

The three of them went back to the hotel to freshen up before they went out for the evening. They were going to a dinner club that had live music, where a popular Senegalese singer was slated to perform.

John was the first one to hit the shower. Jillian thought he had sensed she wanted to ask Marty about Michael, and it was just like him to give them a private moment for just such an occasion.

Marty wasn't really ready to admit it completely, but she said that she liked Michael—"a lot." She couldn't see how anything could come of it, however, with him living on the exact opposite end of the nation once they returned to the States. Jillian had to admit that would be quite a challenge.

"You are right, Marty. There would be nothing easy about such a long-distance relationship, but don't give up on it too quickly. If it's meant to be, there will be a way."

"I guess you're right, Mom. And I suppose if we could make it through the next year or two from a long distance, we may end up working closer to each other eventually."

"You will just have to decide if he is the kind of man who is worth the effort," Jillian said.

"He is," Marty admitted.

"Well, then I think you've answered your own questions, Marty."

"Thanks, Mom. And by the way, how did you know?"

"The same way you knew that I was in love with John and that he was in love with me."

"Oh," she said and smiled.

The next two days felt like they were fast-forwarded, and it was time to head for home via Chicago and attend John Anthony's graduation celebration. It had been quite the adventure, and they couldn't wait to share news of their travels, especially of their family in Italy, with the younger Romanos. One of the first things John planned to do when they got to Chicago was to have a copy made of the photo Pietro had given him, to give to Tommy. He knew that he would equally cherish it.

It wasn't quite as hard to say goodbye to Marty this time, knowing that in a few months she would be back in the United States. It sounded like nothing compared to the eighteen months they had been separated before the wedding. Another group hug bookended their visit, and John and Jillian were on their way back across the ocean.

It would be the most memorable trip of Jillian's life. Some might call it a honeymoon, but Jillian thought every day with John was like a honeymoon. It was more of a "sharing of each other's lives

Kathy J. Jacobson

with one another" kind of trip. It was an experience that drew them into an even stronger type of closeness, as each of them bared a bit of their history, as well as their hearts and souls, with one another on the journey.

Jillian hadn't thought it possible, but their trip had made their relationship and their love for each other stronger than ever, and the memories it created were indelible. They would go on to remind one another of the things they had done and seen, and the people they encountered, many times over in the years to come. It was not just a trip. It was a treasure.

Chapter Fifteen

"Carol, you look fantastic!" Jillian said as she hugged her good friend at the airport.

"I was just going to say the same thing about you two. I don't have to ask if you had a good time. It's written all over your faces," she said, smiling and helping them with their luggage.

Jillian couldn't wait to get home and get the scoop on Jerry, although she wasn't sure that she would be awake enough by the time they arrived home. Jet lag was going to be interesting. She only hoped that John recovered quickly, as he had to start shooting a movie in less than a week.

They returned home, greeted by Lucy, who was ecstatic to see them both. Carol invited them to the kitchen, where she had sandwiches and a fruit salad waiting for them in the refrigerator. It was a thoughtful gesture, and much appreciated. They sat down at the breakfast nook with their plates, not knowing where to begin with their tales.

After they wolfed down the food, they presented Carol with a beautiful wood carving from Tanzania and a scarf from Italy.

"You didn't have to give me anything. It has been a gift staying here. The weather was perfect. The pool was a delight, and the cottage is so comfortable. I haven't felt this relaxed in years!"

"We really appreciated you being here, Carol," John said. "We didn't have to worry about the house at all knowing someone we knew and trusted was on the premises."

"Well, anytime you need a house-sitter, you know my number," she said smiling and looking radiant.

John and Jillian were fading fast, and Carol noticed.

"I'm going to let you two get to sleep. I'll see you tomorrow," she said and hugged them both good night.

John and Jillian picked up their bags. John looked around at the house. "It's good to be home, but it seems so big, doesn't it?

"Yes, because it is big. I was happy when I came back from living in Tanzania that we went straight to inner-city Milwaukee. It was a bit easier to handle."

"I've got some processing to do," he said, "but right now, it's time for bed."

Jillian had set an alarm for a reasonable time, just to help them try to get their sleep cycles back on track as soon as possible. The first task was unpacking—not one of her favorite things—with the exception of their souvenirs. She gathered up dirty clothes and took them down to the laundry room and got a load going. John used to have all of his clothes sent out to a service, but now only his dress shirts and pants went to the cleaners.

She texted Carol to see what she was doing. Carol was just packing up some of her things and would head over to the house shortly. Jillian wished her friend could stay, but realized this was most likely the longest time Carol had been away from her home in years—perhaps ever. Jillian had another one of her feelings, though, that new and major developments might be just around the corner for Carol. She would find out more soon.

"So, Jerry drove all the way down here two weekends in a row?" Jillian asked.

"Yes, it was so nice of him. He stayed with Alan and Bev, although he didn't spend very much time with them," she said, turning a bit rosy with that last bit of information.

"He seems like a special person," Jillian said.

"I think you are correct in that assumption. He's so intelligent, and very respected, but not the least bit snooty. He's so down-to-earth, and I enjoy his sense of humor. I guess we all need that in the field of medicine and academia," she said.

"Yes, we need it, but not everyone achieves it. I think it is wonderful that you two met each other. It's just too bad that you live two thousand miles away from each other."

Jillian then told Carol more about Marty and Michael, and their similar dilemma.

"Except it's three thousand miles for them," Carol said.

"I told her that if it's meant to be, somehow things will work out."

"I hope you are right about that," Carol said, looking thoughtful. Jillian wasn't certain if Carol was thinking about Marty and Michael's situation or her own. Maybe it was both, Jillian thought.

After John and Jillian came home from taking Carol to the airport, they sat down at the breakfast nook table to talk.

"Do you think we should sell our house?" John asked.

The question took Jillian by surprise. "What brought on that question?" she asked.

"I keep thinking about Africa," John said. "Everyone had so little, but they seemed so happy."

Kathy J. Jacobson

"Yes, they know how to appreciate anything and everything that they have."

"I just feel like I need to do something—something that will help people who don't have enough. I just don't know what to do exactly."

"I understand what you mean," she said. "It takes time to discover the best plan. Some people think giving someone money is the answer, but sometimes money isn't the best solution. One of the best strategies is to teach people something that they can do to make their lives better. It's like the little cheese factory we visited. The woman was taught by an American how to make cheese. Now she supports her family and teaches others how to do the same. It's like Pastor Jim talks about sometimes—about our vocation—our work, our skills, our passions—that we can use to make this world a better place, to make it the kind of world God had in mind in the first place."

"Hmmm," he said. "How could I use acting to make the world a better place?"

"I think there are a lot of ways, actually. Think about how you helped that teacher with her class by teaching the children how to act out the story they were reading. Think about how happy you made the people at the nursing home when you did a dramatic reading of *Moby Dick*. Think about how you made that little boy feel last Christmas when you dropped your tray on purpose and made him smile. Think about the television shows and movies that teach others about what is going on in the world, or just plain give them some joy for a couple of hours. I think your profession is amazing."

Jillian could practically see the cogs working in John's mind as she spoke.

"I think *you* are amazing, Jillian," John said softly and put his hand on hers.

Chapter Sixteen

Before Jillian and John knew it, it was time for John to become "Mack." They had gone over his lines once more. John hardly needed any reminders. Jillian wondered to herself if all actors learned their lines so easily.

John had to be at the studio before the crack of dawn for make-up. Jillian told him he should have just stayed up, as it may have been easier than only getting a short night's sleep. She was pretty sure John had barely slept—not any good sleep, anyway. She knew he was both excited and nervous. She didn't blame him. She was pretty excited and nervous herself. Even her usually effective nurse's neck and shoulder massage hadn't done the trick this time for John. She wanted to stay up with him and talk, but she hadn't been able to keep her eyes open.

They were going to Karen and Robert's for dinner that night. Karen had just gotten her assignment for the school she would be working at in the fall, and Jillian couldn't wait to hear all about it.

While John was gone, Jillian also called Pete to see how Kelly was feeling. It sounded like she was feeling well—a bit "fat," as Kelly was used to having a model-like body. And she was tired much of the time. Jillian told Pete to have Kelly call her if she ever wanted to talk.

"She may just do that, Jillian. One of the problems of not telling anyone is that you can't really talk about all the changes going on. But soon we will share the news with everyone, now that we are a couple of months along. We just wanted to make sure that everything was okay before we did. By the way, good job of keeping it quiet."

"It wasn't easy, Pete, although going away for almost a month out of the country certainly helped." She told him briefly about their incredible journey.

Then Pete filled her in on the health club renovations and also a house that they hoped to buy. The house needed a bit of "TLC," and they would have to do some updating, but it was in a good neighborhood, close to his new gym, and the price was right. Pete also thought that he could do some of the remodeling himself and was excited by that idea, as he had once wanted to be a builder.

"We are going to look at it again tomorrow, and if we still like it, we will make an offer," he said excitedly.

"That would be great, Pete. Having your own home would be so nice with your little one coming. When is your next appointment?" she asked.

"On Friday. They are going to do the ultrasound this time. I've never been so happy or excited in my entire life, Jillian."

"I understand that feeling, Pete. Good for you," she said.

"I know you understand it, and good for you, too, Jillian."

Next on Jillian's list was a call to Greta. They had talked about getting together for coffee, but it just hadn't happened before John and Jillian's honeymoon trip.

They met at a coffee house that Greta suggested. Jillian loved the atmosphere, its fair trade-only coffees and teas, locally crafted pottery mugs, and even some fair trade items for sale from Guatemala and Mexico.

Jillian was a bit surprised when Drew walked through the door with Greta. She felt slightly disappointed. She was hoping for some time to get to know Greta better, one-on-one.

Drew must have been reading her mind—which was a "first" in their relationship—as he quickly spoke.

"I'm only here for a minute, Jillian. I just wanted to say hello and be here to tell you."

Jillian didn't have to guess what it was that they had to tell her, as they were both beaming.

"We're engaged," they said in unison, laughing that they both said it at the same time. Jillian could barely believe that this was the same, often stiff, disinterested Drew that she had dated on and off for almost an entire year. She and Drew had clearly not been the right ones for each other, but Drew and Greta—that was a different story entirely! Greta showed her the unique ring on her left-hand ring finger and pointed out the diamond stud in her nose.

"Congratulations," she said and hugged them both. "I'm so happy for you both," and she meant it. In the back of her mind, she still wondered about Drew's family's reaction to all of this, but the two of them would figure it out.

"We want you to be our matron of honor," Greta said, Drew's arm around her shoulder.

"You do? Are you sure?"

"Yes, we are sure. Drew says that if you hadn't told him to invite me out for coffee, none of this would ever have happened. He says you knew that he liked me right from the start. Is that true?"

Jillian told her that she had never heard Drew talk so excitedly about anyone or anything before, and had never heard him say anyone's name about every two seconds in a conversation. She had guessed that he was crazy about this girl. However, Jillian didn't mention that Drew had said that she was "driving him crazy," and not in the flattering sense. Jillian had suggested that he ask her for coffee and have a nice talk, and felt that only time would tell if her intuition had been correct.

"This is the place we met for coffee, Jillian—that first time. We wanted you to see where it all—began, you might say."

"What a nice idea," Jillian said, smiling.

"Well, I'm going to let you two get to know each other. I've got to get back to work," Drew said.

"I love you," he said to Greta, and kissed her on the forehead.

"Back at you," she replied, smiling at him. Then she turned to Jillian, motioning for them to sit down at a small table by the front window.

Jillian found Greta to be a fascinating young woman. She had been employed at the gym the past five years, working her way through graduate school. She was almost done with her doctorate in art history at UCLA. She already had her undergraduate degree in art, and Greta was one of the artists whose mugs were for sale at the shop. She hoped to be an art history professor and teach pottery classes, as well as make and sell pottery on the side. She did other types of artwork, too, but potting was her passion.

They conversed for more than an hour, until Greta had to leave to get ready for work. Jillian headed home to work on her writing before John got home from the set. She had been praying all day that it was going well for him. A first day on any new job was an anxious proposition, but a first movie in many years was especially so.

When Jillian returned home, it was back to her laptop. She was so involved in her writing that she didn't hear John come into the room. Instead, she saw a yellow rose slowly come into her view out of the corner of her right eye. She smiled and turned around.

John was smiling that huge grin of his. Between the grin and the rose, she knew that it must have been a good first day.

"So, let's hear it," she said to him.

He sat down on a chair next to her and described the day. There had been very few snafus, probably because everyone came prepared and ready to make a good impression on the first day, he said. They also had a top-notch cast, with people who were both talented and reliable. They had to do one scene a good number of times, mostly because it was integral to setting up the entire plot of the movie, and they wanted it to be perfect. John mentioned that he had politely asked if he could offer a suggestion after a number of unsuccessful takes. The director was a bit frustrated by that point, so he had said okay. John told him his idea, and miraculously he actually went with it. It was the one that ended up as a wrap.

Jillian silently sent up a prayer of thanks. She was so proud that John dared to do this project after a long hiatus from acting, especially from the silver screen. He was beaming, she thought, inside and out. And because he was beaming, so was she.

"What time are we expected at Karen and Robert's?" he asked.

"Seven."

He looked at his watch and smiled. "Good," he said, pulling her off of her chair and into his arms.

Jillian missed talking to Karen as often as she used to when she hadn't been in school, but she loved even more the enthusiasm that exuded from her friend as she talked about the upper ele-

Kathy J. Jacobson

mentary school in East Los Angeles where she would be working in just two months. She described what she had been told about the neighborhood, the main issues the children faced, and her hopes for her semester. Karen was excited, but with a healthy dose of realistic expectations. Her advisor sounded like a wise woman, preparing her to do good work but also to realize how difficult and challenging this experience would most likely be.

John asked more about the area Karen would be working in once she was acclimated. He wanted to know what might be helpful to the population there. He said he had some ideas circulating in his head. Jillian had, too, ever since their conversation that first night back after their trip. They would have to talk soon and compare notes.

They feasted on a fantastic meal of French spaghetti, fresh-baked breadsticks, and salad with homemade dressing, courtesy of Karen and her phenomenal cooking skills. As their stomachs settled, they shared tales of their respective trips, both of which were outstanding.

Jillian had always wanted to go to Alaska. It was the only state she had not yet visited. John had not been there, either, so they loved hearing about it and seeing some of the photos Robert and Karen had taken.

They all decided that they needed to have another evening or two for sharing. Karen suggested an "Africa Night" and "Alaska Night," complete with local fare from the places they had visited. That sounded like a great idea, and they tentatively set up an evening in a few weeks at John and Jillian's for some Tanzanian cuisine, followed by a presentation in the theater room.

John and Jillian went home that evening full of food and ideas, both of which were very satisfying. They fell into bed when they got home, with John setting his alarm for very early again.

He gently guided Jillian's head to his chest. She could hear and feel his heart beating.

"Jillian," he said and then paused.

"Yes?"

"What did I ever do before I met you?" he asked seriously, gently rubbing her arm. "I can't imagine life without you."

"That's good, because I can't imagine life without you either. I believe you're stuck with me."

"Thank God," he said, turning off the light with his free hand.

"You've got that right."

Chapter Seventeen

The movie shoot was going well for the most part. Every once in a while there would be a glitch, usually related to unco-operative weather or an equipment failure. The actors in the cast had meshed with one another quickly. John particularly enjoyed one of the younger actors, who seemed to look up to him and often asked for his advice. John and Jillian were going to have the actor, Brooks, and his girlfriend, Bobbi, over for dinner at the end of the week.

Jillian's book was really taking off now that she was back from the honeymoon and John was so busy during the day. She thought that by the time he was done shooting the movie, she would be done with the manuscript. Then she needed to decide who would publish it. She would need an editor and possibly someone who would do some publicity.

It was such an exciting time for both John and Jillian, as they were both doing something they loved. The only difference, which made Jillian feel a bit uneasy, was that her venture would most likely cost her money rather than make money. She wanted to be a more contributing member of the household.

John came home that evening with a small, gift-wrapped box in his hand. Jillian looked at him curiously as she opened it. Inside was a business card for a book publisher.

"What's this?" she asked, reading the name on the card.

"Well, I was talking to someone a few weeks ago about your writing. He is a friend of the editor at this publishing company, and said he would mention to her the kind of book you were writing, because it sounded like something she would be interested in. He talked to her the other day, and she said it sounded intriguing and that she would take a look at it. She wouldn't make any promises or anything. She said she would treat it like any manuscript, but she liked that you already had a blog going and a following, and thought that the blog could enhance the book and continue even after it was published. There could also be many other offshoots from a book like that, including lectures at health conventions. So, you are supposed to give her a call sometime soon."

Jillian just stood there with her mouth open. She was married to the most incredible man on the planet, she thought. "Oh, John," she said, "what a wonderful surprise. You are..." She couldn't even come up with the words to describe how she felt about him at that moment. "You are the best," she finally said, unable to produce anything more original, and she threw her arms around him.

"You've done so much for me in my work that I wanted to do something for you in yours," he said.

Jillian just shook her head in disbelief at his thoughtfulness, and at the opportunity that now lay before her. She would be even more energized to finish up her work as soon as possible with this new development. She couldn't wait to get back to her computer. As usual, John had a way of reading her mind.

"Go and write," he said. "I'll scrounge up something for dinner."

Kathy J. Jacobson

He put his arms around her and kissed her, tempting her to forget the writing momentarily. But then he quickly disappeared toward the kitchen, allowing her to get back to the business at hand.

That Sunday John actually had a day off, and they were able to go to church together. Nancy was there with Buck. They were all so pleased to see each other that they all decided to go to brunch together after the service.

Buck was the nicest man, and Jillian was particularly fond of his sense of humor, and most of all, the way he treated Nancy. He was polite and gentle in some ways, yet there was a ruggedness about him that made him attractive. But best of all, he was definitely enthralled with Nancy. Nancy seemed to genuinely care for Buck, but Jillian sensed that there was something that was holding back her heart.

Jillian decided that she would call her friend as soon as she got home and find out if there was some way she could help. She knew quite a bit, from her own experience, about "holding back" and didn't want Nancy to make the mistake that she came so incredibly close to making.

She called Nancy in the late afternoon, thinking that Buck would have to go home and do chores, or at least oversee them. She was right, and Nancy said that Buck had just left.

"Buck is a nice man," Jillian said.

"Yes, he is a very nice man," Nancy agreed.

"But..."

"What about my house?" she asked.

"What *about* your house?" Jillian answered.

"It was the house my children grew up in. It was our... *our* house. I just feel like it is the last bit of my late husband that we have left."

"I understand that feeling," Jillian said. "But Nancy, you and your children will never lose the most important part of Ed—all of your memories of your lives together. You will always have those, no matter where you live or with whom you live. And of course, you have your wonderful children, and now grandchildren—your husband's living legacy. Nancy, what do you think Ed would tell you to do after all these years?"

"Knowing him, he'd tell me to get over it," she said.

"Easier said than done, isn't it?"

"Yes. Very."

"Nancy, do you love Buck?"

"Yes, I do. I have been praying about it for months now, and I keep getting the same answer—that he is a good man, and that he is the one..." she said, her voice trailing off.

"I feel another 'but' coming on, Nancy."

"Jillian, the last time I had someone who was the one for me—he died. It hurt so much I could barely stand it. I don't know if I could go through that again."

Jillian shared with Nancy her own situation with John, especially her fears when he was hospitalized. "Now I can't imagine life without being married to that wonderful man. I came within minutes of leaving the house for good and never coming back. It is a horrifying thought."

"But don't you worry about losing him?" Nancy asked.

"Well, I certainly do not relish the thought, but I just cannot imagine not enjoying whatever time we have—together. It would be a travesty to miss out on one minute of it."

"Well, when you put it that way, it does make sense. I've just been so afraid..." Nancy said, her voice conveying such deep emotion.

"Again, I understand, I really do. But some people are just worth the risk, Nancy. You need to decide it Buck is one of those people."

"You're right," she said, sighing. "Thank you so much for calling, Jillian, and for your insights. I will pray about it and make a

Kathy J. Jacobson

decision soon—one way or the other. Either I'm going to go with this all the way, or I'm going to tell Buck I can't see him anymore. It's not fair to keep him hanging in limbo like I have been doing."

"I will pray for you, too, Nancy. You are a special person, and you deserve much happiness."

"Thank you, Jillian. God bless you, dear."

"God bless you, too, Nancy."

The end of another week came, and John and Jillian enjoyed hosting dinner for Brooks and Bobbi. Bobbi was an aspiring actor as well, a beautiful girl with platinum blonde hair and bright blue eyes. Both she and Brooks were from Minnesota. Jillian found it interesting that they were all native Midwesterners and thought that perhaps this thread of commonality had made John seem more accessible to Brooks.

Brooks thanked John again for all his tutoring, as he put it, throughout the movie shoot, and mentioned to John that he was a great teacher. Jillian smiled at him, as she had told him the same thing on a number of occasions. They discussed the movie, and then Brooks and Bobbi's dreams for the future, which included marriage at some point, they hoped. John and Jillian told them they both gave marriage "two thumbs up."

After Brooks and Bobbi had gone home, John and Jillian sat outside on the new outdoor love seat next to the pool, a recent addition to the patio. John wrapped his arms around Jillian.

"I think I have it figured out, Jillian," he said after a few minutes.

"What's that, sweetheart?"

"I think I've finally found out a way to help others with my vocation. I could open up a free acting studio in East Los Angeles, perhaps somewhere near the church where we served Christmas dinner. People of all ages could come and learn, even if it was only for fun. Heaven knows that few will make it as professionals, but it could be a good thing, don't you think?"

Jillian turned and looked adoringly at him. "I think that it would be more than a good thing, John."

"I'll start looking into how to go about setting up a non-profit. I suppose one has to have some kind of lawyer, and a business person, and an accountant, too."

"Well, let's see," Jillian said, "Robert is a lawyer, Kelly works in business, and Drew is an accountant."

"And then there may have to be some renovations," he said.

"Pete is helping renovate a building into a health club right now, and has always wanted to be a builder. I bet he would help."

"And maybe someday it could be expanded to include other areas of the arts," John said, excitement growing in his voice.

"I know an artist named Greta and a writer named Jillian, who also knows how to dispense some health care," she said, the cogs beginning to turn in her own mind.

"It sounds like the possibilities are endless. It could be something really special," John said.

She turned to him, "Yes, very special," she said. She looked at him for a moment—this man, who had gone from not even speaking to people to going back to work as an actor to mentoring others on the set. And now he wanted to set up a free school to share his craft and talents with others. God's handprints were all over this one.

"John..." She was at a loss for words at that moment. She nodded her head in affirmation of his ideas and the person he had become. "Wow," she finally said softly, then kissed him sweetly.

Chapter Eighteen

Over the next month, John checked off the requirements for forming a non-profit organization during every free moment that he had. Robert helped with some of the legal issues, and what he didn't know, his associates and colleagues elsewhere did. John and Jillian were so excited that John's idea was slowly but surely taking shape. Once they got more information, they would draw up a proposal and then present it at a city council meeting. They got their names on the agenda for an upcoming one, knowing that the sooner they got the go-ahead, the better.

The filming of the movie was almost complete, with just a few minor scenes to shoot. The director said it was one of the easiest groups of artists he had ever worked with, and the project had progressed in record time. He also felt that the exceptionally talented cast had turned it into an even better product than he had ever expected. He knew it would be a good movie, but now he felt it was a great movie.

Jillian had a chance to meet with the editor at the publishing company. Not only did she like the book, they bought it and offered Jillian an agent. She was on top of the world, to say the least.

A contract and an agent were beyond anything she could have imagined when she first came to Los Angeles. Actually, just about everything in her life was beyond anything she could have ever imagined.

Everything was going so well that it sometimes frightened Jillian. She knew, from her own past, and other people's pasts, that things most likely would not keep on this incredible positive path indefinitely. Unfortunately, Jillian didn't have to wait much longer for that assumption to be validated.

Jillian woke up in a sweat at midnight. She bolted upright in the bed, wide awake, her heart pounding and her lungs gasping for air. She wasn't sure what was going on, but she felt that something was wrong—very wrong. She turned to John, who was sound asleep. He had been working so hard on the movie and the acting school plans, and he had to be up again before dawn. She didn't want to wake him up, but the feeling of dread was frightening her to her core. She wasn't sure if she was having some type of panic attack—or worse. Or perhaps she had had a nightmare, and this was her reaction to it. Just to help calm herself down, she turned on the lamp on the side of the bed to its dimmest setting and sat up, trying to take some long, slow breaths.

John turned over and faced her. In a sleepy voice he asked her if she was okay, and half-asleep, reached out for her hand.

"I think so. I'm sorry I woke you up, honey. It must have been a bad dream or something," she said, still feeling a bit shaky. She was just reaching over to turn off the light when her cell phone rang, which startled her even more.

It was a number she didn't recognize, but she felt that she should answer it. Now John was awake and sitting up, looking at her.

"Hello, this is Jillian," she answered.

Kathy J. Jacobson

"Mrs. Romano—thank God," the young male voice said. The voice sounded somewhat familiar, but it just didn't register in Jillian's half-asleep, half-upset head.

"It's Michael—in Senegal."

Jillian's heart sank, and her head started swimming.

"Michael, is everything all right?"

He hesitated. "I'm not sure. They just put Marty into isolation. She has a high fever and..." He couldn't seem to get the rest of his words out.

Jillian could barely think straight and could barely speak herself. She was trying her best not to panic, to be nurse Jillian who comforted many frightened parents in the past, but this time, she was the frightened parent. She looked at John, who was now wide awake with a very concerned look on his face. He searched her face, and she grabbed his hand, tears filling her eyes.

"I would assume they are testing her right away?" she finally asked.

"Yes, they took some blood samples, but it may take a few days. In the meantime, they are giving her fluids intravenously, as she is very dehydrated. So far, there is no sign of hemorrhaging, so that is good. They are watching her closely. We are all watching her closely," he said, sounding upset, but trying to be brave.

"I should come, Michael," Jillian said.

"Why don't you wait a day or two until we have the results of the tests? It could be something else. It could even be the flu. She started feeling bad yesterday morning. We had gone down to the rainforest a couple of days ago, when we both had a day-and-a-half off at the same time. She felt great until we got back, then got really tired and nauseous. She said she thought she was coming down with a bug. But she was in so much pain last night, she said she couldn't even sleep. She said it felt like there was fire going down her back."

"Is that common to Ebola?" Jillian asked.

"The tired and nauseous part is, but not the severe pain. That's what makes me think it may not be the worst-case scenario. I'm just praying it isn't, and deep down I feel like it isn't—or maybe I just don't want to believe that it is. I'm trying to stay positive. I'm going to keep on thinking about the other possibilities and do some more study. I don't know what I'd do if something happened to her..." his voice dropped off.

"Me, either," Jillian said, tears now rolling down her cheeks. She looked at John who was staring blankly ahead. "Call me—anytime. Will I be able to reach you at this phone number, Michael?"

"Yes, I just got this phone last week, and am so glad I did. I can't believe I could call you on it like this. Marty gave me your number right before they secured her. I will call soon with an update. You could look into travel arrangements in the meantime, just in case you need them, but let's pray for the best."

"We will be. Thank you so much, Michael, for calling us."

"I'm sure that someone from the school will be in contact, too, but I wanted you to hear it from me first," he said.

"I appreciate that," she said, wiping her cheek with the back of her hand.

She ended the call. Jillian didn't know what to say. She could barely think straight. Earlier she had thought she had had a nightmare—now she felt like she was living one. She looked at John. He looked sadder than she had ever seen him, but he seemed determined to be strong for Jillian. He pulled her into his arms and held her tight, kissing the top of her head.

"Pray, John," she said softly and earnestly.

"I already am," he said and tightened his grip, Jillian crying softly as he held her.

Kathy J. Jacobson

John was going to call the studio and tell them that there was an emergency and he couldn't come in, but Jillian insisted he finish this project. He said he would talk to the director and see if they could adjust the schedule and finish up his scenes that day, just in case he needed to go to Senegal with Jillian.

In the meantime, Jillian called Alan's favorite travel agent at his suggestion when John had called him to tell him what was going on. She said she could put two tickets on hold until the next evening. Jillian knew that the woman was doing them a great favor, somehow extending the hold period longer than normal. Luckily, they had their shots from their trip early in the summer. Jillian contacted the clinic and got malaria pills, just in case they had to leave the country. One advantage of living in a bigger city was the quick availability of some of those types of items.

Jillian called Pastor Jim and Nancy, asking for their prayers and to put Marty on the prayer chain. She told the pastor that she may be in later at the church, just to sit and pray. Then she called Karen, Pete, and Carol, her best friends in the world outside of her husband, to give them the news. They were all very concerned and empathetic. Carol was the most upset of all, but then again, she had known Marty for many years, and Jillian even longer than that. She said she hadn't done so in a long time, but she would start praying right away. She also said she was going to talk to her colleagues to see if anyone had any other thoughts about what it could be if it wasn't Ebola.

Jillian stopped in at church late in the afternoon. No one else was there, which was perfect for what she wanted to do. She walked into the quiet sanctuary, the light shining in through a modern design stained-glass window, and sat down in one of the front pews. She couldn't speak, just sighed. The words from the book of Romans came to mind—the "Spirit intercedes for us, with sighs too deep for words." She wasn't sure where to start, but trusted that the Spirit, indeed, would help her out.

At the end of an hour, Jillian felt strangely calm. She had one of her feelings again. Something told her that while her daughter was now suffering, that she would eventually be okay. As she left the church, she decided she was just going to "go with" that feeling at this point, and then she drove back to the house.

John came home at seven o'clock, later than originally scheduled, but with the news that his work on the film was now completed. Neither one of them had much of an appetite, but they knew that they had to have something, as their stomachs were growling loudly. They also knew that it also wouldn't do anyone any good if they didn't take care of themselves.

Michael called back about eight o'clock with a report. Marty was still in a lot of pain and finding it difficult to find a way to lay comfortably on her bed. Her fever was still very high, and now she was getting some blisters on her hands in the webbing between her fingers. Again, this was not a typical Ebola symptom. Her nausea, however, was beginning to subside, and she had had a drink with electrolytes in it and actually kept it down.

They were still giving her an "IV," and would continue that until she could eat and drink more regularly. A portable ultrasound unit was due to arrive from another larger hospital, so they could check to make sure she was not hemorrhaging internally. Internal bleeding was the major cause of death in Ebola cases. Michael said that by the next morning—John and Jillian's time—they should know the results of the blood tests.

Michael sounded exhausted, and Jillian was certain that he had not slept at all since they talked last. Then again, neither had she nor John. She decided that they had better get some sleep, as in another twelve hours, they would know what they were dealing with—or hopefully not dealing with.

After the call ended, John made some eggs and toast. He was doing everything he could to be helpful and positive, and Jillian couldn't imagine going through this ordeal without him.

John looked so tired, which made sense since he had only gotten about two hours of sleep before they got the news, then had gone to the set for fourteen hours. He had mentioned that it was the longest day of work he had ever experienced in his life. Jillian felt so bad for him. It must have been terrible to try to concentrate on his lines with all the turmoil going on in his head and heart.

Jillian filled John in on the details of Michael's report as they ate, then she suggested that even though it was before nine, they try to get some sleep. They rinsed the dishes and put them in the dishwasher. They texted Tommy an update and told him they would know the next morning whether or not they were flying to Dakar. They would call him as soon as they knew the answer, one way or the other. Tommy and his family all loved Marty and were very upset and concerned. They were all praying, as was their priest and church prayer group, which John and Jillian appreciated.

They crawled into bed exhausted—mentally, physically, and emotionally. They said a prayer together for Marty, then turned off the light, but Jillian's eyes would not close. John sensed that she could not sleep.

"Turn over," he said to her gently. "It's my turn to be the nurse." He proceeded to begin to massage her neck and upper back, just as she had done for him the times when he was on edge. Jillian was sure it would have no effect, but in ten minutes, she was out like a light, and John was right behind her.

Jillian's cell phone rang at 8:13 a.m. She couldn't help but notice that number as she hit the "accept" button. They were Marty's numbers—her birthday being August the thirteenth. She was praying that that was a good sign.

"Michael," she said flatly, then held her breath.

"Mrs. Romano, some good news! It is *not* Ebola, and she also doesn't appear to have any hemorrhaging," Michael said and let that sink in for a moment. "Unfortunately, we are still not certain what it is, but I have an idea I am going to bounce off one of the doctors. They are still pumping her full of fluids. They will most likely take her out of isolation in six to eight hours, and then you can talk to her or maybe even video chat if she is up to it."

"Really? That soon? Oh, Michael, that would be wonderful. We will be waiting," Jillian exclaimed, with hope and excitement in her voice.

"She is still very sore and hasn't eaten much of anything for days, so she's pretty weak. We will have to see how much activity she will be up for, but she will touch base with you, one way or the other," he said.

They hung up. John could tell that it was good news, but they were still concerned that they didn't know what it was.

"Should we go?" he asked.

"Let's wait until we talk to Marty later," she said. "Michael is going to have her call us or even video chat with us as soon as she gets out of isolation."

"We're going to be able to talk to Marty? When?"

"Hopefully this afternoon sometime," Jillian said, smiling for the first time in days.

John hugged her, seeming even more choked up than she was at the news. John had always wanted a daughter and finally had one. Jillian knew that he would really like to keep her.

Kathy J. Jacobson

A text message came from Michael's phone at 2:20 p.m., telling them to be ready with their computer to video chat at two-thirty.

John and Jillian had been ready all day, waiting with the computer and phone plugged in to make sure they were charged, and not going far from their presence.

At two-thirty, the familiar "ring" came through Jillian's computer.

Jillian stood at the kitchen counter, with John right next to her, anxiously awaiting the visual. Then there it was—that beautiful, smiling face—a bit gaunt and flushed, but smiling nonetheless.

"Hi, Mama," came the familiar, cheerful voice.

"Marty," Jillian felt like she might start to cry, then felt faint and wobbly for a moment. John noticed, threw his arm around her shoulder, held her tightly, then bombed into the screen.

"Hi, Dad," Marty said.

"Sorry—I couldn't wait my turn," he said, trying to lighten the air. With his free hand, he adjusted the computer so both he and Jillian could be seen by Marty.

"How do you feel?" John asked.

"Like I got hit by a Mack truck, but a little better. I'm just really tired, and I don't think I'm going to eat any more fish and rice for a long time. My favorite foods here sound disgusting to me, unfortunately. All I really want is a good cheeseburger and some fries, but I guess that will have to wait until I get home at Christmas," she said.

Hearing Marty say that she wanted to eat, and that she felt like she would actually be home at Christmas, made Jillian feel like crying again. She was really struggling with this call, but Marty seemed to be having a great conversation with John, so she tried to enjoy that. John continued to hold Jillian tightly, and she managed to smile from time to time, and nod her head.

Then Marty said that Michael thought he had figured out what she had, and the doctors were concurring that it was a good possibility. It was called "Dengue Fever," also known as "Breakbone Fever," because it is so painful, it feels like all of your bones are broken.

"I can attest that it is aptly named," she said after she relayed that information. "I've never hurt so much, for so long. My blisters look like they might be going away, though. I think I'm through the worst for now, but Michael has given me the 'good news' that if it's Dengue, I will probably get a rash and start itching soon. Then there are a host of other lovely side effects before it all works its way out of my system. Like Ebola, there is no cure, only treatment with hydration and electrolytes."

"How do you think you contracted it?" John continued.

"Dengue is transmitted by infected mosquitoes. It must have happened when we visited the rainforest. I never really noticed a lot of mosquitoes while we were there, but I did have a bite or two when I came back. I wasn't worried about it because I take my malaria pills all the time. I never gave other illnesses a thought," she said. "I just hope I can finish out my work before I leave."

That was Jillian's Marty talking, for certain—never worrying about herself, only about others and about her responsibilities

"You need to take care of yourself, Marty," Jillian finally said, having regained a tiny bit of composure.

"No worries, Mom, I will. And Michael will make sure I do, too. He has been wonderful. He would be talking to you, but he fell asleep in the chair and I'm not going to wake him up now. I don't think he has slept in days. And speaking of that, I should get some sleep. I'm finally not so sore and can get comfortable enough to actually do that," she said, smiling again.

"Thank him again for us, Marty, when he wakes up. Just text us when you want to chat again. We are so happy you are getting better, sweetie," Jillian said. Then she was starting to lose it again, and John's grip tightened once more.

"We love you, Marty," John said.

"I love you both, too," she said. "*Lala salama.*"

Overwhelmed with happiness and unable to speak, Jillian just nodded. It would be a night of much more peaceful sleep for everyone, that was a certainty.

Jillian turned to John, and he enveloped her in his arms. She didn't know how long they stood holding each other, as time seemed to stand still.

"I don't know what I would have done without you these past few days," she finally said, looking into those warm brown eyes.

"Now you know how I feel each and every day," he said sincerely, and held her again.

Two days later, they video chatted with Marty again. Indeed, she was itching, but at least she could itch in the privacy of her own home now. Their little house had been quarantined until they knew it wasn't Ebola, and she and her housemates were very happy to be back in their own quarters, especially Marty. After she had been moved into a regular hospital room, she had so many visitors that the doctors finally banned them. At one time, twelve people were sitting in her room, bringing her treats of all sorts consisting of homemade food items they thought she should eat to get her strength back. She didn't have the heart to tell them that she could barely look at the food, let alone eat it.

Marty scratched her arm as she spoke. "Ooohh!" she said in aggravation. "It's like having a million mosquito bites all at once. I know it won't last long, but it is pretty awful. I just want to scratch my entire body, and I can't. I will have a new perspective and empathy when my patients come in to me in the future with pruritus," she added, using the medical term for itching.

While Marty was talking to them, there was a heavy knock at their house door. One of her roommates answered it. There stood a sweaty man, saying he had a delivery of food for them. At first, they thought it was someone trying to sell them some food, but the man said that it was already all paid for and that he was just sent to deliver it.

"Just a minute, Mom and Dad. Someone is at the door with food for us, but no one ordered anything."

"I did," John said suddenly.

"You did—what?" Marty asked.

"I ordered food for you. I'm glad it's finally arrived. Go check it out and let me know if they brought the right thing," he said, a sly smile crossing his face.

Marty walked over to the door and talked in Wolof to the young man who had two boxes of food at his feet. She peered into them and let out a squeal of delight.

"Oh, my gosh!" they heard Marty exclaim. She told her friends to tip the man and she would pay them back in a minute. She rushed back over to the computer screen.

"Dad, you are the best! Cheeseburgers and french fries!" Marty looked stunned, but thrilled.

"You need to eat and get healthy, Marty. You'd better get at it before it gets cold. I hope that they are not that way already," he said, as the restaurant he ordered them from was on the other side of the city.

"We will enjoy them even if they're cold. Again, you are the best," she said, getting a bit emotional, which was not usual for Marty, but under the circumstances, was appropriate.

"I love you, Marty," John said.

"I love you, too. I love you both! I'll talk to you again, soon! Cheeseburgers and french fries!" she exclaimed again, smiling, as the screen darkened.

Jillian could barely speak again—for a record number of times in the past two days. As Marty's face faded out, she turned to John. She looked into his eyes and just shook her head. Finally, she could speak again. "As our daughter just said, you are the best, John D. Romano," she said softly, then she kissed him unreservedly.

They held each other, Jillian feeling like the weight of the world had been lifted from her shoulders. She felt like as a feather, and she noticed another thing—she was truly hungry—for the first in quite awhile, and said so.

"Any requests?" John asked.

"How about—cheeseburgers and french fries?" Jillian asked, smiling.

"Like daughter, like mother," he said, his huge grin showing up for the first time in days.

"Amen," said Jillian.

Chapter Nineteen

John and Jillian walked hand in hand around the neighborhood one beautiful evening in October, six weeks after Marty came home from the hospital. As they passed the familiar sights, they discussed the incredible journey they had been on thus far.

The movie had wrapped up on time, which made the director and producer exceedingly happy. John's work had been praised by both, and the word that he was "back" as an actor and was a changed man in his disposition was spreading quickly on the Hollywood grapevine.

The movie had been released just a few weeks before, and Jillian got her first taste of a premiere and a red carpet. She had been nervous about tripping, especially with all the flashbulbs popping around her, but her prayers were answered and she stayed upright. It helped to have John at her side, smiling at her from ear to ear, and being congratulated all around them.

The movie's reviews were fantastic, and talk of Academy Award nominations were in the air for best picture and many others. John got kudos for his role as "Mack." It was a supporting role, but integral to the story. Brooks also received excellent reviews in his role, and thanked John profusely, certain that it was his tutelage that helped him achieve such high praise.

Karen was two months into her semester of student-teaching and was loving it for the most part. There were tough days once in a while, when she wondered if she was making any difference at all. But overall, it was a great experience. She was a natural in the classroom, and many of the children seemed to see her as a mother figure. They were naturally drawn to her caring and kind ways. She embraced the situation wholeheartedly, as she and Robert were never able to have children of their own.

Robert was working with John and Jillian, putting the finishing touches on making the acting workshop become a reality. He, too, seemed energized by volunteering his time and expertise. He mentioned more than once that, for whatever reason, it didn't seem like work. The project was becoming a passion for everyone who became involved.

The city council had happily approved their request to build or renovate, thrilled that anyone—let alone a celebrity—was interested in doing something positive in that particular neighborhood.

John and Jillian found a small building to buy that would work nicely. It even had a space that would be perfect for a stage. Pete was going to help them with renovations when he could, as was the foreman working on Pete's gym project. He had overheard Pete talking about it one day and wanted to know more. Once he got the specifics, he wanted to join in and do something important with his skills, outside of his normal routine.

Nancy had decided that Buck was indeed "worth the risk," and had finally given him another real chance. The two seemed to be enjoying the new level of their relationship. They, too, expressed interest in helping with John and Jillian's project. Buck said he would like to donate money and could help with some of the renovations, too, pronouncing that he was "handy with power tools." He wished he could help in a more important way, but Jillian told him every type of help was important, and that one never knew what possibilities might arise in the future, even for a rancher.

Alan and Bev, not wanting to be excluded, asked how they could help. Jillian thought that Bev wanted to do something simply because of how happy her brother Jerry was, now that Carol was in his life. On Carol's last call to Jillian, she stunned Jillian by announcing her intentions to retire from the university. This was going to be her final year teaching at the University of Wisconsin, having shaped the lives and careers of thousands of nurses over three decades as an instructor. And perhaps the most amazing part of it all—after the spring semester was over, Carol was planning to move to California! Jillian could barely believe it. Jillian was ecstatic that her best friend would be so close by.

Jillian had finished her manuscript, and *Where Broken Hearts Go* would be released soon, just in time for the holiday book-buying season. After the new year, Jillian would begin a book-signing tour, and then if the book was well-received, she hoped to do lectures at libraries, churches, and perhaps even some medical facilities and social service agencies. The blog was going strong, and her readers were excited that the book would be on the shelves soon, as was Jillian, whose writing dreams were finally coming to fruition.

Drew and Greta were planning a Thanksgiving weekend wedding. They had chosen that because they felt so thankful for finding one another. Jillian was indeed slated to be the matron of honor and was looking forward to the event at Greta's parents' home in Encino.

Maria had opened her Italian bakery and deli in downtown Libertyville, and so far it had been a huge hit. Many people were inquiring about orders for the upcoming holidays, wanting the traditional recipes their mothers and grandmothers used to make.

Maria had also wisely tweaked some favorites into what she termed "waist-watchers"—healthier versions of the original selections. She also had some vegetarian and gluten-free offerings, which were appreciated. She was a savvy business-woman, in addition to her cooking skills.

Kelly was beginning her sixth month of pregnancy and was starting to become very uncomfortable. She would be on maternity leave for three months after the delivery, and she joked that it should be double that time. When she had gone in for the ultrasound, she and Pete found out that they were expecting twins—a boy and a girl—with a due date in early February. Pete had cried when he told Jillian the good news face-to-face. He said he felt like his life had made a complete turnaround, and again, thanked Jillian. But she pointed to the sky and told him that she wasn't the one to thank.

Marty was improving day by day. She had lost weight, but was gaining it back slowly but surely. She was losing some hair when she combed it, but had been assured that the problem should stop in a couple of months. Luckily, she had a lot of hair to spare. She still couldn't stand her favorite Senegalese foods, much to her chagrin, but she and Michael had found the restaurant where the cheeseburgers and fries came from and had gone there twice since the order had been delivered to her door. She mentioned, however, that nothing would ever taste as good to her as the food that had been delivered when she was sick. Jillian thought that was because it had been sent with the "secret ingredient"—love.

Marty was also relieved that she was back on schedule in her work, and would be able to get her research and reports done before her time in Dakar was over, which should be shortly before Christmas. She had made a "360" in the past six weeks, much to the relief of all those who loved her. She mentioned that she had never appreciated her health, or life in general, as much as she did at this time—now that she had been given another chance.

Jillian thought about all the incredible things she had witnessed in the last year, and the many turnarounds. She felt she knew first-hand about complete transfigurations. Her own life was one, as was John's, and it seemed that all around her she saw incredible examples of people she loved who were either taking—or were being given—another chance.

As they ended their walk, Jillian and John headed up the driveway toward the Storybook house. When they neared the part of the driveway where Jillian had been given that note from John months before—the note that suggested that John was the right person for her to love and made her reconsider and stay—she suddenly stopped.

"Is everything okay?" John asked, turning to her and holding her by the arms, a look of concern on his face.

"It's more than okay," she said, lifting her hand and stroking his face gently. "I just needed to take another good look at the *right person*, the one who gave me another chance."

John smiled that huge grin that she loved so much and said, "We were both given another chance—for new creation—as you always say."

She looked into the eyes of her loving husband, nodded her head, and said, "New creation." Then she kissed him, loving him with all of her being and looking forward to all the future might hold. Jillian knew that no matter what they might face, good or bad, it would be okay, because they would face it together.

The End

Enjoy this excerpt from third book in the NOTED! series.

A NEW NOTE

John came into the kitchen with a stack of scripts in his arms, then dropped them onto the counter. This had become a weekly ritual ever since his movie had premiered.

"I was going to ask you what your plans were after dinner tonight, but I think I have my answer," Jillian said, eyeing the pile of papers.

John sighed. "It's going to be an all evening affair again, I'm afraid," he said, as he hugged her. "I'd rather spend it with you," he said, and kissed her forehead.

"I got a lot done today, so I could help you go through them," she said.

"You've been staring at a computer all day, and you want to read scripts all night?" John asked, still holding her.

"As someone once told me, as long as I'm with you, I don't care where we are or what we are doing," she said, looking into his deep brown eyes.

John shook his head and put his fingers gently under her chin. "How did I get so lucky?"

"I was just wondering the same thing," she said, and then kissed him.

The script reading session was long and frustrating. John couldn't believe that in all the scripts he had perused over the past month, there wasn't something that stood out. Sometimes the two of them found themselves laughing out loud, trying to imagine John actually playing a particular part, or wondering how something so mediocre could have gotten this far along in the process.

They were planning to have three piles on this night—yes, no and maybe. John was looking for something thoughtful and well-written. He had always been a stickler when it came to the writing, and had been spoiled after working on *O.R*, which had a team of award-winning writers. Writing could make or break a television show or movie, no matter how talented the actors.

Most of the movies were stories with mass appeal, but had little else to offer. At this point in his career, John was looking for something special. He was least interested in the romantic comedies, although Jillian enjoyed reading the parts of his love interests. John mentioned that they had to stop acting them out, however, or they would never get done.

At 2:00 a.m., John let out a weary sigh and put the last script on the "maybe" pile. Unfortunately, they only had two piles at the end of the night—"no," and "maybe."

Nothing really struck either of them as "just right," but new offers were coming in almost every day. Luckily, John didn't have to make a decision on any of the current ones immediately, but he would definitely turn in the "no" pile the next day.

John also planned to find out who the intended directors were for the maybe pile. The best script may not reach its potential under the wrong guidance, and a clash of personalities could ruin a project as well.

"Enough," John said, putting his arm around Jillian's shoulders as they sat on the couch. She put her head on his shoulder and closed her eyes.

"There must be something better out there, something meaningful," John said, caressing her arm.

"You mean you really think there's something better out there than *Sad, But True?*" she asked teasingly, referring to a romantic comedy script that had gone quickly into the "no" stack.

"Talk about an appropriate title," he said, rolling his eyes.

Kathy J. Jacobson

"But John, it has such memorable dialogue," she continued. *"I can't remember my phone number. Can I have yours?"*

He surprised her by flipping her onto her back until her head rested in his lap. She found herself looking straight up into his eyes. *"Too late, you already have my number,"* he said, reciting the line, then kissed her sweetly. Afterward, he gently pulled back, his face just inches from hers.

"See, I told you it was good dialogue. It worked, didn't it?" she said in a soft, playful tone.

He just smiled, and kissed her again.

The next afternoon John came bounding into the kitchen, a script in his hands.

"I think this is it, Jillian!" he exclaimed. "Will you read some of it and see what you think? Carson Stone is directing it and asked for me— to play the lead male role," he said, sounding like he didn't quite believe it.

"Wow—Carson Stone. Let's have a look at it. And John, you shouldn't be so surprised. You are an amazing actor, and it's time you accepted that fact," she said, putting her hands on his chest.

"You're only saying that because you're crazy about me," he said.

"It's true, I *am* crazy about you, but give yourself some credit," she said, then kissed his cheek.

"I'll try," he said, a dreamy look upon his face.

"Breakfast nook? Library? Couch?" Jillian asked, suggesting places for the reading.

"We'd better stay away from the couch," he said, teasingly.

"Okay, to be safe, let's stay in the kitchen," she said.

"I'm not sure any place is safe with you, but it's the best we can do," he said, as they both slid into the two wooden benches of the breakfast nook and faced each other.

The story was a suspenseful drama concerning the Alaskan pipeline. It reminded Jillian of *The China Syndrome,* a hit movie made in 1979 about a near nuclear disaster. Like that movie, this one would have a large cast of characters. The leading role John would play would be that of a scientist. Of course, he would have a love interest in the movie, a veteran reporter sent to investigate his claims.

Jillian knew, especially after reading through all the scripts in the past month, that it was inevitable that John would have to kiss other women, and perhaps even more than that. She was working on mentally preparing herself for the situation. This movie would have quite a bit of kissing in it and one bedroom scene between John and the female lead. At least it wasn't very long— but it was there—in "full living color," as her mother used to say.

Jillian wondered if they had anyone in mind yet for the female lead and asked John.

"So, who gets to kiss you?" she asked after they read through a good portion of the script.

"I guess that is still up in the air. Alan said Carson had someone in mind, but he hadn't heard back from her. If that person doesn't do it, they might do auditions. I guess they are trying to assemble a fairly star-studded cast," he said.

"It seems like a great story, John. It's meaningful, suspenseful, and of course, there's a bit of romance for those of us who enjoy that. It seems to have very intelligent dialogue, and might help people think a bit more seriously about environmental issues. Scripts like this one, along with a top director, rarely come around," she said.

John nodded his head in agreement. "Exactly my thoughts. I think I should do it, if you are okay with that?" John asked.

"John, you don't need my permission," she said. She could see the excitement in his face and it made her feel good inside.

"I know, but I'd like your blessing," he responded thoughtfully.

"You'll always have that, John," she said. "Whatever makes you happy, makes me happy," she said, meaning it.

John took her hands in his, then brought them to his lips and kissed them.

"I sure do love you, Mrs. Romano," he said.

"That's good, because I sure love you, Mr. Romano," she responded. "Now, you'd better call Alan. I would bet he's sitting with the phone in his hand, just waiting for you to call."

Jillian was right about that, as Alan answered on the first ring.

"Tell them to send over the contract, Alan," John said, beaming at Jillian across the breakfast nook table, still holding one of her hands in his free one.

"Ah...sure. I will. Ah..." Alan was stammering on the other end of the phone. It wasn't exactly the reaction John was expecting from his long-time friend and agent.

"Is there a problem, Alan?" the smile beginning to fade slightly from John's face.

"Ah... they heard back from the actor who will play the female lead," he said.

"So, who is the lucky woman?" John said, trying to tease Jillian, and wondering why Alan was acting so peculiar.

He got his answer a moment later. John turned as white as a sheet and Jillian thought he might pass out. John ended the call, put the phone down on the table and just stared ahead, looking straight through her. Jillian felt worried for a moment. The possibility of John having another brain tumor was always something that lingered in the back of her mind.

"John," Jillian said in a concerned tone, squeezing his hand. "What's the matter?"

He just said two words, ones that smacked her right in the face and would continue to ring in Jillian's ears the rest of the night and into the next few days.

"Monica Morgan."

Questions for Discussion

1. Jillian narrowly escapes making a major life-changing mistake. Sometimes we are able to avoid mistakes, other times we head straight into them, sometimes willingly, sometimes unknowingly, sometimes with false hope. Share your experience with making, or avoiding, a life-changing mistake.

2. What do you think the future would have looked like for John and Jillian had John not returned that day to ask her to stay?

3. Do you believe that there is such an entity as a "right person"? If so, do you think it is ever too late to find him or her?

4. John and Jillian are in a very vulnerable situation at the beginning of this story. They are experiencing extreme euphoria after extreme distress and sadness. They are feeling deep emotions and strong physical attraction, yet manage to use restraint. To what do you attribute their self-control? Do you think that things would have worked out as positively had they given in to their desires?

5. Jillian isn't the only one who has experienced heartbreak in the past, or encountered less-than-ideal relationships. John had a "high-maintenance" relationship with Monica Morgan, the woman who eventually broke his heart. Why do you think John, and many people, stay in such relationships?

6. One of the first positive moves in John's life seems to be his reconnection to people whom he loves, and who love him. First, it was his nephew, Tommy, and his family. Then it is an old friend, Leo. Leo is not only happy to see John, but also notices immediately that he is "different," i.e. happy. Later, people in John's profession, such as directors, notice positive changes in him. Have you ever seen such transformation—in yourself or in others? To what, or to whom, did you attribute the change?

Kathy J. Jacobson

7. John and Jillian often experience times of "comfortable quiet" with one another. Comment on this.

8. Along with beginning a new relationship, John is also starting over in other areas of recent "failure," such as biking (his last experience before buying his new bike was a bloody and humiliating accident) and acting (his last time on stage he had experienced trouble remembering his lines.) Each renewed venture seems to build on the last. Have you ever had a similar experience?

9. Jillian is often pleasantly surprised by John's attentiveness and thoughtfulness. These are two of the attributes she loves most about him. What attributes do you look for and appreciate in people who are important in your life?

10. Jillian mentions that what makes certain foods special (whether it is a family recipe or a special order like John ordered for Marty in Senegal) is the "secret ingredient"—love. What do you think about that idea?

11. Jillian and John's contact with the nursing home residents positively affects both their lives. What are some ways you have been positively influenced by more mature adults in your life?

12. Jillian is just beginning to understand the reality of the life of a celebrity. Have you ever met a celebrity? How did you feel or act? Have you ever had celebrity status of your own? How did it feel? Do you think you would enjoy a "steady diet" of a celebrity's existence?

13. What did you think about Edith's advice for a long and happy marriage?

14. Both Jillian and John have their own vulnerabilities and issues. Jillian has trouble accepting compliments and sometimes puts herself down. John is often very hard on himself and is insecure, even though he is considered a handsome and talented actor. Comment on this. What are your vulnerabilities and issues?

15. Drew meets "that Greta" and is instantly annoyed by her. Later, this feeling changed drastically. Have you ever met someone and had strong feelings about them (good or bad) and then had those feelings change over time?

16. The "bug" for acting returns for John slowly but surely in a number of ways (i.e., at the nursing home, in the classroom in Tanzania.) Not only do these experiences reinforce his love for his craft, but they also guide him into new ways of sharing his skills and vocation with others. Have you ever had a similar experience?

17. Do you believe that John and Jillian's relationship progressed too quickly? Why or why not?

18. If you were to celebrate a life-changing, monumental event, like a marriage, who would you want to have present/celebrate with? Would you enjoy a "honeymoon" like John and Jillian's?

19. Just when everything seems to be falling in place in John and Jillian's lives, a near-tragedy occurs. Jillian cannot imagine going through this scary ordeal without John in her life. She feels later that no matter what comes her/their way, they will be okay, because they will face the future together. Have you ever had to deal with a difficult or scary situation? Who was "there" for you?

20. There are many "firsts" for both John and Jillian in this book. List some of them. What "firsts" stand out in your own memory? What "firsts" do you look forward to in your life?

Kathy J. Jacobson

Author's Note/Acknowledgments

The past year has been one of most exciting ones of my life. I have been thrilled by the response to *NOTED!* and happy that others have come to know and love Jillian, John and their friends, and want to continue with them on this journey called life. I hope and pray that each person who reads my books will be touched in some way, experiencing God's grace in the characters' stories, and in their own.

A huge thank you to my family—husband, Jeff, daughter, Kirsten, and sons Spencer and Jens Jacobson, their significant others—Rob, Emily and Carly, my cousins Judy and Pam, the Jacobson clan, and my hospice and church families for their ongoing love and support. A special thanks to Terri Ellis and Nancy Fulton-Young for reading the manuscript. I couldn't do this without all of you.

About the Author

Kathy J. Jacobson has worked in various forms of ministry over the past twenty years—from youth and Christian education coordinator, to campus ministry, rural parish ministry to hospice chaplain.

She lives in the beautiful "Driftless Area" of Southwestern Wisconsin with her husband, Jeff. They have three "children"—all "twenty-something." She is an avid traveler, with most memorable trips to the Holy Land, Papua New Guinea, and Tanzania. She loves music, the theater, and sports, but her true passion is writing. *On Another Note* is her second "faithful fiction" novel.

Check out the entire NOTED! series.